FIC   Herriges, Greg.
       Someplace safe

13.95

DATE			

SOMEPLACE SAFE

SOMEPLACE SAFE

GREG HERRIGES

ST. MARTIN'S PRESS   NEW YORK

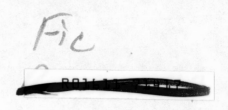

Design by Laura Hammond

Library of Congress Cataloging in Publication Data

Herriges, Greg.
  Someplace safe.

  I. Title.
PS3558.E753S6   1984   813'.54   83-16004
ISBN 0-312-74418-8

First Edition

10 9 8 7 6 5 4 3 2 1

FOR CARMEN, WITH LOVE

SOMEPLACE SAFE

CHAPTER

I

t was one of those nights.
One of life's little jokes.

Life's jokes are hardly ever funny, because you're usually the punch line.

On May 15, Friday, everybody was at what they call the "Last Dance" at Harrison Godfrey High School, in Chicago. That's my school. It was named after some judge that died about a million years ago, and he never did anything to get named after him, so they named a school after him. So anyway, it was a big night for us seniors, on account of no more dances after this one. Except the Prom. Hardly nobody goes to the damn Prom anymore, because you have to be a millionaire to afford the tickets and flowers and tux. So it really wasn't the last dance, but they called it that anyway. Don't ask me why.

It was kind of cool that night, even though it *was* May. I was standing with a few of the guys, sort of shivering and watching the couples come out on the front of the steps for air. In Chicago, it doesn't matter if it's almost summer and near June or anything. It could be *August* and it might snow. You always hear radio disc jockeys say, "If you don't like the weather, wait a minute and it'll change," which isn't very funny (in fact, it's stupid), but it's true. The guys and me are just shooting the shit and making fun of the other guys and their dates for taking a stupid school dance so seriously. One guy, Ron Schullman, came out the front door with his date, Candy Lewandowski, wrapped around his arm like she was stuck on permanently with Crazy Glue. Or Ugly Glue. (You've never seen Candy.) It's funny, but you can tell in about ten years from now you'll see Ron and Candy, or somebody like them, coming out of the door of some country club and waiting for some car hiker to bring them their new Porsche. You can just tell that kind of stuff. I don't care what anybody tells you, high school dances are mainly practice for country club life.

"Nice ass," Rick says. Rick is one of the guys I was standing with.

"Who? Who's got a nice ass?" I asked. There were about a dozen girls around by then, and I didn't see a nice ass on one of them.

"Ron. Ron Schullman," he says, very straight-faced. "Ron Schullman has the finest ass at Godfrey High." Then he gets this real high falsetto voice and lisps, "Oh, God! Why won't Ronnie let me in his jeans? Yoo-hoo! Ronnie! I just wanna come between you and your Calvins."

Rick, he was just kidding. He's no fag. But he can play one pretty good. He sure can sound like one when he wants to.

The other guy we were with with was Kevin Reid. We're all in a band together, and in fact we'd auditioned to play for the Last Dance, but they didn't choose us. The student government representatives are the creeps who select the entertainment, and they don't like us much. See, they think we're too weird, on account of we never play two places with the same group name. Once we were the Panty Hose, and once we were the Charles Manson Quartet. When we auditioned for this job, we called ourselves Frog Eggs. Rick stole about fifty frogs from the biology labs and let them go while we played our first number. They were jumping on the amplifiers, on the stage, and out in the audience. One jumped right into Nancy Goldbaum's blouse, which just goes to show that we had some pretty smart frogs in that school. *Every*body wanted to jump in Nancy Goldbaum's blouse, even if she was a bitch, personally.

Kevin was standing next to me and sort of stomping the ground because it was getting colder every minute. He didn't look too happy. He barely said a word all night, now that I think of it. He'd just had a tragedy in his family, though none of us wanted to talk about it much. Especially Kevin. I don't blame him.

The door kept opening, and the sounds of Flasher, the group that got the job that night, came stinking into the parking lot. They sounded like Abba, that Swedish group. Pretty songs, like. Gooey songs that you could gag from. Rick kept bugging Kevin, saying why didn't he go in and talk to the band, that maybe they'd let him sit in. Kevin just smiled and said he'd rather cut off part of his anatomy. I won't tell you which part. Then we heard this car come screeching around the corner behind us, a Trans Am, and this guy Jerry Kalimahoupoulos and some other kid I'd never seen before stuck their heads out the windows. They wanted to know if we were playing tonight. They were drunk. Rick told 'em yeah, we were going to play just as soon as our equipment got there. Right out in the parking lot. Rock around the headlights. Jerry had a bottle of Jack Daniel's, and the other guy had some hash and a hash pipe. We climbed in the back seat and passed the bottle around a few times.

I don't drink much hard liquor, and for very good reasons. The first reason is that it *burns* too much when it's going down. I'll bet if you were to drink Liquid Plumber it would feel the same way. It would probably clean your system out pretty good, but it would feel exactly the same. The second reason I don't drink hard liquor is because it doesn't taste good unless you put it in something else. And also I tend to throw up whenever I drink anything stronger than beer. None of those reasons stopped me *that* night, though. I was depressed, is how come why. When I'm depressed, I'll do just about anything as long as I have some company.

"Any action in there?" Jerry wanted to know.

"Are you shittin' me?" Rick said.

"Wait a minute," I said to Rick, trying to get him to play along. "You didn't tell him about Karen Kassel unbuttoning her blouse to the drum solo."

"No big deal," Rick said, taking a hit from the pipe. "You seen two tits, you seen 'em all."

Jerry's eyes popped out. He's got these big old eyes that look like tennis balls when he's excited. "R-e-a-l-l-y?" he said. "Karen Kas—"

"Relax, Jerry," Kevin told him. "They're just putting you on."

Rick hit Kevin in the ribs because he spoiled the joke. Jerry

3

Kalimahoupoulos will believe anything. He's Greek, and we tease him a lot about spinach pie and not standing behind us. We always say that in gym class, not to stand behind us, on account of him being Greek. But he's no fag; he just believes whatever you tell him, is all.

I'll tell you the truth, this was not a high point in my life. Actually, it was about as low as I ever got, though sometimes I think I might still get lower. I know I wasn't *acting* sad or miserable, but that's because I learned not to show my true feelings. You learn that kind of stuff. Probably because of teachers and TV anchormen. Sometimes teachers and TV anchormen can have some pretty bad news for you, but they always give it to you like they're inviting you to their son's birthday party. So I blame them. Really, if Dan Rather had to announce World War III tonight, he'd say it matter-of-fact-like and then go to a commercial. Teachers, too. I had one that told us about the Holocaust, about people having the gold yanked out of their mouths and then getting thrown in incinerators, and he never once even flinched. Never once! So I've been taught well. Thank you, Dan. Thank you, Mr. Zavin. (That was the history teacher's name.)

We sat in Jerry's car for about an hour, the whole time trading sips from the Jack Daniel's bottle and taking hits from his friend's hash pipe. (I never did learn that guy's name.) The radio was on and at one point they were playing those corny oldies, like "Your Graduation Means Goodbye," or whatever the hell that song is called. You know the one. They always play it around graduation time to make you get sad if you have a girlfriend who's going to a different college than you. If I had a girlfriend, she'd *have* to go to a different college than me, 'cause I'm not going at all, I don't think. But I think they *want* you to be sad, is the point. It's like at Christmas. Last Christmas I was listening to a disc jockey we have here in Chicago. He thinks he's very clever and funny because he has all these prerecorded voices of jerks who say dumb things, and he pretends to talk back to them. He's been doing that for the last fifty years, and everybody's grandmother would rather commit suicide than start a day without him. Last Christmas he played this song "Noel," and it was all about some guy who sings "Noel" for all the little girls without pretty dresses and all the little boys without teddy bears, and he keeps singing about all this stuff these poor kids don't have at Christmastime, *just so you'll be sad*. And it works. If I were a real poor kid and didn't have any of that stuff, I might not miss it, unless some freak played a record to *remind* me I didn't have it. Then I'd feel *terrible*.

So this radio station was playing the graduation song just to depress people, and Rick and Jerry and me and Kevin all started singing along with it at the tops of our voices. Only, we didn't know the words. We had to make them up:

> *"Your graduation means goodbye,*
> *I'm so upset I think I'll poke out my eye,*
> *You know that I'll be true,*
> *Who else would puke on you?"*

Boy, were we drunk. We were so drunk that at one point Rick told Jerry to slow the car down, and you know what Jerry did? He jammed on the brakes and swerved the steering wheel, even though we were parked. He thought we were on the road or something, that's how wasted he was. Rick laughed so hard he wet his pants. He kept saying, "I'm gonna piss! I'm gonna piss!" And that's exactly what the bastard did. All over the back seat. I ran out of that car so fast you would've thought I was on fire, like one of those Buddhist guys who soaks himself in gasoline and then turns himself into a roman candle.

Then everything was one big fuzzy blur. I just remember a lot of laughing, and Rick running around the car pissing on everybody while he was singing the graduation song. But one thing made me stop laughing real quick. It was Kevin. Remember how I said he didn't look so hot that night, on account of a personal tragedy that nobody wanted to talk about? Well, while Rick was pissing on Jerry's car, and while Jerry was doubled over in hysterics, I caught this very clear glimpse of Kevin's face; he was leaning on another parked car, and he was crying. I saw these tears just streaming down his face, but nobody noticed except me. Kevin's got a nice face, and I'm not queer or anything, but I just like his face.

The reason he was crying, I guess, was because about two weeks before, he came home from school and found his mother dead in her bedroom from an overdose of Demerol. She killed herself. Just about everybody in town knew she was having an affair with her partner. She taught acting, and at one time she was a pretty accomplished actress—Roberta Reid. Maybe you've heard of her. Yeah. She was nearly famous. I liked her, because she used to cut the crust off the sandwiches she made for me. I hate crust, and so she'd just cut it off real neat before she gave it to me. Also, I liked her because her and Brandon—her acting partner, who was real good-looking and sophisticated—used to take Kevin and me with them to fancy joints when they went out. I mean, it was no secret about them or anything. It sounds weird, maybe, but she used to turn me on quite a bit. She was extremely sexy and had beautiful legs and the works, and she was quite physical in the way she communicated. Whenever she hugged me, like an affectionate hug, I'd get embarrassed, 'cause her tits and everything would flop practically in my face. Once, even, Kevin and me found a sexy dance video tape she'd made with Brandon—it was almost X-rated. We watched it about twenty times. I used to have fantasies about her frequently. Until she died. When she died, I thought mostly about how she cut the crust off my sandwiches. It was all hushed up and everything—her death. And Kevin never said a word about it. But there he was, little Kevin, crying his goddamn guts out while we were being crazy. I just couldn't stand it.

Then I started thinking about that "Noel" song—kids with no Christmas toys, and that graduation song, and a few of my own personal problems (which I won't go into right now), and I just started running. When you're really, *really* drunk and stoned at the same time, your vision sort of narrows to a little circle in front of you, like a TV set on the blink. Your legs get all rubbery, and you don't know where you are. I just ran.

There's a big fountain in front of Harrison Godfrey High School, and it squirts night and day, with big floodlights to show it off. I jumped right into it. I cut my leg pretty bad on the cement around it, because I couldn't see, let alone jump. All I remember is tons of water coming down on my head and being blinded by the floodlights. There was a big crowd around me then, laughing their asses off and shouting things and tossing pennies and making wishes. I just thought I was drowning. I sort of hoped I would.

6

After a while I got used to the coldness of the water and the strangeness of the scene, all those kids shouting. So I just sat there in the fountain, water pouring all over me. I must have been there about a year or something before two old guys pulled me out. I didn't know what was going on. I didn't know who the hell they were. All I knew was I wanted to stay there, and to be left alone. I took a swing at one of the old guys who was trying to pull me out. I missed, of course. He slapped me in the face about twenty times, and once this ring he was wearing hit my tooth and I thought all my teeth had gone down my throat. I kept saying, "Get outta here, goddamn it. Your fucking graduation means goodbye, you sonofabitch."

They got me out, though. I was being carried by these two big guys somewhere. I figured I was being kidnapped or something, that maybe they were deviates who would rape me and take all my money. You read about that in the paper all the time. You do. Chicago is a pretty violent place. I thought I was the next victim, and that you'd read about me the next day on page seventeen of the *Sun-Times*:

DRUNKEN YOUTH ASSAULTED BY SICKOS AND ROBBED IN FOUNTAIN

That's what my mother would have to read, with all the ugly details thrown in and continued on page seventy-eight. She'd have to read about how I got my throat slashed with a butcher knife, or my head smashed with an ice pick while some old forty-ish guy committed buggery with me. (That's what they call it when a guy does it to another guy. They call it *buggery*. It sounds like something an exterminator ought to do, but that's not what it is. It's when some old guy does it to you.) And right next to the article about me would be an ad for sweaters at Marshall Field's or some goddamn thing. Lovely.

I started thinking, while they were carrying me off, about all the things I'd never have a chance to do, like make a record with my band, or get it on with Nancy Goldbaum. It's really hysterical, because I couldn't *stand* Nancy Goldbaum; I was just in love with her stupid body. I wouldn't even be able to go to my own gradua-

7

tion. I didn't care a whole lot about that, though. All I cared about was my mother having to read about what they were going to do to me. It would probably even be on the ten o'clock news, if they found me quick enough. If not, then they'd have to wait until the next night. But they'd show it. The same kind of people who make "Noel" records and graduation records also make the news shows. Anything to make you sick. They'd probably get a big close-up of my bloody face and my pants down, so you'd get the idea that I'd been raped. Bugged. Bugged by some old bugger who probably had *kids* my age. And then they'd go to a commercial for Cheerios and you'd see a bunch of happy kids eating breakfast while I lay dead in the goddamn morgue. That's how the world works. You get used to it after a while.

10:00 P.M. News
Official Script

(*Camera opens on a news guy with bad skin, holes in it from like acne when he was a kid. He's got makeup on and everything, but it doesn't help, it just makes his ears look too white, 'cause they never put makeup on your ears. There's a screen behind him showing a slide of a stickman drowning in a high school fountain with blood on his face and his pants down. The crooked-looking guys are running away from the scene.*)

Anchorman (*facing the camera good naturedly; it's his son's birthday*): Good evening. My son, Bartholomew, is seven tonight. The top story at this hour involves the tragic buggery and murder of a Harrison Godfrey senior, Lenny Blake. Lenny had been attending the Last Dance, though it really isn't the *last* dance, when, as witnesses tell it, a good friend peed on him and sent him running madly toward the school fountain, where he was accosted by two buggers who beat and then bugged him brutally. Seven hundred ice-pick wounds were counted on his poor nearly graduated body. The blood was sickening. The wounds were six feet deep each, beginning in his head and coming out his feet. Police officers said it probably hurt a real lot and that if his mother found out she'd proba-

8

bly gag on her dinner. We hope she doesn't. Sources close to the boy report that he was planning to record a hit record someday, as well as jump all over Nancy Goldbaum at the earliest and most promising moment. And now, a word from Cheerios, the delightful *fun* breakfast cereal that makes you glad you're alive to enjoy it, unlike poor Lenny.

I was so drunk and hurt that I wrote the whole report in my head as these two bastards carried me into a dark office and rested me on a chair. I pretended to be unconscious, but I was waiting. I was ready for them. I figured what I'd do was, I'd come to real quick and do a kung fu chop and break their stupid necks. One of them was fumbling all over the wall for a light switch. I saw my opportunity and, quicker than I thought I could move, considering the lousy shape I was in, I jumped at them.

Something hit my groin and the next thing I knew, I was sliding over a desk, knocking things and papers onto the floor. Then the lights came on. I'd slid clear across the goddamn desk and landed on the floor next to some framed pictures of a bunch of ugly-looking kids. Boy, were they ugly. They looked familiar, like somebody I knew but couldn't put my finger on. Then I looked up and I saw who'd been carrying me. It was no bugger. It was Mr. Atkins, the principal.

We just stared at each other for about a month. I could see blood running down the front of my shirt from my mouth, and I wiped a few drops on my hands. Mr. Atkins stared holes though me while his suit dripped water on the carpet. It was pretty much ruined, the suit. His face was all twisted on account of he was pissed off or something. He had this one little blue vein that stuck out on his forehead, and it throbbed a whole bunch. His hands were at his sides, squeezed into fists, and if you looked real close, you could see them shaking, on account of him being pissed off again, I guessed.

I scratched my head and looked around the office at the crummy art work on the wall, the cheesy furniture that didn't match. Then I sat up, took a deep breath, put the pictures of the ugly kids back on his desk, and said, "Handsome. Handsome kids. They yours?"

Mr. Atkins, he didn't say nothing. He just glared at me.

It was going to be a long night.

9

CHAPTER 2

You could hear the music from the dance way up in Mr. Atkins' office. It was terrible. That group, Flasher, was playing "Let's Get Physical." Things had already gotten about as physical for me as I wanted them to. I could just picture all the kids dancing and making dance lines and thinking they were having fun. Christ. I don't know; high school kids are supposed to be like on the dirty edge of becoming adults, but you'd never know it judging by the kids at Harrison Godfrey. They were like a bunch of stupid infants. Look, who except a half-wit would take a dance contest seriously when every night on TV they talk about nuclear war in Europe? For all they knew, a missile could've been headed straight for Chicago, ready to blow up every home, every school, every *designer jean shop*, for God's sake, and they're dancing to "Let's Get Physical." I was pretty drunk just then, but I think I'd have to get a lot drunker before that kind of stuff would stop bothering me. A lot drunker.

"He's sick—he's a sick boy," Mr. Atkins was saying to the assistant principal, Mr. Morrow. He was the other guy who helped carry me in. Maybe that's why they call him the assistant. I was still on the floor by the desk, watching Mr. Atkins pick up some papers that I'd knocked down. Then, as if he'd just noticed it, he rolled back his shirt sleeve and showed off this little bitty scratch he'd gotten back at the fountain.

"Look! He hit me!" he said, which was really a laugh, because here I was on the floor losing about a gallon of blood a minute from my lip, my nose, and my ankle, and he was upset about some little scratch on his wrist. It made me want to laugh, but when I smiled, it hurt too much, so I just tried to ignore it all.

Then something that wasn't very funny at all happened. Two cops came running in, like maybe there was a crazed maniac waiting inside who had to be shot. One of them, a real mean-looking guy, kept his hand on his gun like at any minute he might have to use it.

Mr. Morrow hung up the phone and said she'd be right over. He was talking about my mother.

"Did you have to call *her?*" I asked, from the floor. "Jesus, did you have to—"

"*You* shut *up!*" Atkins said.

So I shut up. But I really wished he hadn't called my mother. In the first place, my mother practically lives on Valium because she has a bad colon, and in the second place, she'd just gotten divorced from my dad and wasn't taking it too well. She could get upset if the *mail* was late, or if a *light* bulb burned out. She's my mother and all, but she's totally incompetent in situations like the one I'm telling you about.

One of the cops, the mean one, took Mr. Atkins aside and said something in his ear. Maybe they want to take the gold out of my teeth before they throw me in the oven, I thought. They would have made great Nazis, honest. Then Mr. Atkins nodded and went over to Mr. Morrow and whispered something in *his* ear. I didn't know what the hell was going on. Maybe they were going to meet for drinks after they got rid of me. I started thinking that maybe I would have been better off with a deviate. With deviates you can at least reason.

Mr. Morrow came over to me and tried to get me on my feet. He was about as gentle as a gorilla.

"I'm gonna throw up," I told him, so he dumped me in a chair. I really thought I was going to throw up.

"He says he's going to throw up," Morrow said to Atkins.

"Don't!" Atkins said.

How do you like that? Don't throw up. Sure, I'll just hold it. Okay, I won't throw up. What a bastard. He was probably just worried about his tacky carpet. Believe me, I would have done him a favor if I'd've puked all over it.

So then I found out what they'd been whispering about. This one cop, the mean one, came out of Atkins' private bathroom with a bunch of wet towels and started wiping the blood off my face. They weren't so dumb. They didn't want my mother to see how hard he'd hit me when I was in the fountain. I kept them going, though. I mean, I really got back at them. Every time they wiped my face a little too hard with the stinking towels, I sort of held my stomach and said, "I'm gonna throw up."

"You can't!" Atkins shouted.

"Whad'ya mean I can't? Sure I can! I can throw up if I want! It's a free goddamn country. You show me a rule that says I can't throw up, and I won't. Otherwise, I'm gonna puke all over your goddamn ugly carpet."

He made like to come at me, but I knew the score by then.

"You hit me again and I'm gonna sue you and the school board and these two cops. And I'll call the newspapers. And I'll throw up, too!"

That stopped him. One thing school guys hate is when you say "sue" and "newspaper." (They're not too wild about "vomit," either.) They'd rather cut their goddamn wrists than have a scandal in the newspaper. I'll bet there are cases all over Chicago and other big cities where students got *killed*, practically, only they never hit the paper. Kids get knocked around in school a lot, even though they got laws against it. It's true. I've seen it. A lot of times they're able to con the kid's parents by calling it discipline. Everybody respects that word, but I don't. Not when it's used by school guys, because what *discipline* in a school really means is abuse, or torture. You may think I'm exaggerating, but I'm not. If you're a parent, and if I were *you*, what I'd do is, every time a school official used that word in connection with my kid, I'd call a lawyer. And a newspaper. And the radio stations. Then, if the kid felt like it, I'd have him throw up, just for good measure.

I started to fall asleep sitting there. I could hear the cops' portable radio clicking on and off. Once it was about sending some other cops over to Division Street, where there was a man who shot someone in a bar with a shotgun, and once it was about a fire with injuries. Once it was about some poor slob who fell on the third rail of the "L" tracks. When that happens, it's good-bye Charlie. You get fried. In just under thirty minutes, about three people had gotten killed somehow. It was depressing. If I were a cop, I'd quit. Or go crazy.

My mother walked in about an hour later, and by then my cuts were turning into scabs, so most of the blood was gone. She looked terrible. After the divorce she cut her hair real short and took est, which is a load of crap, in my opinion, because it's always the sickest people who get involved in it. Not that my mother's sick, but she isn't well either.

Atkins sat her down at his desk with this very calm, stern air. He told her about how I went crazy in the fountain and had to be taken out by force, and he even showed her the scratch on his goddamn wrist. What a child he was. Then came the bad news. I was expelled. I wouldn't graduate. Then came the really bad news. I was under arrest. The charges were public intoxication, disturbing the peace, and threatening to puke, or something. I don't know.

My mother, she was crying and trying to look brave, but Atkins really had her intimidated. He told her he had my name on a list of drug users in the school, and he brought up the business about the stolen frogs that got loose during the band auditions. He was wrong about that; it was Rick who stole the frogs, but I didn't want to get him into trouble, so I stayed shut up. The drug thing was a lie, too. I don't take drugs. I mean, I'm not even crazy about grass, but once in a while I smoke a joint. I know I shouldn't, but I do occasionally. What had me worried was, a few weeks before, I thought I'd put a few joints in my locker one morning. But when I opened it after English, the joints were gone. I figured maybe I'd been wrong; maybe I'd put them someplace else and just lost them. I wasn't so sure anymore. It could be that there was a locker search that day, and that Atkins had found them. I sure as hell hoped not, though.

Then he told my mother that I was a sick boy. Sick, sick, sick. And that I needed professional help. He said I was a drug addict, and that he had proof. Uh-oh, I thought. I was almost *positive* then that he was the guy who stole my joints. The sneaky bastard. The

13

cops started to read my rights to me, and that's when my mother really came through.

She picked up the telephone like she owned the place and called her attorney. Right in front of Atkins. She said, "Hello? Irv? I wake you? Margaret." My mother's name is Margaret. "Lenny is being arrested for . . . for—What's he being arrested for?"

"Getting wet," I said.

"You shut up!" Atkins said.

"Don't you tell my boy to shut up!" she said. Atta girl, Mom, I thought. For a nervous lady, she was doing fine. Except she was hysterical.

Then she listened on the phone, and the cops' radio kept squawking. She held her hand over the whadayacallit, the mouthpiece, and turned to me. "Irv wants to know if they hit you."

"Yeah. I got a chipped tooth," I said. "They hit me about twenty times."

Atkins was going crazy on account of he lost the upper hand. "He was resisting—"

But my mom cut him off. "You shut up!" she said. She was shaking something awful and kind of crying, too, but she was good. "I want to fill out a complaint," she went on, talking to the cops then, "for aggravated assault and battery." She was listening to Irv and repeating what he was saying. The whole time she kept wiping her forehead with her hand. She does that when she freaks. "Call the newspapers, Irv. Call them and get a reporter out to the— Which district are you boys from?" she asked the cops.

The cops and Atkins went into a discussion, like a huddle. You could tell they watched a lot of Monday night football. When they came out, they said the charges would be dropped. But I was still expelled. My mother picked up her purse and sort of helped me out of the office. I was limping kind of bad because of where I'd hit my ankle.

It was a horrible scene. She drove me to Grant Hospital, where they took X-rays of my leg. It was swollen like a balloon by then. It was very embarrassing, too, because I had to sit in the emergency room with just this little white gown on, and you could see my ass when I stood up. I had to wait about two hours until they had time to take me, because all these much worse emergencies kept coming

14

in. One guy had been stabbed; they carried him in on a stretcher, and the blood was all over his shirt. Just like me. Then—and this is the awful part, I probably shouldn't even tell you—they started running all over the place, all these doctors and nurses, because some baby had been shot in the head. They took it to emergency surgery, and I could hear them in the little curtained room next to me. They were swearing and trying to stitch it back up, but it died. I knew it died when all the commotion stopped.

My mother was out front in the lobby, swallowing Valium like candy, and I was waiting on this table in the back part of the emergency ward, between a dead baby and a guy who'd been stabbed. I felt like dying. How does a baby get shot in the head? I mean, why would somebody *do* that? I know you're supposed to feel sad when something like that happens, but I was angry. I was so pissed off, I remember wanting to shoot everybody who owned a gun. They finally took X-rays and everything was normal. If you call what I just told you *normal*.

I found out what'd happened to the baby, though, just before I left the hospital. I asked a nurse. I said, "Who would shoot a baby in the head?" She told me it was an accident. "Yeah, sure. Accident," I said. "Don't tell me—a guy was trying to get it to stop crying, so he hit it over the head with the closest thing, and it happened to be a gun, and it went off accident-like, right?" She said no, that somebody was cleaning it in the apartment below and it went off. I said "Bullshit," because it sounded like bullshit to me. Well. Now the guy's gun is clean, at least. I hope he's happy how clean his gun is.

It took me a long time to fall asleep, because all the pictures of the night kept flashing through my head. I saw Kevin crying, and me getting beat up in the fountain, and stupid old Atkins at his desk (probably with my three joints in his coat pocket, the crook), and that little baby. I should never have gone out. I should've stayed home and watched the Friday night movie and made some popcorn. But I didn't.

CHAPTER 3

When I woke up, it was late in the morning. I tried to figure out what day it was. It was Saturday, but it took me some time to realize it. My mom and me live in a condo, and my bedroom faces east. I get all the sun in the morning, and today it was real bright. My head felt like Peter Townshend had just broke a guitar over it. I wondered if all the stuff I've told you about was a dream or if it really happened. Then I felt my ankle. It was real, all right.

I stayed in bed for quite a while, just thinking. It seemed kind of funny that everything had happened just because I went for a little dip in a fountain. I started thinking maybe I was *meant* to jump in the fountain, like maybe it was arranged that way. That sounds weird, I know, but sometimes you have to consider things and wonder. But the part that really made me think, the thing that really got me, was somebody shoots a baby and I get wet, and then *I'm* the one who's sick. I know I got a lot of problems, I really do. For instance, I'm scared to go out on the street. I'm afraid I'll get mugged or killed. That probably isn't normal. But I see stuff in the papers all the time, and it amazes me that so many people ignore the headlines and go outside anyway, where maybe the next John Wayne Gacey is. And nuclear war. I worry about that *all* the time. I keep thinking about the radiation coming in the window and making my skin fall off. I saw this one movie about Hiroshima in history class, and all these people kept losing their skin on account of the nuclear radiation.

Then I sort of dumped the idea that it was *meant* to happen, the

16

night before, because it's hard to believe in fate when you don't believe in God. I don't believe in God, most of the time. Sometimes I do, but only on Christmas when they show *A Christmas Carol* by Charles Dickens on TV. Otherwise, I don't. I like Scrooge. I really do. He turned into the nicest and saddest one of the whole bunch. It's kind of hard to like Bob Cratchit, because he's such a wimp. I mean, hey. If you're poor, then don't have so many kids. Use a little birth control, of if you're Catholic or a musician or something, use a little rhythm, why don'tcha? "God helps those who help themselves." Mrs. Cratchit should've told Bob no more often, and then she wouldn't've got knocked up so much. I can only feel sorry for somebody up to a certain point.

But I got other problems. I do. Take for example I'm an only child. That's a problem sometimes. Only children are like *born* sick; I've read articles in women's magazines about it. Like they make up friends they haven't got, or they're lonely all the time or something. I never made up a friend, but I do get lonely a lot. But when you get right down to it, I'm glad I haven't got no brother or no sister. One kid in a nutty family is enough. I mean, it wouldn't be fair to them. If I had a sister, for instance, then she might be like my mother, all worried all the time and everything, and then to have no father living at home, it just wouldn't be worth it. So in a way I'm glad I'm an only child, though I don't like it much, either.

Also, I'm a cynic-like. That's no good, when you're seventeen and a cynic-like. It means you don't believe in anything. Me, I don't believe in anything except rock and roll, maybe, and if you look into it, even that's a rotten business. And being a cynic means you probably also got an arrogant face. I've got one. A lot of my teachers have told me so; they hate me on sight. Even walking down the street, complete strangers sometimes give me the finger, on account of the arrogant thing I've got. Sometimes they just give me dirty looks, but a lot of the time they give me the bird, too, so what I do, I try to look *nicer* whenever I remember to. It's very fake, this *nice* look. It's like I try not to wrinkle my forehead or raise an eyebrow, and I smile. But then there's a problem with being nice. Everybody just thinks you're simple-minded if you walk down the street smiling. And they take advantage of you.

Once—and this happened just last winter—but once I was in a

Winchell's donut place on Clark Street, on the North Side. It was a Saturday, and I took this long walk and just ended up there. I was hungrier than hell and I didn't feel like a hamburger or anything, so I thought it would be a good idea to get about six donuts and make a pig of myself. The place was loaded with weird people who didn't have a lot of money, you could tell. Mostly they just smoked; they didn't eat anything. I was at my table. I'd just sat down when this crazy lady started motioning to me with her hand. She kept putting her hand to her mouth like she was eating, but she wasn't. This was a day I remembered to look nice. I smiled a lot. So she kept putting her hand to her mouth and looking at me. I finally said, "Would you like a donut?" and she started nodding her head like crazy. So I gave her a strawberry-coconut donut, and that left five for me. I bit into this chocolate one next, and then this guy at another table, he says, "'Scuse me. You got a cigarette?" And so I put my chocolate donut down and gave him a cigarette. Then he wanted a match. By then, all the crummy-looking people in the joint were coming up to me and asking me for stuff. One guy, he wanted a quarter. I asked him for what, and he said he wanted a cup of coffee, so I gave him *my* cup of coffee and got up and left. I wasn't smiling anymore, and as I was walking out the door, the guy who wanted a quarter gave me the finger. You can't win.

It was pretty late in the day, but I was still in bed. I was wearing my pajamas and this be-bop hat I got down on Lincoln Avenue. That's where all the blues clubs in Chicago are. Every once in a while my mother would come to the door and tell me Rick was on the phone, or that Lisa, this girl I know, was on the phone. Rick said something about how our band had a job next week, and Lisa didn't say what she wanted. Lisa's mother owns one of those night-clubs on Rush Street that you always hear about. I didn't want to play with the band, and I just didn't feel *handsome* enough to talk to a girl at the moment. I told my mother each time that I didn't want to talk. Then it was my father on the phone, and I told her I didn't want to talk to him, either. When I get in a mood, I just don't want to talk to anyone. I picked up my guitar and started playing it in bed. Sometimes I can play for hours and just forget where I am.

What I sort of wished, I wished my parents weren't divorced. That's another problem I forgot to list before. I thought it would be

18

nice if we could all sit down together and iron things out. But even when my parents *were* together, all they did was fight. I remember one horrible fight they had in the morning when my dad was on his way to work. My dad, he's a banker. He was leaving for work one morning and they started fighting about something. I don't know what, something stupid, you can bet on that. That fight lasted all the way down to the lobby, where my mom followed him. All the neighbors and the doorman and everybody saw them screaming at each other. It was highly embarrassing. For days I used the garage exit whenever I had to go anywhere. They weren't meant for each other, my parents. Most people who get married just weren't meant for each other.

I got hungry around five o'clock in the afternoon. I put down my guitar and walked into the kitchen to see what we had in the old refrigerator. I knew it wouldn't be much, because my mother, since the divorce—when she cut her hair short and started going to law school—stopped being much of a home keeper, or housekeeper. She was always going on about women's rights and all that, which I personally can't stand, and so we ordered in food a lot. About a hundred times a week we had Chinese or pizza. I was turning into a sweet and sour anchovy. I started thinking about that, that change in my mother, and it made me kind of worry because she was beginning to look a little bit like Billie Jean King. She didn't play tennis, though. She did aerobic dancing, which is worse.

So anyway, I walked into the kitchen and I heard these voices coming from the living room. Sounded like men's voices. I grabbed a slice of cold pizza from the fridge and walked out there to see who it was.

I wasn't ready for this. It was my father, and a counselor from school, Dr. Kollbisk. They stood up when they saw me. I just stood there with pizza in my mouth, not chewing or anything, I mean.

"Lenny," my father said. He was kind of surprised to see me up and around; you could tell. "Lenny, how are you feeling?"

He didn't yell at me or nothing about getting kicked out of school. I still had pizza in my mouth, but it hurt to chew, from where Mr. Atkins had hit me. It took me about an hour to chew that goddamn pizza, boy. I nodded and tried to swallow. But you can't swallow cold pizza unless it's chewed well. It like cuts your throat.

19

"You know Dr. Kollbisk, don't you, Lenny?" my mom said. I just nodded. I hadn't got anything to drink in the kitchen and I felt the hiccups coming on. Then they told me Dr. Kollbisk might be able to get me back in school before graduation.

"Don't waste your time," I told him, with my mouth full, and then I left the room. The last thing in the world I wanted to think about was going back to school. I closed the door behind me and got back in bed. All of a sudden I wanted a beer. I called up Rick to see if he could bring some over, but he wasn't home. When you need somebody, that's when they're not there. About a second later there was a knock on my door and I was starting to get pissed. It's not that I didn't appreciate my parents' concern. I did. It just seemed like a little late to start thinking about making a sane boy out of me. See, Dr. Kollbisk, he's the psychologist at school. He handles the nuts.

It was Dr. Kollbisk at the door. He said, "Can I come in, Lenny?"

I said sure, sure he could. If I would've said *no*, I would've sounded like a baby. He sat on this chair by my desk and started looking around the place. I got back in bed and picked up my guitar.

"This is a nice room," he said. He didn't know where to begin, you could tell. But those psychological guys always *act* like they're at home, and like they haven't got ulterior motives. I can see right through them.

"Thanks," I said, playing a few chords. I just played soft-like. You can't hear an electric guitar too loud unless you plug it into an amplifier. Dr. Kollbisk was eyeing everything in my room, checking the place out, and playing with a canister of Mace which I keep on my desk for emergencies. Then he stopped playing with it, read the label, and put it back real gently, like he thought it might explode in his face. He sort of stared at the windows for a while. He had a very thin face, tired-looking, and a beard. He sort of made you feel like he had X-ray vision, the way he just stared at things.

"May I ask—would you think it rude if I asked you why you have aluminum foil on your windows?"

He thought it was weird, you could tell. Psychological guys always go for what they think is weird first.

20

"No special reason," I said. "I like it like that."

Just in case *you* think I'm weird, too, I do it because it keeps the creeps in the other high rises from looking in with binoculars. Or telescopes. If you think I'm exaggerating, you just go visit somebody on Lake Shore Drive in Chicago and see if the bastard doesn't have a telescope or a pair of binoculars in his living room. They all do it. At night, if you look out the window, you can count about a thousand people spying on each other. It's sick, but they do it. Also, I read that Elvis used to do that, put up aluminum foil, whenever he went to a new hotel. Everybody thought he was nuts, too, but I don't personally blame him. *They* go around spying on you in your own home, and if *you* put up aluminum foil to keep them from doing it, then *you're* the one who's crazy. That's the secret. All the crazy people try to convince the sane ones that *they're* crazy. I'm used to it.

Then, after he looked around the room a few more times, he told me I play the guitar good. Well. That was nice. He probably didn't know a guitar from a vibrator, but it was nice anyway. He was an antsy guy. He couldn't sit still. He started walking around the room and tripped over one of my fire ladders that I keep rolled up under the windows.

"What's this?" he wanted to know.

"It's a fire ladder," I told him. "Rope ladders, like you see on TV shows when a place is burning to a crisp and people have to escape. If there's ever a fire in this place, I'll be able to get out quick. I got one for my mom, too, but she keeps hers in her closet. She shouldn't. She should keep it rolled up right under her window, in case of an emergency or something.

He seemed surprised-like. He said that if there was a fire, I should take the stairs, because I was on the eighteenth floor and the ladders wouldn't reach.

"That's where you're wrong. I got it all figured out." I took him to the far window and peeled some of the aluminum foil away. "See? Right down there, next to our building, is another building. It's ten stories tall, and that's how far the ladders reach. When I get down there, I just jump to the roof of that other building and I'm safe. See?"

He said he saw. I taped the aluminum foil back. Then I showed him my fire extinguishers. I keep them on the walls in my bed-

21

room. And my smoke alarm. I got a smoke alarm right near the door. He sort of smiled.

"Think two extinguishers will be enough?" he asked, joking-like.

"I got another one in my closet." I opened my closet door to show him.

He cleared his throat. He had a frog in his throat all the time. "Let me get straight to the point, Lenny," he said. "I've talked to your parents about what happened to you last night, and it seems to me you got the raw end of the deal."

I said, yeah; I got the raw end of Mr. Atkins' hand, too, and the chipped tooth to prove it. He said he wanted to help make sure I could graduate, and that he thought he could do it.

"I don't want to graduate," I told him.

He was still walking around the room. That guy couldn't sit still. "Sure you do," he said.

"No I don't," I said.

"Lenny, think about your parents for a second. Your parents are quite worried about you right now, and—"

"Wanna bet?" I said.

He just got this blank look—like he'd just run out of X-ray vision—and said, "Pardon?"

"I said they're not worried about me. Oh, sure—they don't want me to be in trouble or anything. But the reason they want you to get me back in is so they don't have to tell other parents that their kid got kicked out of school. It's true."

Then he said that I was speaking out of bitterness, that the divorce must have been rough for me to go through. I just laughed. I walked to the door of my room and opened it. You could hear my parents yelling at each other from the living room. My dad was saying that my mother was incompetent as a parent. My mother was saying that *he* didn't care enough about either one of us to pay enough alimony or child support.

"You're a lying, devious bitch!" my father said. I closed the door and got back into bed.

"I'd rather have them divorced, believe me." I think he got my point.

Dr. Kollbisk was about to say something. I could see it coming a mile away. He started walking around again, and this time he picked up my baseball bat that was leaning against the wall. He

22

swung it once or twice. He was showing me what a great athlete he was.

"You like baseball, don't you, Lenny?" he said, swinging once more, like he thought he was Reggie Jackson.

"No. I hate baseball. It's *boring.*"

He said then how come I have a baseball bat in my room, if I think it's boring?

"That's in case somebody tries to break in, so I can knock their goddamn head off. Haven't you ever heard of home invasion?" You'd think he never heard of home invasion or anything.

"You know," he said, putting the bat down, "there's such a thing as being *too* careful."

"No there isn't. I watch the news. I read the newspapers. Home invasion happens all the time. Some guys come in and steal your stuff and tie you up and rape you and then slit your throat. Don'tcha read the papers?"

"Why, certainly, I read the papers, but I—"

"Well, all *right*, then! First they take your stuff, and then they bugger you or something. You really ought to carry Mace," I told him. "Do you?"

"No. I don't see the need—"

"Oh, there's need, okay. Believe me, there's need. Take mine. Go ahead."

He was a little confused. "No, thanks, but—"

"Go ahead," I said. *Please* take it with you. I got more. Please."

He picked it up and was about to put it in the inside pocket of his sport coat. You had to tell this guy everything. Some people, I don't know how they've survived in the city as long as they have.

"Not like that," I said, getting out of bed to show him. "Put it in your right-hand pocket, and then keep your hand on it. Then if somebody tries to mug you, pull it out quick, and point it right at his face, so he chokes to death. You just keep spraying, and when he's good and Maced, you run like hell. Got it?"

"Got it," he said. At least he listened. Most people don't listen.

Since he listened to me, I figured I should be polite and listen to him. He only wanted to talk about me going back to school, though. He told me about the value of education, which has nothing to do with it, since high school doesn't have anything more to do with education than Jell-O. But I saw his point. His point was

23

that I couldn't get a job without a diploma, which is true. You can't get a job *with* a diploma, either, but if you graduate, at least you have the diploma. He wanted to know what I wanted to do with my life. I told him living it would be enough. He meant a career, though. What career did I have mapped out. I said I didn't have one mapped out. So he tried to get me in a conversation about what I wanted to do.

"Maybe I could be a musician," I said.

"Maybe," he said.

"Maybe I could do what you do, help nut cases." It sounded like something I'd be good at. I'm used to nuts.

"Not without a college degree, you won't," he said. Everything was diploma or degree.

"Fine. Then I won't."

"And I don't just work with *nuts*. Take yourself, for instance. I'm trying to work with you."

Then I laughed. "You don't think I'm nuts?"

He said no, he didn't.

I watched him for a while. I wanted to see if he was just humoring me. I don't think so, though. He *did* take the Mace, which showed he had some sense.

"Mr. Atkins thinks I'm nuts," I told him. "He said it to my mother—that I'm sick, sick, sick. 'Cause I jumped in the fountain. Hey, you're the doctor. Who do you think is sick? The guy who jumps in the fountain, or the guy who beats up the guy in the fountain?"

He said he'd just talked to Mr. Atkins at his home, and that he'd worked out a deal with him, which is why he came over to see me. He was like one of those union negotiators. The trouble with negotiators is, half the time you don't know who he's negotiating *for*. For example, he never did tell me who was nuts—the guy who jumps in the fountain, or the guy who beats up the guy in the fountain. But like I said, I owed it to him to listen, so I let him spill his guts.

"Here it is: you *may* be able to graduate. Under certain conditions."

"I gotta get a lobotomy, right?"

He didn't laugh. He was a tough audience. I started thinking maybe that really *was* one of the conditions.

24

"No lobotomy," he said, "but you would have to see me three times a week for the next two weeks, regular office visits. Next, you are *not* allowed on campus *except* for those visits. If you do that, if you accept that part of it and don't miss any visits, you still have to hand in a sizable project."

"Like what?" I asked. I wondered just what he meant, *sizable*.

"Well, I've talked to your parents, and they tell me you're on the creative side. You like to write songs and poetry. I thought maybe some writing, to explain why you do the things you do, and to communicate your feelings, which—it seems to me—you don't quite do often enough." His X-ray eyes were working again. That guy could see through you or something.

"What kind of writing? I mean, what do I have to say?"

"Exactly what you want. Just as long as you express your feelings and do it in some legible form."

"Anything I want to say?"

"Anything," he said.

I got up from my bed and opened the door again. My mother was in hysterics, crying. She was saying how she wished she'd never met him, my father. I closed the door. I could tell it made Dr. Kollbisk uncomfortable, but I had to giggle anyway. Here were these two grown divorced people blaming each other because they ever *met*. My parents are nuts. I like them, but they're still nuts. Even so, I wasn't making their lives any saner by getting kicked out.

I asked Dr. Kollbisk who'd read it, what I wrote. He said only him and my English teacher, Mr. Simons, who was an all-right guy. He smoked grass with us on a class picnic.

I started pacing back and forth. I do that when I'm trying to make a decision. Dr. Kollbisk said, "You've had enough experiences in school and enough opinions about them to use as material, don't you?"

"Shit! Yes. Are you kidding? I could write a book."

He said good, because that's exactly what I'd have to do. The project was two hundred pages long—book length.

"What?" I said. He must have been crazy. "Whose lousy idea was that?"

"Mine."

"Oh," I said.

That's my assignment. I gotta write this goddamn book.

25

CHAPTER 4

et me tell you a story. Once there was this very average guy who lived in a very average town and lived this very average boring life. One day he got this newspaper slid under his average door that warned him he was going to get robbed if he went out, or worse. That a building might fall on him as he walked down his very average street, or that maybe, if he went outside, he was going to get his guts blown out by a shotgun blast, and then it went on to say that if he made it home, with his intestines hanging out, he'd find his very average wife and snotty kids cut to pieces after having gotten raped and tortured. Only, he didn't believe the paper. All his friends saw the paper, too, but like him, they were average slobs and they didn't believe it, either. So he puts the paper down and then—get *this*—he eats breakfast, talks to his wife about her est class or her aerobic dancing class, and *then* he turns on the TV while he's putting on his tie. On the TV he sees a bunch of dead people being carried out of their homes after they've been killed and raped and mutilated. They show some guy who was crossing the street who got run over by a new Mercedes. They show all of it. All of the blood and guts and death and shit, and then, do you know what this very average guy does? He *whistles*. He puts on his hat, kisses his wife good-bye, pats his snot-nosed kids on the head, and the asshole goes to work.

While he's at his desk at work, his average wife answers the average front door and gets raped by two big guys who make the kids watch, and then they rape them, too. All this is happening and the

26

average guy is still at his desk at work. He doesn't know his wife and kids have had their throats slashed (even though the papers and the TV warned him), so when he calls and they don't answer, he figures they went to McDonald's or someplace for lunch, like in the commercials. He pictures his kids laughing and playing with Ronald McDonald, and actually, they're killed. And buggered. So when it comes time to go home, he walks to the bus stop, looks at his watch, feels an average pistol pushed up against his back, and he still doesn't believe it's happening to him. He turns around, the jerk, and gets shot in the stomach. The mugger takes his money and then kicks him in the head. So this average bleeding-to-death guy crawls home with the inside of his stomach hanging out all over the street, and when he gets there, his average wife and kids are dead and brutalized. And you know what? He's *surprised*. Then he dies. The next day, all his friends and neighbors see this guy in the paper and on TV, and you know what? *They're* surprised, too. Then what they do, after reading about it and seeing it on TV, they kiss their average wives good-bye and pat their average snot-nosed kids on their heads, and—this is the hot part—*they go to work*.

If you were Helen Keller or somebody it would be different. Then I wouldn't blame you for not paying attention. But it's right in the goddamn paper every goddamn day and people think it's like soap operas or something, that the stuff doesn't really happen. I live in Chicago. In *Chicago* people don't even believe it, but every morning it's right there. They don't make that stuff up. It's real. Out of about two million people in the crummy city, I'm willing to bet that over *half* of them will someday pick up a gun or rape somebody's mother or sister or kid or grandmother, even. They're going to do it. And then everybody related to the victim will be surprised.

I woke up the next morning thinking about all this, which is nothing out of the ordinary for me; I wake up most mornings thinking about this stuff, only this time I decided to prove my point. I got dressed and took the elevator downstairs to get a paper. I figured maybe I was wrong. Maybe there's one day I can go into the lobby, get a paper, and when I open it up maybe there won't be one depressing story. I mean, if everybody seems to think that stuff *isn't*

27

average, then okay. I'll pick an average day and go down and see who's right. Me or them.

Down in the lobby, our doorman, James, was helping some rich-looking couple get their luggage in their new Jaguar. There were three pieces of expensive-looking luggage, and the guy who owned them was young and strong, but he made James put the goddamn luggage in the back seat while he held the door. It figured. I see it all the time, but it still makes me mad. The lobby was sold out of papers, so I walked down to Oak Street and picked up my paper at a stand. Then I went to the Bagel Nosh for breakfast. I remembered to keep my right hand in my pants pocket, on my Mace. Rush Street isn't too bad in the morning, but I'm the guy who reads the paper. I'm the only guy in the whole world who *believes* I'll get shot just like everybody else.

I got orange juice, cheesecake, a bagel, paid for them, and then went upstairs where they got these windows that look right onto Rush Street. I decided I wasn't going to look at the paper until I got home, safe in my room, with the goddamn door locked. Besides, why ruin breakfast? If you read the paper *before* you eat, then you got a reason to run home. I was having a very leisure-like breakfast when this drunk guy came walking upstairs with another guy who wasn't so drunk, but he had on these black pants—bell bottoms— and these pointy type shoes. I knew it was trouble. I kept my mind on my cheesecake, and then one of 'em, he touches me on the shoulder and says, "That's a big table, ya know. That's for more than one person. Why don't ya take one in the back, you sonofabitch."

I put my hand on my Mace and ignored him. But he pushes me again. I looked up, put my fork down, and stood up. I didn't look nice, either; I looked angry, and arrogant. But this guy was either too drunk or too stupid to notice. I was all shaky-like, and I was about to pull out my canister of Mace, when this big truck driver–type gets up from his table and walks over and pushes the guys away and tells them *he's* having breakfast with me, and would they like to try to make *him* move? Christ, was I shaking. The drunk guys, they just walked away and said how we were mother-fuckers. Then the truck driver type, he brings his coffee over to my table and sits down. I sat down then, too. He just sipped his coffee.

"Hey," I told him. "Thanks. Ya know? Thanks."

"Don't mention it, kid," he says. "Next time that happens to you, you *move*. They could have killed you. Don't be no hero."

"You're right, you're right. Jesus. Thanks."

I was pretty lucky, that guy being there, until I finished my breakfast. When I finished my breakfast, he kept buying me more coffee so I'd stick around. He kept telling me what was my hurry. Then he starts to talk about this apartment he's got down the street, and maybe I'd like to come home with him to see these records he's got. To *listen* to them, he meant. I told him no, I couldn't. I really couldn't. And then he wants my phone number. I was being picked up. He was a faggot. I'm not saying I wasn't grateful on account of he saved my life, but then he wanted to—you know. You know what he wanted to do. I got up real fast and said I had to catch a train. He said he'd drive me, but I was already halfway down the stairs by then. When I was out on the street, I looked back up at the big round window of the Bagel Nosh, and he was watching me. So I waved, just so I wouldn't look stupid or something, and he waved back. Then I ran like hell. I even forgot to take my paper with me. But I didn't care. If I hadn't left when I did, you would've read about me in the late edition, under the buggery section.

I stopped for a paper at the same stand I got the first one, and then I kept running home. I ran right past James, the doorman, and just said, "Hi, James." I was lucky 'cause there was an elevator waiting for me. James said, "Hey, Lenny," and waved, but the door shut before he could say anything else. I was relieved as shit. My heart was pounding and my trigger finger was all sweaty on my Mace. When I got to the eighteenth floor, I opened the door to our condo, ran to my room, locked the door, and threw the paper on the bed. I real quick turned on my TV and switched to channel thirteen. Channel thirteen is where you can watch the lobby of my building. You can see all the people come in and everything. I just sat and watched it for about an hour, to make sure the guy from the Bagel Nosh didn't follow me. Then I opened up the paper on my bed, and this is what I found:

WOMAN RAPED; FORCED TO BREAST-FEED BABY

A twenty-seven-year-old woman was the victim of home

invasion and rape Friday night in her Streamwood home. Carol Jennings, of 4353 Marble Oaks Terrace, opened the door of her home after repeated ringing of the front door-bell. Two unidentified men then invaded her home, severely beat her husband, and then forced the young wife and mother to have sex with them while breast-feeding her baby, age seven months. Police are looking for two Caucasian males, of about thirty to thirty-five years of age, driving a white late-model Chevrolet.

That was on page two. I kept wondering if they made her husband watch while that was happening, and if they did, how did he feel? Me, I'd commit suicide if somebody ever made me watch something like that. Even if the woman wasn't my wife. Then I started thinking what must have been going in that poor woman's mind. And afterward, how was she going to go on with her life? A bunch of friends and relatives would probably make sure she went to a shrink, and they'd keep telling her to forget, and that life goes on. But how could she forget? And if life goes on, then isn't there a chance that more terrible stuff will happen? Maybe worse? But how could it get worse? Maybe that's how she'll get by. Maybe she'll figure how could it get worse? I don't know. All I know is I jumped in a fountain and the principal of my school thinks I'm sick. They say, "Tell us how you feel, Lenny. Write us a book. Express what makes you sick." This is what makes me sick. And I was only on page two.

On page seven, I found this one:

NUN MUGGED; IN COMA

At seven-thirty Friday night, on North Milwaukee Ave., a forty-three-year-old Sister of Loretto was accosted by an unknown black male in the 2700 block area. Sister Agnes Marie was forced to the ground, where she was brutally given repeated kicks to the head. The assailant fled on foot with the nun's purse, which contained a small amount of cash and a daily missal. Sister Agnes is in stable condition, though in a coma, at St. Michael's Hospital. Police have no other clues in the robbery.

30

I got depressed again, so I looked at channel thirteen a bit longer and watched a bunch of people coming and going in the lobby. I could tape channel thirteen and call it *My Lobby* and sell it to ABC. Really. It would probably get an Emmy. One guy down there, he didn't look kosher. He kept hanging around, and I saw James help some more people with bags and stuff out of their car. I didn't know if he saw the guy, so I picked up the phone and called James's desk. It took a while, but he answered.

"Lake Shore Square," he answered. That's the name of our building.

"Hello. James? It's Lenny. Lenny Blake."

"Hey there, Lenny. I saw you a while ago run in like you was on fire, babe. Those girls just won't leave you alone, huh? Heh-heh!"

James, he's a great guy. It wasn't girls I was running from, but I didn't want to tell him about that. I wish it *would've* been girls.

"Yeah," I said, kind of hurried, 'cause I couldn't see the guy in the lobby camera anymore. "Hey, James, is there a guy with like a cap on and a short jacket in the lobby? Didja see anyone like that about a second ago, by any chance?"

James, he looked up at the camera then and smiled. "Sure I did. You watchin' the Lobby Show again, Lenny?"

"Yeah. Yeah, I am. Look, the reason I ask—"

But all of a sudden James started waving at the camera and making faces. Then he started dancing-like and tipping his hat. He's the funniest man in the world. He's the only guy who could crack me up while I'm being serious. No shit. James could start dancing and making faces while I'm being murdered and I'd still laugh.

"How'm I doin', Lenny?" he said into the phone.

"Fine. You're doin' fine, James. Listen, the reason I ask, about that guy with the short jacket, I mean. He looks a little suspicious. Whad'ya think?"

James, now *he* started laughing. "I'd say he's about the most *suspicious* man I ever seen, Lenny. He only owns three goddamn condos in this here building. He used to own the whole friggin' building before it was converted. You want I should arrest him?"

That was a relief. I mean, I felt stupid, but I'd rather feel stupid than be sorry any day. I did feel pretty stupid, though.

"Lenny? You still there?"

31

"Yeah. Sorry about the false alarm, though, James. Just being careful."

"You can never be too careful, Lenny," he said. He thinks like me. He's a doorman. He knows. Then he said, "You got a number you can lay on me, Lenny? I gotta work the whole day, and I can't do that straight. Not a whole day. No sir."

What he meant by a *number* was a joint. I don't give him tips—I give him presents. He likes grass the best. I told him I'd bring one down in a little while and he said thanks. Then he hung up. I was about to turn the set off when James did something very funny in the camera. I won't tell you what. Use your imagination. He sort of made me feel a little better after reading the paper. Good old James. It made me feel sad about him being a doorman, but he did okay. He knew what bullshit it all was and he was happy anyway. I admire him, I really do.

I left the TV on then. The TV is sometimes good company if you're feeling lonely. I was feeling lonely. There's no sound or anything on channel thirteen, but sometimes it helps just to have the picture in the room with you. I watched for a while longer and I saw this real little girl go out the front door with her mother. She had just taken some gum or something—maybe it was just sticky candy—out of her mouth. She was trying to throw it away, but she couldn't get it off her hand. Her mother was out the door by then, and this little girl kept trying to wipe off the gum on the wall, but it wouldn't come off. It was hysterical. When you're a very little kid, about the only thing you have to worry about is whether you can get the gum off your hand or not. James must have saw her too, because the next thing you know, he went over to her, took out his handkerchief, and wiped the gum off her hand for her. Then she smiled and skipped out the door. James, he couldn't get the gum off his handkerchief, so he just rolled it up and threw it away. That's the kind of guy James is. He'd give you his handkerchief if your kid had gum all over her hands.

I started turning the pages of the newspaper again. I didn't have anything else to do. Besides, that was only two stories I found. If those were the only two stories like that in the whole paper, I would've been surprised. I would've been *glad*, naturally, but I would've been surprised.

On page fourteen, in a small article titled "Decapitated Boy Found in Mother's Home," I got to read how some twenty-one-year-old lady went home to visit her mother in a housing project and found her eight-year-old brother pushed in a closet with no head. It was a very small article, and it never did say if they found his head or not. It just said the mother was being charged with child abuse and neglect. What—did they think his goddamn head fell off because she just *neglected* him? Christ, the law. The law never gets things straight. What they must do, they must feel sorry for the parent because now the kid is dead, and so they give 'em a ticket instead of sending them to the electric chair. I don't like the electric chair. But shit, I don't like eight-year-old boys being found without their heads, either.

Then I started wondering how she cut his head off. It's sick to wonder about that stuff. I know it is. But what are you supposed to do? Not think about it, like everybody else? You know, just because you don't think about something doesn't mean it goes away or gets any better. So I thought about it. I started thinking about how the whole scene happened when that twenty-one-year-old lady came home to visit her mother:

Scene

(Twenty-one-year-old black lady goes to visit her mother in a housing project. Among the poor black people who come and go, looking a little unemployed whether they got diplomas or not, is a well-dressed former mayor with a fox coat and a grocery bag full of chitlins, whatever they are. Everybody ignores the mayor, because she calls everybody "brother" and they don't want to hear her say it.

Door opens.)

21-year-old woman: Hi, Mama.

Mother: Hey, sweets. You finally come visit yer old mama after livin' with them white folks fo' the last three years?

21-year-old woman: Sure 'nough. Ackshully, I come home to see Junior, too. Where be that li'l alligator? He playin' with the street gangs that sell dope?

33

Mother: Nope.

21-year-old woman: Well then, he be followin' the rats around the hallway?

Mother: Nope.

21-year-old woman: Well. I do declare. He be watchin' the TB?

Mother: Uh-uh. Ain't got no TB.

21-year-old woman: I give up. Where he be?

Mother: He be in the closet.

(Twenty-one-year-old woman opens closet door and finds boy with no head. Look of alarm comes into her face.)

21-year-old woman: Mama! Junior be here, but his head don't be! Where it be? It be in the pantry?

Mother: Nope.

21-year-old woman: Well then, it be under the—

(Two policemen and the former mayor come to the door checking on a report of a boy with no head.)

First cop: All right, lady. That your kid with no head?

Mother: Um-hmm. I always says that boy so forgetful he 'bout forget his head if it wasn't attached. He done forgot it, anyway.

Second cop: Well, you should watch your son more carefully. We're taking you in for child neglect. Soon as you find the head, we'll drop the charges.

21-year-old woman: It be in the microwave?

Mother: Nope.

Former Mayor: When you get back, sister, will you please show me the best way to prepare chitlins under glass? And come election day, don't you all forget who fixed your toilets so they work.

21-year-old woman: It be in the toilet, Mama?

Jesus. Child neglect. I turned the pages slowly after that one, 'cause I was scared what I was going to find next. Nothing on page sixteen. Nothing on page seventeen. On page nineteen, though, there was one about an eighteen-year-old who played Russian roulette after watching the movie *The Deer Hunter*. It told where he lived and all, but I'm not going to put that part in. I figure if anybody ever reads this, I should save the family the embarrassment of letting everybody know who had such a dumb kid. Usually, you know, when you play Russian roulette, you do it with one bullet in a revolver, which is stupid enough. It's sick enough that way. But this kid, who was nearly my age and everything, he played Russian roulette with a fully loaded *automatic*. Guess what happened?

Then, right below that one was a story called "Hero Stabbed Chasing Robbers." It was all about some guy who was watching a purse stealing incident on the "L," and he got brave and got stabbed for it. He's in serious condition in some hospital. It reminded me of what that faggot told me that morning, "Don't be a hero." He may have been a faggot, but he was right. Heroes get it more often than the chickens in the world.

I'd had enough of the paper. It was an average day, just like I told you. It was an average paper. Who's right? Me or them?

You figure it out.

CHAPTER 5

fter I turned off the TV, I threw away the newspaper. But not before I cut out the grossest stories. What I have is, I have a whole collection of stories like the ones I showed you, and I keep them filed in a secret place in my room. I probably shouldn't keep them, because they just depress me, but I don't want to forget to be careful. Someday, if I have kids or something, and when they're old enough and start asking me what it was like in the good old days, I'll just hand them the file and tell them to stop reading when they feel like throwing up. You shouldn't lie to kids.

Then what I did, I picked up my baseball bat and took some practice swings at my bed. If you keep something in your room for protection, you should practice with it once in a while. You just stack your pillows up and pretend they're a home invader, and then you lift the bat clear over you and pretend you're smashing the guy's goddamn head. You should do two quick swings at a time, in case you ever miss him on the first one. You won't have time to check if you got him good if it ever really happens to you. And it probably will.

I promised James I'd bring him a number, so I rolled two at my desk. I'm not saying where I keep my grass, because as soon as someone reads this they'll probably try to bust me. But I keep it in a place that nobody would find in a million years. I figure when they send the cops out here, they'll search the place like crazy, tearing apart all my stuff and everything. They could bring dogs, too. They do that sometimes. But even the dogs won't find it. Then I'll sue them for destruction of property and false arrest. Then I'll smoke a joint.

I'm a pretty good joint roller. It's not because I smoke a lot of grass—I don't. I just smoke it once in a while when I feel in the mood. But I roll them for all my friends, so I stay in practice. Also, I got pretty steady hands. If I had the grades, and if I hadn't got thrown out of high school, I could have been a surgeon. Except I can't stand blood. If they ever wanted me to operate on anybody, they'd have to take all his blood out first. But then he'd be dead, so what would be the point? If I could stand blood, and guts, *then* I'd be a good surgeon. But I can't.

I took the elevator down to the lobby and waited for James to finish this conversation he was having with some fat guy who lives in my building. I was just waiting by his doorman's stand. He's got a little desk there and he reads stuff when it gets slow. James is a pretty educated guy. I mean, he may just be a doorman and everything, but that doesn't keep him from reading and finding out about things.

The fat guy, he was talking to James about food. It figured. Here's this fat-assed sucker who you'd think would be ashamed to *admit* that he eats, because of the way he looks, but instead he's talking about it as if it's the only thing he ever does. It probably is. I don't like fat people much. If you've ever seen a fat guy eat, you'd know why. They like to pretend that they're all the time on some kind of diet, but don't let them fool you. Baskin-Robbins shops all over the world are right this very minute filled with fat people who just got through telling their doorman or somebody that they're on a diet.

James finally got rid of the slob and came over to where I was standing by his little desk. I slipped him two joints in his pocket. You couldn't even tell.

"Lenny, my man. Thank you. You saved my ass today, babe."

"Don't mention it," I told him. "Pretty slow day, huh?"

James, he just said, "Shit." But he said it like it was all whispered, like, "Sheeeeeeeeeeeeeet." He said, "It ain't got nothin' to do with slow or fast. It just *is*. How're those women treatin' you, hmm? They ever catch you this mornin'?"

37

"No. And I wasn't running from *women*," I said, looking around the lobby to make sure we were alone.

"No? Who besides women chasin' you? You ain't gone over to the other side?" Then he laughed. He just laughed his ass off. What he meant about going over to the other side was turning into a fag. He was just kidding, though. James kids me a lot.

I asked him if it was all right if we went someplace and smoked a joint together. He looked around, kind of careful-like, and then nodded. I followed him outside into the garage. The garage is dark and nobody can't tell if you aren't just smoking a cigarette in there. James, he lit one of the joints and took a big hit off it, and then passed it to me. You ought to see James smoke grass. He does it better than anybody I ever seen. He doesn't make a big star trip out of it, he just does it very polished and refined. He keeps all the smoke in his lungs a long time and then exhales it back up his nose and then out his mouth again. He does it very good. Well.

"What you been up to, Lenny?" he says, after he's let all the smoke go.

"Nothing. I got kicked out of high school for good two nights ago, though."

James's eyes got big and he looked real hurt all of a sudden. "No!" he says. I nodded. "Why? How come? You was 'bout to graduate, wasn't you, Lenny?"

I told him the whole story, then. I told him about jumping in the fountain and about Rick pissing on everybody and about Kevin crying and his mother committing suicide. I even showed him my chipped tooth from where Mr. Atkins hit me.

After he listened (and he listened good; James is the best listener in the world—it's like he cares), he shook his head and passed the joint back to me. "Lenny," he said, "Lenny, you got to get your education. I don't care how and I don't care about no Mr. Atkins, but you just *got* to get you your education, babe. You understan'?"

I said yeah, I understood, but it's hard telling James about Harrison Godfrey High School. James kept saying how I had to get my education. I told him yeah, I knew, and that there was a counselor at the school who was trying to help me graduate. He said that was good. Then to like switch the topic, I said, "Hey, James. Do black people ever tell white-people jokes? I mean—you know. White

38

people are always telling jokes about black people, and I kind of wondered. Do black people tell jokes about white people?"

James just about bust his gut. "Sheeeeeeeeet!" he said. "That's about all we ever *do* do."

I asked him if he could tell me one.

He thought for a minute, put the joint out on the inside of his shoe, and then started: "See, Whitey, he take up sky diving 'cause he hears it's the greatest feelin' in the world, just fallin' through the sky—no buses, no taxicabs. An' 'cause all the other Whiteys do it, he want to do it too. That's the way Whitey is. One Whitey do it, all the other Whiteys want to do it too. Like designer jeans."

I was laughing already. "That what you call us? Whitey?"

"Sometimes Whitey, sometimes honky, sometimes fey-Whitey. You interruptin' my story."

I told him I was sorry, that he should go on.

"So Whitey, he don't got time to learn things right, to do them the *right* way. He just hand over a whole fistful o' money and say drop me out the plane. The guy keeps tellin' him he got to learn the ins and outs, but Whitey want to do it *his* way. Just like everything else. So they take Whitey up in the plane and he lookin' out the window at the ground way below, and he say, 'Drop me now,' so the man drops Whitey and Whitey go fallin' way, way down. As Whitey be fallin', he lookin' around and enjoyin' hisself, 'cause now he's like all the other Whiteys he seen in them beer commercials. Then he figure he gone far 'nough, so he pulls the cord. Nothin' happen. But Whitey, he ain't ruffled 'cause he knows he got an emergency parachute. He pulls the cord, and nothin' happen again. Now he be shittin' bricks. As he fallin' he sees the damnedest thing. He sees another Whitey come shootin' up from the ground with all kind of smoke and flames comin' out of his ass. As he passed, he says to the other Whitey, 'Excuse me. But do you happen to know anything about parachutes?' And the other Whitey, he say, 'Why, no, I don't. Do you happen to know anything about Coleman stoves?'"

That was a good one. Old James laughed and laughed at his own joke till he was all out of breath and cryng. You should've heard him sound like a white man. I suppose that's the way us white people sound to black people, like newscasters or something. It was funnier than shit listening to James.

Then things got quiet in the garage. Sometimes, if you're a little buzzed, time starts acting crazy and you can't tell if you've been in one place for a whole year or only about ten seconds. I said to James then, "James, you know the way you saw me running into the building today?"

"Um-hmm," he says.

"I wasn't running from any girls."

"No?"

"No. I was running from a fag. He tried to pick me up in the Bagel Nosh."

James looked serious. He knew I wasn't kidding now. "Really? You want to tell me 'bout it, babe?"

I told him about it. I told him how first the guy saves me from practically being killed and then he tried to get my phone number. James, he said to be careful.

"I *am* careful. Jesus, I'm just about the most careful guy in the whole world!"

"Not about the subtle things you ain't, Lenny. Not about the subtle things."

I asked him what did he mean.

"You careful 'bout the *once-in-a-while* things. The big things that you read about. You ain't careful 'bout what you don't see, but what's there."

"Is that true, James, or are you just trying to spook me?" I thought maybe he was kidding around and just trying to spook me or something.

"I ain't kiddin' you, Lenny. It just gonna take you some growin' up before you start to see the things below the surface, with people, I mean. How every cat got an angle. After you been around a while longer, you'll see it."

Then neither of us talked for a while. I was thinking about what he'd said, about seeing the stuff you don't see. It made sense, but it's very confusing trying to learn about what you can't see, and then being stoned on top of it. That didn't help.

"Tell me somethin', Lenny," James said. "You miss your daddy now that he don't live here no more?"

40

"No."

"Ahh—well. Well. I see."

"They always fought too much when he was living with us," I said, to sort of explain. It sounds pretty cruel to come right out and say you don't miss your own father. But I don't think I did.

James kept saying, "Well, well, well."

Then I said, "James?"

"Yeah?"

"Never mind," I said.

I thought maybe I was asking too many questions. But James said, "No—go ahead. What was it you was gonna say?"

"Well, it's nothing, really. I was just wondering how come everybody in the world is so fucked up and mean. You know? Doesn't it seem to you sometimes that everybody in the world is fucked up? And mean?"

James thought for a minute. He likes to consider before he gives you an answer.

"There's a lot of mean people out there, Lenny. Lot of 'em. But you can't let them keep you from seein' the good people. You let 'em do that, then they win. Don't never let those mean mother-fuckers keep you from seein' the good." He stopped, like he had something real important he was looking for in his mind. Then he started again. "Look at you, Lenny. Down inside, you good. Real good." Then he started smiling all of a sudden. "You just a little *strange*, is all."

"Yeah? You think I'm *strange*? Weird-like? Sick, maybe?"

James laughed. "I *teasin'* you, babe! Sure, you good. One of the best. And you heard that from James T. Wilson. He don't shit nobody, sweetheart."

I felt like hugging him. I honest-to-God did.

We sat around for a while not saying anything, and there was this kind of glow. I mean, it was dark in the garage, but it was like there was this glow anyway. This might sound sick, but for a second I sort of wished James was my father. I don't know. That must have been some heavy grass we smoked. Sometimes I wonder if they don't put something else in it. I could just see James and my mother married. Shit!

Somebody all of a sudden started honking their horn. They

wanted James. That's what they do when they want James if he's not there. They start honking their goddamn horns, like he should come running to wait on them. James started to get up, only I said, "Don't go, James. Let the bastard wait."

"Can't do that, Lenny. It's my job."

"Oh, yeah," I said. I sort of forgot it was his job.

"You be okay now?" he asked, dusting his pants off from where we'd been sitting.

"Yeah. I'll be okay. I'm just gonna stay here for a while."

James left. Every once in a while a car would come down the ramp and the big garage door would open, but I was sitting kind of far back against the wall and nobody could see me. I didn't want to go all the way back up to our apartment, because I was too tired. Too stoned. Sometimes after I smoke that stuff I get scared to go out in public. I mean, even more scared than I usually am. Grass makes me paranoid. And boy, when I'm paranoid, that's like Terror City. I start getting afraid of stuff that isn't even there. I get scared about stuff that happened about ten years ago that I thought I'd forgotten.

Like once, once when I was very small, maybe four or something, I remember sitting in my dad's car. We lived in the suburbs then, before it was hip to live in the city. My dad was mowing the grass in our front yard and I was right there in the driveway playing with the car, in the front seat, pretending I was driving. We lived on kind of a busy street in Highland Park, and these cars would go by the house real fast, because the speed limit was like forty-five or something. Somehow—and I don't know how this happened—but somehow I put the car in neutral and it started slipping down the driveway. Our driveway was like on a hill, and the car started sliding right out to the street. I remember this all very well, because when you almost get killed you always remember it. I tried pressing on the brake with my hand, but that didn't help. I kept sliding into the street. My dad must have seen me then; he came running toward the car and opened the door and shoved me over. He threw on the emergency brake. All that time I was certain I was going to die. I'm not even sure if I knew what that meant, to die, but I was sure it was going to happen to me, whatever it was.

There in the garage I sort of saw myself slipping into the street, backwards, in my dad's car all over again. I kept saying, real soft-like, "I don't want to die. I don't want to die." I said it over and over again. Boy, was I stoned. Then another car came by, and the big garage door of the building opened, and the May sunshine lit up the entrance. Then I remembered where I was. But I still didn't want to get up. I thought maybe James would come back if things slowed down, and then maybe we could talk some more.

I learn so much from James. I learn about a zillion times more from him than I ever did from any teacher. It's true. James should have been a teacher. Instead, we got all these other guys being our teachers, guys who don't know their asses from a hole in the ground. They let these old stuffy farts be our teachers and then they make James—who really understands things—they let him be a doorman. It makes me so mad. There ought to be this law that every year they make everybody switch jobs. Then maybe they'd find out who's good at what. And if that happened, and Mr. Atkins ever had to be our doorman, I'd give him such a hard time. I'd give him so much shit. I'd make him carry my luggage to our car all the time, and I wouldn't tip him. I'd bring luggage everywhere I went, even if I didn't need it. I'd honk my horn and make the bastard jump.

I sat down in the garage for about a hundred years, watching the cars come in and go out. I was so sleepy. I didn't get up until I got the munchies so bad I couldn't stand it anymore. But then I was kind of too scared to go back up to the apartment. I didn't want to get on the elevator with anybody. I wanted to get on one by myself. Just because a person lives in your building doesn't mean they won't get smart with you, funny-like, in an elevator. So I took the stairs. Eighteen goddamn floors. Thirty-six flights. I was almost dead by the time I got to the top. But I was safe. At least I was safe.

CHAPTER 6

went straight to the refrigerator and started taking everything out that looked like it could be eaten—along with some stuff that looked like it couldn't. There was a can of olives, two-day-old chow mein, half a bottle of Coke, a bag of stale donuts, some leftover take-out chicken (mostly the little pieces that nobody wants, because when you bite into them they're practically all cartilage and yucky stuff like veins or muscles, or whatever those dark, stringy things in chicken are), and peanut butter. I didn't care. I was so hungry I ate it all anyway. Then, when I was going to put the chicken back because it was just too gross to handle, I got lucky and found a package of salami, left over from World War II or something. I ate that too. Marijuana makes you eat anything. You could open up your refrigerator and find a hubcap to a Buick and you'd throw some mustard on it and eat it. I felt better then.

But I couldn't get off the idea I'd had down in the garage, about James being a teacher. I did a lot of thinking and I figured out that there are about only ten types of teachers. James wouldn't be any of those types, because James has a brain. He's decent. Teachers aren't. They don't have brains.

See, every school—and I'm *sure* of this—has just ten types of teachers:

1. The School Drunk (Sometimes there's more than one. Sometimes there are twenty of them.)

44

2. The Lecher
3. The Horny Female
4. The Sadist
5. Fags and Lesbians
6. Mr. Renaissance
7. The Robot
8. The Ex-Nun
9. The Wimp
10. The Leper Kisser

That's it. That's what we got at Harrison Godfrey High, anyway.
But I'm sure it's the same all over the country. Probably all over
the world. And you can tell something about *all* of those types—
they'd never make it in the outside world. Even *they* know that.
That's why they became teachers. Let me tell you something, in
high school it's 1940 *all the time*. None of those people have any
idea that the world's changed since they were little. That's why we
can't learn nothing from them. We can learn to be *like* them, but
we can't learn nothing worth really knowing. It can't happen.

If you learn anything at all, it has to be from a job, or from
someone like James, or maybe in college. College is better than
high school, but just barely. I've read college catalogs on account
of they make us, and at least there they keep the courses up with
the world. But in high school we're still doing fire drills. We're still
having pep rallies. Come on. I mean, come on! Fucking *pep
rallies*. They get us all together and play the school alma mater
(which is also from 1940) and then the football team comes out and
the cheerleaders come out, and the coaches speak in the microphone and everybody cheers together. You listen to a high school
coach speak sometime and you tell me if you'd want your kids
being educated by them. Shit. I'd rather let my kids hang around
with *bums*.

They let those ten types of teachers I just told you about teach us
math and English and history and science, and if we do real good,
they make us join the Honor Society or something, where there is
absolutely nothing that has anything to do with honor. Crime,
maybe. Yeah. The Honor Society is filled with the most dishonest
kids you'd ever want to meet. They cheat on tests, or they're the

45

ones who're ratty to some little simpy kid who isn't popular, or they just go around kissing teachers' asses. That's all the Honor Society is.

If you got kids, I'm not kidding you, you get in there and look at the books they've got for them. "Copyright 1792" or some goddamn thing. In English, your kid is learning to parse a goddamn sentence instead of *reading* or *thinking*. If he or she is writing anything at all, it's some dumb essay with rules about narrow your subject, and transitions. You think Charles Dickens could parse a fucking sentence? He turned out all right, didn't he? Sure, because he dropped out of school when he was eleven or something. Tell F. Scott Fitzgerald not to write a run-on sentence and he never would've made it through *The Great Gatsby*. He was no schmuck.

History is the same thing, too. They make you memorize a lot of dates and facts about generals and stuff who died about a thousand years ago. But they never tell us about what went on in the Korean War, or what it was like to live here during World War II. They'll just show you a film strip with a bunch of bombers over Germany. I want to know what movies people were watching, or how that gas coupon thing worked. Everyday stuff, you know? Who was popular on the radio? What did the wallpaper look like? Did they have laundromats? I don't give a flying turd about what Eisenhower did or which treaties he signed. Who the hell cares?

Science and math—I don't care about those subjects anyway. That stuff never changes, but they *could* at least give you practical examples about what good the theories and all are and when you're going to use them, if you ever do. I don't think you do. Me, I just bought a calculator and copied a friend's homework. I don't care about science or math. It's science and math that made the atom bomb, so I stay away from it.

I was thinking about all this school stuff at the kitchen table. I was so damn mad. What I was maddest about was that none of those teachers make going to school *fun*. They could. If they knew how, they could. What they make fun is being kicked out. I was facing a Monday of nothing to do except see a shrink for an hour, and I was *glad*. That should tell you something. Something is wrong if I'd rather go to a doctor for my head than go to school. I know what a lot of adults would say. They'd say there was something wrong with *me*, not school. And that might be true, or at least half true. I think I got things wrong with me. But just 'cause there's stuff wrong with me doesn't mean I haven't got ears and eyes and can't see what's going on.

I made a list then, right at the kitchen table, of all the teachers who shouldn't be teaching. The first on the list was Mr. Binder. He's the *School Drunk*. What this guy does, he comes to school looking like he just came out of an alley. He teaches English, but all he does, he puts the assignment on the board and just sits there, looking real worried, talking to himself and writing notes on scraps of paper that he throws away. If the principal or somebody comes in the room, he gets up and pretends he's been talking to us about adverbs. And he smiles at the principal and pats him on the back, and as soon as the principal leaves, he slumps back in his chair and looks worried again. Then, about noontime, he goes out to his car and starts drinking. When he comes back, he uses mouthwash and cologne, like he thinks he can hide the smell. But it's so obvious; his eyes get red, and then he smiles a lot and nods and talks to himself. He does the same routine every day. I've known him for four years, and he does the same thing every day. They should fire him. Why don't they? He could do something else—and even if he couldn't, he's still got no business with young kids.

And the *Lecher*, that's Mr. Laffow. He presses up against the girls all the time. I think there've been complaints about him, but he always gets out of them. One girl, Donna Nessen, she told me that once Mr. Laffow kept her after class and turned the lights out. They just sat there and he held her hand and recited poetry to her. Jesus! What a creep. He's the kind of guy you read about in the papers. Someday he's going to go over the line and some girl will get raped. I'm not kidding.

And the *Horny Female*, that's Miss Proost. There are all these rumors about how she's been living off and on with different guys from the school. Not teachers, but students. Once she even made a pass at *me*. (Talk about desperate.) I had her for math when I was a sophomore, and she kept me after class to go over some papers with me, but then she couldn't find the papers. She wrote down her address on a slip of paper and said I should come over sometime and she'd tutor me for free. I told her thanks a lot, that I'd do that if I was having any trouble, and then she said not to wait until I had trouble. She was kind of playing with my pants when she said that. Right at the zipper and everything. She was quite crass about it. I never went over there, though. She looked like a manikin, first of all, and second, older women rarely attract me. Their legs always have those veins in them, and they wear polish on their toenails. I can't stand women who wear polish on their toenails. I don't know why they do it. Maybe they think it makes them look pretty, but I don't think it does. I think it makes them look like they were so bored they painted their goddamn *toes*. I'm not making any accusations, but my phone rang at around midnight for about a week after that incident, and every time I answered it, whoever it was hung up. After about five nights of that, I looked up her phone number, and then when the call came at midnight, I called her, and when she answered I hung up. I didn't get any more calls after that.

The *Sadist*, well, that's almost *all* of them. All teachers like to embarrass you if they get the chance. That's sadistic, all right. But one in particular, the guy I wrote down on this list, is Mr. Small. What's really funny about Mr. Small is, he is. Small, I mean. He's a gym teacher who has a thing about lifting weights. About all year long all he does with his classes is weight lifting, and if a weak little kid comes into the class, he makes him do all the hardest weights. And if the kid says he won't, he forces him, or hits him. I know one kid who he hit and broke his arm. Of course the whole thing was whitewashed to make it look like the kid attacked him, but he didn't. We all knew that poor little kid didn't attack him. He just refused to lift a big weight and he got his arm broke because of it. That's *discipline*, Harrison Godfrey style.

The *Faggot*, well, we got two real screaming faggots. We got Mr. Henderson, who teaches music, and Mr. Cochran, who teaches history. That's a funny name for a faggot, *Cochran*, but there's nothing funny about him. Mr. Henderson you don't mind so much because he's kind of a fat guy who leaves you alone. He has real wavy hair that looks like he puts spray on it, and he swishes a lot, but mostly he leaves everybody alone. Mr. Cochran, though, he hangs around the gym a lot. Especially at shower time. He pretends he's there to get in some swimming during his free time,

48

but he's there to see the boys come out of the shower. He doesn't fool me. It's bad enough in the boys' locker room, having to be naked in front of everybody, and everybody pretending not to look, but really looking. Everybody wants to see who's bigger than who, if you know what I mean. Guys'll deny it up and down, but in the locker room they all compare. I'm a little self-conscious about it, because the truth is, I'm not very big in that department. But it's even worse when you know some guy is a faggot and he's watching you.

I know this kid, Gary Mendel, who swears that Mr. Cochran used to touch him too much in history class. You know, a little pat here and there. He used to write things on his papers about him being good-looking and all, and having a good build, but Gary never told his parents, because it's *embarrassing* to have a fag come on to you. It's sort of like it makes you a fag, too. I told him he was crazy, that he should tell somebody, but I don't think he ever did. I don't blame him. I know now how he felt. I didn't want to tell my mother about the faggot at the Bagel Nosh. You could tell James that kind of stuff, but not your own parents. Anyway, what made the whole thing with Mr. Cochran worse was Gary Mendel was in *my* gym class. Mr. Cochran must have looked up Gary's schedule, because every day at fourth period he'd be in there, just waiting around, naked, when Gary and me came out of the showers. Gary used to push me in front of him so he could sort of hide behind me, but I pushed *him* first, because I didn't want any fag staring at my you-know-what. Besides, I'm small that way. I told you. But Gary was tremendous. About the biggest I've ever seen. Not that I looked deliberately, but you can't help noticing. You can't. Mr. Cochran was into big things, you could tell. He never gave me a second glance, but poor Gary. He'd come out of the showers *blushing*, for Christ's sake. And there would be Mr. Cochran pretending to dry himself off. He'd always say hi to Gary, and Gary would mumble something and practically *run* to his locker. He got his gym period changed a few weeks after that, and Mr. Cochran stopped coming around.

That queer stuff, that's easier to spot in men than it is in women, unless you're real used to it and understand something about lesbians. There might be, for instance, some woman teacher in the school who nobody would suspect in a million years of being gay, but she is. It's mostly easy to spot the *butch* kind of lesbian. They're the easiest to tell. I couldn't swear to God about this, but I *think* the entire women's gym faculty is lesbians. Yeah. Some of 'em even live together and let everybody know about it. They mostly have those Billie Jean King haircuts and are very into being assertive. (That's what worried me about my mother and *her* new haircut, and the est bit and how she's always blaming men for everything.) The girls at school talk all the time about how two or three of these lesbian gym teachers watch them undress and follow them into the showers. That would drive me nuts if I had a daughter and I knew she had to take gym in a public school. I'd know that a bunch of fat lesbians were looking at her naked every day. With a boy, he can protect himself. But with a girl, she doesn't even *suspect* that something is funny until it's too late, most of the time. I could be careful-like and qualify that statement about the whole women's gym faculty, but I'm not going to. I really think that ninety percent of them are queer. The thing about women nowadays, they act like they got a *right* to be queer if they want, even if they're gym teachers and see your kids naked. It's like you can't *do* anything about it, and should be embarrassed or something if you even want to. That's the world in the eighties. Perverts got rights. They give rights to perverts but not to kids. What sense does that make?

One of the most sickening types of teachers, who is probably about the most harmless but is still sickening, is *Mr. or Mrs. Renaissance.* This is the guy who is so respected and loved by both teachers and kids that you could get sick. He knows everything about everything and has three thousand diplomas (usually *framed,* in his office) and he runs Fine Arts Week at school. He makes it seem like he was once personal friends with Leonardo da Vinci, like they grew up together. He's usually quite handsome but old, with gray hair on the sides, and that's Mr. Bellamy, at our school. He dresses in designer suits and spends all his vacations in Europe being distinguished. He speaks about seven hundred languages and loves opera. I hate opera. The thing I hate most about opera is that first of all, nobody knows what the sloppy fat broad is singing, and if they do, it's because they read it in a review somewhere. They use all those fake voices that are supposed to be sophisticated or something, but what they are really is corny. There's nothing more corny in the world than an opera. Bunch of characters running around in stupid costumes singing while they're being killed, or about to be killed. And they were all written about a hundred years ago. Maybe longer. If you *say* you like opera, it's supposed to like let you into this exclusive club-like, and it's supposed to make you better than somebody who likes rock and roll, or country and western. Or cocktail lounge music. The funny thing is, I bet in about five hundred years from now, when people want to seem better than other people, they'll be listening to some schnook sing Barry Manilow songs. Or Bruce Springsteen. I just bet you.

The *Robot*, that's Mr. Samuels. He does everything by the book. He calls attendance like he was programmed as a little computer for it. Most adults, they had childhoods, but Mr. Robot was a transistor when he was born. Every day he says the same things. "All right, class. Today we open our books to chapter seventeen, 'Molecules and Other Boring Shit.'" He always calls you mister or miss. He's the kind of guy who—if the school bulletin said to execute your class after a test—would collect the test papers and then he'd pull out a gun and start shooting everybody—in alphabetical order.

Most of the kids, they'd tell you he was boring. But they'd also tell you how organized he is, like that makes up for him being a machine. The one thing people want you to be these days is organized. It doesn't matter if you have a personality, or if you pay attention to the pimply unpopular kids. All that matters is *Did you do it by the book?* You can't *see* that kind of stuff being bad for you, but it is. It teaches kids a very bad lesson. It teaches them that being human isn't important. Being a walking computer is important. I can't stand Mr. Samuels. I'll bet his wife can't stand him. If he has a kid, he'll be the one who grows up to be the next mass murderer. Just to get some kind of *emotion* out of his crazy father. What he'll do is, he'll kill about thirty people and hide them in the attic, and when the police catch him, Mr. Samuels will make him clean up his room and file everything where it's supposed to be filed before he goes to jail or the electric chair. The kid will be dragged away by twenty cops with riot gear on, and he'll be pulling on Mr. Samuel's shirt and suit, saying, "Just show some fucking

51

emotion first!" And then Mr. Samuels will straighten his shirt and tie and say, "Don't forget to keep your cell neat."

These robot guys are crazy. They're the craziest people in the world.

This list I was making was getting me depressed. Whenever I even *thought* about the people who run that high school, I got depressed. If you were forced every day to *see* those teachers, not listen to them, not even that, but to just *see* them, you'd understand what I'm talking about. You'd see how terrible it is to be a high school student in a big city. Maybe there's a little town still left somewhere where they've got nice teachers who the kids like, people who go to their jobs to make sure that the kids have fun and *smile* once in a while. I don't know. I don't think there's a place like that left. All there are probably, are people like the ones I'm telling you about, who aren't even nice to look at. Their clothes are old and wrinkled, or their pants are too short, or their hair is greasy or dyed, or gone, and their faces show you that they're bad people. That kind of stuff has got to show up on your face after a while. That's probably why teachers are so ugly.

I was still at the kitchen table, still writing the list, but I crumpled it up and threw it away before I even got to the *Ex-Nun* (that's Miss Rafferty) or the *Wimp* (that's Mr. Reynolds, Mr. McCallister, and Mr. Benson), or the *Leper Kisser* (that's Dr. Kollbisk, and he'll read this anyway—so it's probably better not to go into it). All I know is, James would be the best teacher in the world. But he can't, because he doesn't got the degree for it. So they make him park cars and open doors. And I'm not saying kids should drop out. I'm not saying that at all. All I'm saying is parents should get the hell inside a school and make sure the idiots don't ruin their kids, if they aren't ruined already. Make sure they got new books, decent food, and that the bastard teachers at least make them smile once in a while. If you don't smile once in a while, you might as well be dead.

CHAPTER 7

woke up Monday morning, took a shower, and was in the middle of putting on my jeans before I remembered that I didn't have to go to school. When I remembered that, I felt better. Sort of. I didn't have to show up at Dr. Kollbisk's office until ten, and it was only seven-thirty. So I went out into the living room to read the paper, but something was funny. Some woman's coat was draped across the sofa, and some shoes that my mother wouldn't wear in a million years were sitting on the floor by the coffee table. Also, there was a whole ashtray of cigarettes that were different than the kind my mother smokes, and there were two glasses on the table. I looked around the rest of the apartment and there wasn't no one around. My mother's bedroom door was closed, though.

I grabbed the newspaper from the hallway where the doorman leaves it, in front of the door (if someone doesn't steal it first), and I was so nervous I almost left the place without my Mace. I went back and got it, shaking-like, and grabbed a jacket and left. Mucho fasto. I got on an elevator with about forty women and men all dressed in the same navy blue pinstripe, something I ordinarily would *never* do. Usually, I'd just wait for another elevator, but I was angry and shaky. My mother was a lesbian.

When I got down to the lobby, all the business guys and women raced out of the elevator, right in front of me, like I was the hired help or something. If you wear blue jeans, and if you're on an

53

elevator, it's like a signal that pinstripe guys and ladies should run you over and step on your feet and be rude.

"You *mind?*" I said to this one balding kind of guy. He'd stuck his stupid little fag-type attaché case in front of me and cut me off. I couldn't get off that elevator for love or money. He just gave me a dirty look, but I walked out in front of him. Who do those people think they are? God?

I sort of hoped James would be on duty, but he wasn't. It was some other guy I barely knew, and he was busy ass-kissing all the business guys, opening the door for them and tipping his hat. I walked outside and it was kind of warm, and the sun had been up for a while, and for about the first time I could remember I was glad to be outside. No joke. I was just glad as hell about being out of that apartment.

I couldn't even think straight. I started wondering where I could pick up some coffee and sit down to read the paper and figure out what to do now that my mother was queer. I started thinking that what I should've done was left a note for her saying I wasn't coming home until she didn't bring no more lesbians with her. Goddamn women's movement. Goddamn it.

I walked to the Oak Tree restaurant, past what used to be the Playboy Club. There were Continental buses loading up with people going to O'Hare Airport. Everything was moving and jumping—taxis, pedestrians, garbage trucks—everything. You got to move at the pace the city does or else someone notices you, and once someone notices you anything can happen.

When I got to the Oak Tree, it was jammed. People were waiting in line to sit down, so I walked south past the Newberry Library. That's a library where you can't get in unless you got a pass from the President or somebody. I thought about catching a bus a couple of times, but they were real full and you'd have to stand with a million funny-smelling people you didn't even know, so I kept walking. I walked all the way until I was at Lincoln Park. There was a little Greek restaurant that wasn't crowded, so I went in and ordered a cup of coffee to go. Some of the people stared at me and I just pretended not to notice how rude they were being.

When I got my coffee, I turned to go, but some old guy called after me, "Hey, Mac—"

I turned around real arrogant. "What?" I said.

"You dropped something."

He was right. There was my Mace, on the floor.

"Thanks," I said. Boy! The second time in one morning I was almost without my Mace.

Then the guy, he can't shut up. He can't just leave it at that, nice, kind of. He's got to stick his nose in my business. He says, "You got a permit for that?"

I just picked it up and ignored him. I was on my way out when he says again, "You got a permit for that?"

"What's it to ya?" I said. Then he flashed a badge and gets up. Fucking Ada, he was a cop. He took me over to a corner and everybody was staring at us.

"Let's see that stuff," he says, kind of low-like. I showed it to him.

"You under cover?" I asked him. He just kept reading the side of the canister. "You under cover or something?"

"What's it to ya?" he says. He said it back to me. Me and my big mouth. If you're smart, don't ever get wise with a cop. That's lesson number one. I'd rather get wise with a Mafia guy than a cop. Cops don't let you get away with it. Especially if you're a kid.

"Wha'dya doin' with this stuff?" he wanted to know. "This is real tear gas."

"Protection," I told him, but he wasn't too convinced.

"You go to school?"

"Yes sir," I said. They like to be called *sir*. They like to get their asses kissed a lot. I didn't care. I'd kiss his big fat ass if he'd just leave me alone.

"This is dangerous stuff, ya know that? It's also illegal unless you got a permit. You got a permit?"

"No. I mean, no sir. I don't got a permit."

"I could take you in for this, ya know that?"

"No. I didn't know that."

Then he put it in his pocket and told me to get lost. Jesus Christ. He wanted me to just walk out of there with no Mace or nothing.

"Officer," I said. I was being very polite, but I won't kid you. I was pretty upset. First my mother and now my Mace. "Officer, listen. Please don't take my Mace. Please. I mean, it's not safe out there without something. You know. You probably got a gun, but all I got is my Mace. Please don't take it."

He looked at me kind of funny then, with his head tilted, like. "What? What're you talkin' about?"

I said, "Let's not talk here. Get a cup of coffee to go and we'll talk outside. Please."

He looked at me a long time, like I was insane. Then he went back and paid his bill and ordered coffee with cream and sugar. He shouldn't've ordered sugar with his coffee, though. Sugar's no good for you.

When we were outside, I could talk to him better. There weren't a whole lot of people staring at you all the time. Inside, we looked like a cop and a criminal, but outside we just looked like an old guy and a young guy.

"What is it?" He wanted to know right away. He was suspicious as hell of me. He must've thought I was going to try something funny.

"Look," I said. I was still a little shaky. "I live on Lake Shore Drive. Bunch of kooks and weirdos every day, you know? I walk to school. Even more weirdos. Yesterday some fag tried to pick me up in the Bagel Nosh." I hated to have to tell him about that, but I wanted my Mace back. "It's the only protection I got. Please, can I have it back? *Please.*"

He just kept staring at me, like he was sizing me up or something. I didn't say anything more, but I must've looked suspicious as hell. He asked me where I was going. I said I was going to the park to read the paper. He said he'd go with me. We walked to the park and he told me to sit down at the first bench we got to. I started to wonder if maybe he was a pervert. He didn't look it, but sometimes you can't tell.

"I'm gonna give this back to you," he said.

"Thanks!" I told him. "Thanks, officer."

"But I want you to keep that goddamn thing in a place where it won't be falling all over the floor in front of no detectives. I'm just doin' my job."

"I know that. I really appreciate it, no kid—"

"Where do you go to school?" He was still checking me out. Cops, they always think they're being had.

56

"Harrison Godfrey," I said, wondering when the hell he was going to give me my Mace back.

"That's a good school," he said. I don't know where he gets his information, but I hope he knows a hell of a lot more about crime than he does about schools.

Then he took my Mace out of his pocket and gave it back to me. "You know how to use that stuff?" he asked.

"Yeah. Somebody tries to mug or beat you, you pull it out and spray it down their goddamn throat until they choke to death."

"Make sure the nozzle is pointed at them. Keep your face covered. And don't use it unless it's self-defense. You use that stuff unprovoked, you could end up doin' time."

I told him I knew that. But I didn't. I didn't know you could go to jail for Mace. Isn't that something? All these crooks and rapists have guns, but the innocent people can go to jail for just having Mace. It figures.

He started sipping on his coffee and asking how old I was. When I told him I was seventeen, he took out his wallet and started showing me his kids. He had a seventeen-year-old daughter who was *gorgeous*. I asked him if she had a boyfriend, and she did. All the beautiful girls, they already got boyfriends. Then he asked me what I was going to study in college. I didn't even tell him I was *going* to college. Adults, they assume. I made up some story about how I wanted to be a chemical guy—an engineer.

"Oh, that's good. That's good," he said, sipping his coffee. "Good money in that."

I told him, yeah. I wanted to work for Dupont or one of those places. Invent new stuff to help the energy crisis. He said that was good. We shot the shit for a few more minutes and then he had to leave. He was a nice old guy. Nice as hell, when you got to know him. He probably just got drunk at night at a neighborhood tavern. He probably didn't do anything constructive with his time, and he probably believed the whole shitload of lies that everybody else believes. But he was nice, anyway. He gave me my Mace back and showed me his daughter. He was okay.

I opened my paper and started to read it. It almost took my mind off my mother and how she'd become a lesbian. Right off the bat, there was a story about a thirty-two-year-old woman postal deliverer who was kidnapped and murdered in broad daylight in Arizona. A bunch of Indians grabbed her while she was delivering the mail. They murdered her in public while a whole bunch of people looked on and didn't do anything. That's what worries me. Just because you're on a busy street doesn't mean you'll get help if anybody decides to kill you. Then came the sad part. This woman had a husband and a five-year-old kid. What the hell was the guy going to tell his kid? That his mother was killed by Indians? And what's that poor little kid going to do without a mother? I started thinking—at least his parents won't get divorced and he won't have to find out his mother became a lesbian. But that's no comfort. Poor kid. Poor guy. What a world.

I looked at my watch and it was eight-thirty. There was a whole lot of articles about Poland and the President, and then—on only page three—there was a headline:

WOMAN RAPED, THROWN FROM
MOUNTAIN TWICE—LIVES

It was all about some poor woman who was in a forest preserve with her boyfriend when these three guys killed him and took turns raping her. It was awful. I almost threw up my coffee. In fact, I did a little. Some came up, but I forced it back down. I pretended I was spitting, so I wouldn't look too sickening. Then I read about these guys—who turned out to be *security guards*—they threw this woman who they'd raped off a mountainside. Then they went down to make sure she was dead, and she wasn't. So you know what these security guards did? They raped her *again*, and threw her off the mountain *again*. Sweet guys. And she lived! They found her three days later and she was still breathing. She stayed alive by licking dew off the grass. That poor woman. I'll bet when she gets better she'll wish she was dead. And then cops wonder why I carry Mace. Like it's a surprise or something.

I looked around the park to make sure there were no crooks or rapists. There weren't. There were just a bunch of flabby people jogging with those Walkman radio headphones. Probably listening to opera, for crying out loud. Then I started thinking, any one of them could be a rapist or a murderer. Just because you jog doesn't mean you're normal. I kept my trigger finger on my Mace—just in case.

Lincoln Park is okay. You got the zoo there, and this little lake where in the summertime you can rent paddleboats. In the morning, buses come right through the little roads in the park, filled with more of the pinstripe people like I told you about on the elevator that morning. It's funny; I watched a bunch of guys drive to the park and they leave their cars there, and then they get on the LaSalle Street bus so they don't have to drive in the Loop. I never knew that's why there are always so many cars parked there. But that's why.

That commuter crowd, they're like a bunch of wind-up dolls. They get out of their cars, look at their wristwatches, and they all have these short little haircuts and most of them wear big clumsy-looking wing-tip shoes. And mustaches. Most of them got mustaches. I watched them all, thinking about how they all probably had wives and kids. Some of them looked pretty young, so you knew their kids were in a day-care center, and their wives were either in law school or had some business job. All day long they don't get to see the people they really like. The business guy, he has lunch with some other business guy, and they have meetings with other pinstripe people. The wife, she has lunch with a client or a professor, and because they never get to be with their own family, they probably both got affairs. If I ever have a wife and kids, what I want is to at least spend time with them. I don't mean just on weekends, but every day. What good is it to be married and have kids if you don't get to spend most of your time with your family? But it's money. They need the money.

Then I stopped watching the commuters and started reading the advice columns. Ann Landers. If you live in New York, or if you get the *Tribune*, then you got her sister, Dear Abby. I read it because it's so stupid, the advice column. Complete strangers write to this woman for advice instead of calling up a friend or somebody they know. I think they do it just so they can see their personal problems in the paper. And boy, do those people have problems. There's always some story about this woman who claims she's got a perfectly normal marriage except her husband wears panty hose under his pants, or something like that. And Ann always has some

59

real sarcastic and bossy remark to make, like she knows it all. To-day was a story about a woman whose boyfriend makes it with another man, his friend. It reminded me of my mother. What the hell was I going to do about my mother? I couldn't even *imagine* talking to her about it. It was too embarrassing. But I didn't want to live there anymore. I can't stand lesbians. I don't like that stuff going on in my own home. Maybe I should write to Ann Landers, I started thinking. I could just see me writing to Ann about my mother.

Dear Ann:

My mother and father were recently divorced on ac-count of all they did when they were married was fight and practically kill each other. Now that they're divorced, my mother goes to law school, takes est classes, looks like Billie Jean King, does aerobic dancing, and has a lesbian friend sleep with her in the house. I am a seventeen-year-old male who can't stand lawyers, est, aerobic dancing, or lesbians. What should I do? Should I tell my father? I don't think he'd understand. About the only person who would understand is James, our doorman. Should I tell James not to let the other lesbian up? Should I burst into my mother's room when they're together and yell, *"Now cut that out!"* Please answer soon, because I was kicked out of school last week and I got nothing better to do than hang around the park and read your column.

Sincerely,
BORED BUT STRAIGHT

Then Ann would answer.

Dear Bored But Straight:

Listen, buster, you have no right in your mother's af-fairs. So what, you don't like est or lawyers? People don't like a lot of things, like est, muscular dystrophy, aerobic dancing, or cancer; but they live with them, don't they?

60

And how do you know your mother is having a lesbian affair? Maybe she just likes to sleep with a close friend. You ever think of that, Sicko?

And then she'd do an ad for her new book, *When to Let a Boy into Your Pants, and Other Pointers.*

My counselor at school once told me I should go into journalism, but I never would. Advice columns is one reason why. Another is that I'd be the guy who had to write all those sickening stories like the one about the lady who got killed by a bunch of Indians. It's bad enough reading about that stuff, but writing it would make me go insane. And if you're in journalism, you're supposed to work your way up to your own column, and then you can write all this crap that's supposed to be clever but really isn't, because you've heard it all before. Those guys are almost never original. They're almost never entertaining. And it's always the kind of stuff you walk away from saying, so what? And if you're successful at it, you're supposed to have lunch at the Billy Goat Tavern on Lower Wacker Drive, with all the other big shots who aren't clever, or funny, or entertaining. The Billy Goat is this awful little restaurant that serves greasy hamburgers and has a bunch of guys yelling and a lot of famous writers who think they got to be *seen* being famous. All the Chicago big shots hang out there. I've been there. It's just like high school; the popular guys like to hang around with other popular guys, and they like everybody else to *see* them hanging around with other popular guys. Grown-up fucking men acting like kids. I hate it.

It was getting close to ten-thirty when I looked at my watch, so I started walking to school. It was so weird; I was about the only kid in the whole world who wasn't in school. Nobody my age was on the street. It was kind of nice, because I felt like I was allowed to see all this stuff that everybody else misses and doesn't even know goes on. But in another way it was terribly lonely. It was like I was a criminal or something. I was, in a way. Being kicked out is something like being in jail. I guess that's why they did it to me. To put me in jail, kind of.

They wouldn't let me in the goddamn school when I got there because I didn't have a stupid pass. The hall guard was another robot, and there was no talking to him, so I just stayed outside and waited until the period changed. There were a bunch of gang-type kids out there, smoking and stuff, and yelling remarks to me in Spanish. They kept calling me *white boy*. I hate that white-boy crap. Latinos, a lot of them are white too. But they don't think so. They think of themselves as different from white, which I can understand, but I still don't like it. I don't go up to them and say, "Hey, Spanish boy." But some guys probably do. A lot of white people are very ignorant and they probably call them spic and stuff. That's probably why Latinos do it. I just wish they wouldn't.

Then the bell rang and they let us all in and I went straight to Dr. Kollbisk's office. The receptionist lady made me sit down in a chair until his door opened and some pathetic girl who was really a mess walked out crying. He looked at me and said, "Next!" He thought that was funny. He thought that was hilarious. "Next!" he said, again. Jesus. I felt just like one of the pathetic kids when I walked in and he shut the door. There's a little glass windowpane to the side of the door, and everybody who walks by can see you're with a nut doctor. They probably do it that way on purpose. Just so everybody knows who the nut cases are. And I'm not knocking Dr. Kollbisk or anything, but if he's such a hot shrink, how come that girl was crying when she left?

"How's the boy?" he said when the door was shut. He meant me. He forgot to say *white*. How's the *white* boy.

I told him I was fine. "How come that girl was crying?" I asked. I realized I was probably getting personal, but I really wanted to know why she was so upset. "She in trouble, too?"

"Let's concentrate on one thing at a time, why don't we, Lenny." He started putting files away and taking other files out. He didn't want to talk about it, you could tell. When he got my folder out, he opened it up, took a pen from his shirt pocket, and sat down behind his desk.

"How's the book coming?" he wanted to know.

"Book?" I didn't know what the hell he was talking about.

"The one you're writing—part of the agreement, remember?"

"Oh, yeah. The book. It's coming fine." I'd forgotten about the book. I hadn't even started it yet, hardly.

He didn't have a couch like most shrinks had, and it's a good thing. I can just see me lying on a couch while a bunch of gapers looked in the window at the sick boy. What I noticed all of a sudden was his cologne. Dr. Kollbisk must've taken a bath in cologne that morning. It sort of made me want to ask if I could open the door, but I didn't want to, because I was afraid somebody outside might hear what we were saying. I could barely breathe in there. It was a cheap cologne, too. Not the kind you buy at Water Tower Place, but the kind you buy at Walgreen's if you don't have a lot of money.

"I talked to Mr. Atkins this morning," he said.

"Did it make you sick?" I said. I was playing around, but psychology guys got no sense of humor.

"I was talking to him about your chance of graduating, and it looks very good, I'm pleased to say. You'll have to sit for your exams, though." Then he opened another folder and took out a whole stack of papers and handed them to me. "These are your homework assignments for the rest of the semester. You just hand in the assignments to me on the dates specified, and I think everything will be all right."

"I gotta do homework, too?" The agreement we made had nothing to do with homework. It was like buying a used car, sitting there. All of the extras were being added on.

"Think you can handle it?" he asked. There's something sadistic in the way teachers treat you when they hand you a bunch of work. They like want to *floor* you, make you moan or something. I didn't moan, though.

"Sure I can. You don't have to use your brain to do homework. All you have to do is be willing to be bored."

Then what we did, for nearly the whole hour, we talked. About *nothing*. I couldn't believe it. He didn't even give me a lot of inkblots or word association like shrinks are supposed to. They're supposed to get into your subconscious or something. I'm glad he didn't. I don't want nobody messing with my subconscious. *I* don't even like to mess with my subconscious. I figure if it's deep down there, there's a reason for it. Leave it alone, is my theory.

All he did the whole time was talk, talk, talk. He kept saying *gestalt*. Everything was the *gestalt*. He kept mentioning my *problem*, like I had some kind of problem or something and everybody else was okay. I stared out the window a lot and watched the kids walking by. I saw this guy Leo Ferranatti, who's been in high school for like the last ten years but hasn't graduated yet. He steals protection money from the little freshmen, and at the age of twenty-two or something is so popular they elected him president of the class—and then *I* got problems. I watched Mr. Laffow go by, that lecher I was telling you about. But it's me; I'm the guy with the problem. I felt like I was in that movie, the one where the insane guys run the mental hospital. You always see the real sickos in the movies, you see how they think *they're* normal and everybody *else* is crazy. That's pretty much the way I feel about the world, like I'm the only normal person walking around, so maybe I really *am* sick. I don't know. All I know is something's wrong with my goddamn gestalt and I don't even know what the hell it is. It sounds dirty.

So Dr. Kollbisk finally let me and my gestalt the hell out of his office, and I sort of hung around a bit in the hallway during passing time. I stuck my homework assignments in the back pocket of my jeans and took my jacket off 'cause it was getting hot. I watched all the kids talking and screaming in the hallway. I listened to some of the stuff they were saying and it was all bullshit. You go to a high school sometime and listen to what the kids have to say between passing period and it's all bullshit. You'd think that after being bottled up for almost an hour listening to some jerk babble about nothing, that they'd have something heavy to say when they finally got out. But they don't. Mostly they swear. I don't think there's anything wrong with that if they say something else, too, but they don't. One kid was starting to climb the stairs with some friends, and all he kept saying was "Fuck! Fuck!" and "No fuck!" What sense does that make? *No fuck.* That doesn't even make sense.

I was just hanging around watching the cattle when I noticed something else that bothered me. It's like that bit about the weather that the radio announcers say, like I told you about—the weather, remember? With me it's different. With me it's *If nothing bothers you, stick around. Something will, eventually.* What I noticed was all the kids were dressed in brand-new pressed clothes like you see in television commercials. Really. A lot of the kids come from poor families and stuff, but they must spend a fortune on their clothes.

And they don't dress like real kids. City kids—they're funny. They dress real neat in old people-type fashions. Not suburban kids so much. But city kids, they do it. They wear Izod sweaters and shirts. And pointy shoes. Jesus. They probably most of them don't have enough money to pay the rent, but they dress slick. Me, I was just wearing a sweat shirt and a pair of Levi's. I don't go for fashion. I mean, where does it get you? Who are you trying to impress? Half the people in the world—you watch them—they think they're on TV all the time. Like that kid who yelled "No fuck!" The bastard thought he was on TV. He just wanted to be noticed.

I was on my way out of the building when someone tugged on my sleeve. "Hey, Lenny!" It was Lisa Mankewicz. She's this girl. This girl who I was buddies with and whose mother owns the nightclub. She's terrific-looking.

"Hi," I said. "Hi. What'cha doin'?" That was stupid. It was a stupid thing to say. She was going to school. It was obvious. Everybody goes to school except me.

"How've you *been?*" she wanted to know.

I told her I got kicked out. She said she knew. She said everybody was talking about it.

"Yeah? What're they saying?"

"Oh, everybody knows. Everybody—about the fountain and all."

"Yeah? But what are they saying about it?"

"Not so much," she said. She was really a pretty kid. God. She was almost beautiful, in a high school kind of way. "Not so much. Just that you got wrecked and jumped in the fountain and that Mr. Atkins and Mr. Morrow beat you up and took you away and the cops came. Everybody thinks you're in jail."

"Yeah? That's what they think?"

"Uh-huh."

"Well, just between you and me, I think *they're* the ones in jail. And Atkins and Morrow, they didn't beat me up."

"Then how come your lip is cut?"

"Huh? Oh, that. Yeah, well—they hit me. They hit me, that's for sure. But they didn't beat me up. Honest."

Lisa, she's a peppy little thing. I mean, she's real *animated*, you know? Like there's a whole bunch of movement in her face. It keeps moving all the time. She looked great. I don't know. Some-

65

times a girl can hypnotize me all of a sudden even though I've known her for years and she's never been able to do it before. Lisa—she's got great little legs. She's not real tall, but great legs. Nice little ass and everything. All at once I wanted to kiss her more than anything in the world. What I wanted to do, I wanted to pull her in a stairwell and just hug her or something.

But you can't *do* that kind of stuff. If you're a guy and you want to kiss a girl, you have to wait for them to do it or else you don't know if it would be okay with them. Sometimes you might *think* a girl wants to kiss you, but all girls act like you think they want to kiss you. It's just the way girls act. Most of the time they'd rather eat worms than have some guy kiss them. Besides, as it turned out, all she wanted to do was find out if my band was playing at her mother's club that week. I told her it was the first I'd heard of it— that maybe Rick knew, 'cause he handles the business—but that I didn't feel like playing or opening for anybody, not even the Beatles. Not even if they brought John Lennon back. She seemed disappointed-like, but hey. I didn't feel like playing, that's all.

"So," she says. "I gotta run. I got a math quiz. Are you back in now?"

"Me?"

"Yeah. You back in?"

Then something happened that really pissed me off. That guy— that *jerk* who'd gone up the stairs yelling "No fuck!"—he was coming back down the stairs yelling at the top of his lungs "No fuck!" again. What an asshole. Here I was trying to have a conversation with Lisa, and he comes down *no-fucking* all over the place. I thought about Macing him right then and there, but then I remembered what that detective told me, about doing time. So I didn't. I'm not going to jail because some asshole only knows two stupid words.

"Me?" I said again. "No. No, I'm not back in."

"Well," Lisa said, looking very concerned, and she meant it, I knew she did, "are you going to graduate and everything?"

"I don't know. Maybe. They won't tell me for sure." Then the passing period was almost over and Lisa and I were the only two kids left in the hall. She kept saying how she had to run, but she didn't. She just stayed there, and she seemed like she wanted to

66

talk, but she was nervous or shy or something. That wasn't like Lisa. Not the Lisa *I* knew, it wasn't.

"Look," I said, getting nervous because I knew she was going to be in trouble if she didn't get to class, "look. We should really talk. You know? Maybe sometime you and me—"

"What're you doing after school?" she asked. The answer to that was no mystery. The same thing I'd be doing during school.

"Nothing," I said.

"Well, why don't you meet me. We could go out and talk. I mean, if you want to."

I told her yeah, that was good. I'd like to. She said to meet her at two-thirty near the fountain. I said maybe someplace else. I didn't want to get near that goddamn fountain. She said yeah, she forgot. How about the corner of Lincoln Park and Burling, she said, and I said that would be great. Then, she was about to go, and what she does is, she kisses me on the cheek and tells me to take care. Then she ran to class. I was sort of stunned. I mean, I'm no farmer. I don't go out of my mind just because a girl kisses me on the cheek, but she did it so nice. And she told me to take care. Not like everybody else tells you that, but like she really meant that I should take care of myself. Jesus. I wondered why I'd never noticed how great Lisa was before. Some things you just don't notice.

I had about three hours to kill and no place to kill them. When I got back outside, I couldn't figure anything out. I couldn't figure out what to *do*. When you're in school, you don't have to think. You just follow the program. But when you're kicked out, you have to make up your own program.

And I couldn't tell if I was happy or sad. I was both, really. I was sad about my mother being a lesbian and about having no place to go, but I was happy about running into Lisa and seeing her later. What I had to do, I had to take care of business. (I hate that expression, because it's what Elvis used to say, and even though he was cool at one time, he was also a bit of a jerk, so I don't like using his phrase. If it was his phrase, you can bet it's a dumb one.)

I knew I had to find somewhere else to live, because I'd never be able to cut it in Lesbian City. So I decided to catch the LaSalle Street bus (just like all the pinstripe people) and see my father down at the bank he works in. I didn't know if I was going to tell him about Mom or not, but I thought it would be a good idea for us to have lunch together. I thought he'd probably be happy that I took the time out to come down and see him. Maybe he'd let me live with him. He's got a new apartment and everything, in Sandburg Village, and I wouldn't take up a lot of room. I'd just need some aluminum foil and a little place for myself. I was thinking that it might be nice, just me and my father. Unless he started bringing men home, or something. But I didn't think he would. Men, they got to be *born* queer. With women it's different. I think. I *think* it's different for women than it is for men. Jesus. That's all I needed. All I needed was for my father to be a queen.

should've never gotten on that goddamn LaSalle Street bus. I should've walked. But it was pretty far to downtown and I hadn't eaten nothing and I didn't want to take a cab. In cabs you got to share a ride now and you never know who's going to get picked up next. You could get stabbed or something right in the back seat and the driver wouldn't even notice. The only time he'd notice is when he'd come to where you were going and he wouldn't get his tip. He wouldn't get his tip, of course, because you'd be dead. But I took the bus, which is worse. Almost.

At noon, nobody decent is on the bus. You don't even see those pinstripe people you do in the morning; they're all at work already, is how come. What you see is derelicts and real poor people in cheap clothes. Old guys with unpressed pants. Lots of brown pants. If you see somebody with brown pants on, and he's wearing black shoes, then you know he's got no money. No job. No hope. I don't know. I don't know where those people are going, because they almost never get up to get off. It's like all they do all day is ride on the bus. One guy in the seat ahead of me was crazy. He was the type who's lost it—permanently. He talked to himself, *laughed* to himself in this real evil kind of way, and he kept saying, "Fucking bastards," to almost everybody who walked by. Somebody would walk by and he'd say something to them that you couldn't understand, and then he'd laugh, and then he'd say, "Fucking bastards."

He always turned to me when he said that part, like we were in on the joke together. I would've changed seats, but they were all taken.

I looked out my window, just for something to do to take my mind off the crazy guy, and I saw a bunch of hookers on LaSalle and Division streets. They were wearing pink and purple outfits like from *Star Wars* or someplace. I thought that was kind of funny, seeing hookers in broad daylight like that. Maybe they were shopping for groceries. Hookers have to eat, too. I mean, something for nourishment, for a change. Usually you only see hookers at night, except for on North Avenue by all the factories. There you see them when work lets out and they wave to all the cars, only they aren't really *waving*, if you know what I mean. Working girls. They're not so bad, really. But there must be something wrong with them to be hookers. They're okay, though. But something's wrong with them.

What took my mind off the hookers was these two punks who got on the bus with a real loud radio, about as big as a washing machine. The song they were playing was "Stairway to Heaven," by Led Zeppelin. If there's a song in the world that I hope I never hear again, it's "Stairway to Heaven." So now there's a crazy guy who talks to himself and two punks on the bus and I was wondering, What next?

What was next was this Mexican girl sitting by herself on the opposite side from me. She was all by herself until some greasy-looking foreign-type guy with a dirty black suede jacket sat next to her. He smelled. I could smell him from where I was sitting. What he started to do was, he started pushing up next to her. I was watching the whole thing. It made me so goddamn nervous watching it, because I knew I was going to do something if it didn't stop. Then he like put his arm around her, on the back of the seat, real accident-like, and he started stroking her hair. She kept squirming in her seat and trying to get closer to the window, but there wasn't any more room left. I was going crazy. I knew I'd hate myself for the rest of my life if anything happened to that poor Mexican girl, so I got up, took out my Mace, and I was about to blind him with it when *she* got up and walked to the front of the bus and stood near the driver. I put my Mace back real fast and pretended to walk

70

to the front of the bus, too. That was a good thing that girl did. But she should've done it sooner.

So I was standing up front holding on to one of those poles when my buddy, the crazy guy with the brown pants, started walking up the aisle. He was laughing a lot, and when he got next to me he put his face right up next to mine and said, "Fucking bastards! Aren't they all fucking bastards?"

It was pretty embarrassing. On top of everything else my stomach was starting to growl. At top volume. Then I did something I shouldn't have done. I told him, "Yeah."

He started laughing then and slapped me on the back and kept saying, "Fucking bastards." He was probably the grandfather of the kid back at Harrison Godfrey who kept saying, "No fuck!" Those two should get together, I thought. They could have one hell of a conversation. They should get on *Meet the Press* or one of those shows and have some guy interview them. Dan Rather or somebody. William F. Buckley. William F. Buckley could ask both of them some faggy-sounding question with a lot of intellectual stuff about the shift to the right and the failures of the liberals. And then he could ask them to respond and they'd say, "Fucking bastards!" and "No fuck!"

My stop wasn't for a while, because we were only at Wacker Drive. The crazy guy kept slapping me on the back, like I was a hell of a buddy of his, so I told him, "You ought to go on *Meet the Press*, you know?" He laughed real hard then. He didn't know what the hell I was talking about, naturally. "You should talk to William F. Buckley, really." He kept slapping my back. So I said to him, "Fucking bastards," and that made him laugh so hard he fell right in a fat woman's lap. She started pushing him off, but she couldn't, because he was laughing too hard. I got off the bus then, even though it wasn't my stop. I figured I could walk from there. I just couldn't spend another second on that goddamn bus. And that was just *one* bus. Multiply that times three thousand and you'll know what Chicago is really like.

If you've ever tried to walk anywhere in the Loop at noon, you probably hate it as much as I do. You can't, that's why. It's like getting sucked up in some river, only the river is wall-to-wall people. Once they start moving, you have to move with them, and then there's always a line of more people coming from the opposite direction, like a stampede, and I'm always on the fringe. I'm always getting stuck between the two groups. I turned around a few times to make sure that crazy guy from the bus wasn't following me, and every time I turned around, people would step on the back of my shoe, or knock me in the back with their attaché cases.

In the street, none of the cars or trucks were going anywhere. They were at a standstill. Taxi drivers kept honking their horns and swearing at each other, and like every ten minutes or so they got to move around another inch and then all the lights would turn red again. I got to my dad's bank just before I almost had a nervous breakdown. No wonder executives drink so much.

As soon as I walked in, I got that feeling I always get whenever I go somewhere—*I shouldn't have come here.*

My dad works for American State Bank. He's a vice president, but that doesn't mean we're rich or anything. We're not. He's just a vice president, and they've got about a thousand of those at that bank. Maybe two thousand. Besides, the lawyers took most of the money in the divorce. He told me how much it cost, but I forget. It was a lot, though. Lawyers always take a lot.

I walked up to a receptionist—I think she was a receptionist, but you can't tell so good who's who at that bank—and asked to see Mr. Blake.

"Which department?" she asked, real hostile. She didn't like the way I was dressed, you could tell. Everybody in the bank but me was wearing pinstripes or tweeds. I just had my sweat shirt and my jeans.

"I don't know which department. He's a vice president," I said.

Then she said, "What is it you want to see him about?"

"Lunch. I want to have lunch with him."

"Do you have an appointment?" she asked, picking up a phone and pushing a button.

"No. No, I don't."

She pushed the button again. "Who may I say is calling?"

I wanted to fool around with her, give her a phony name. I almost said I was Alexander Haig, but I decided not to. "Lenny. Lenny Blake. I'm his son."

She looked at me like she didn't believe me. You could tell. She gave me one long dirty look. She didn't even ask me to have a seat. Boy, was she a bitch. That's probably the kind of woman my mother's little "friend" is, I thought. All lesbians are snotty as hell. I didn't think this one was a lesbian, though. She had painted toenails and looked like one of those women you see in *Cosmopolitan*. They're not lesbians so much, they're just ice-cold bitches.

She told whoever it was on the other end of the phone who I was and that I wanted to see Mr. Blake. And then she hung up and walked away, so I sat down. I waited and watched all the money people walk all over the place. They had Muzak going and the air conditioning was too cold and every once in a while somebody was paged. There were no magazines to read. I shouldn't've come here, I told myself. But there was no place else to go. I couldn't go to school, I couldn't go home, and I shouldn't've been there. I shouldn't've been *any*place. That's when you know you're in trouble.

I waited thirty-five minutes before the receptionist came back, and by then there was a whole line of people waiting for her. She disappeared after she talked to each one, and an hour later, I still hadn't seen my father. When she came back, I walked over to her desk and said, "Excuse me, but I asked to see Mr. Blake an hour ago."

"He's with a client," she said.

"Yeah, I figured. But did you *tell* him? I mean, does he even know I'm here?"

She looked up like I was boring hell out of her. "I *left* the message with his secretary. He'll be with you as soon as possible."

"No, he won't," I told her.

"Pardon me?"

"I said, no. He won't. You should have told *him*, not his secretary."

"Are you telling me how to do my job?" she said. She was like an insane woman. She could've easily murdered someone; you could see it in her eyes.

"No one's trying to tell you how to do your job," I said, almost like an apology. I was trying to keep her cool, because she was

73

starting to sound a little hysterical. Some people at the next desk were staring at us. "No one's trying to tell you that, but—"

"Well, *thank you*," she said, very cynic-like. *"Thank you very much."*

Christ, what a lousy temper she had. She was a crazy woman. Must've had a very rotten personal life. But that wasn't my fault. She ignored me then and asked a guy with gray hair behind me if she could help him.

"Wait a minute. I was first," I said, but it was like I wasn't there.

"May I help you, sir?" she asked the gray-haired guy again.

I leaned over her desk then and said, pretty calmly for the way I was feeling, "I want you to have someone tell Mr. Blake I'm here. I want you to do that right now." I was practically whispering, and I said it very slow to keep her nerves from exploding or something. But it didn't work. She hit the goddamn ceiling.

"I told you he's with a client! You're upsetting me and I won't take it! I've had it with your rudeness and—"

"Hey, shut up, will you? Try to keep your voice down, why don't you? Come on. Everybody's staring."

"I'm going to call security in one more minute," she said.

"But I'm Mr. Blake's son, I tell you." I really was whispering now because this little crowd had formed around us. It was very close to the most embarrassing thing that's ever happened to me. I could feel myself blushing, and all of a sudden I had to go to the bathroom. That's what happens when I get extremely nervous. It makes me have to go to the bathroom.

"I don't care if you're the Pope's *brother*," she said, at nearly the top of her lungs. "Mr. Blake is with a *client*. Do you understand English? Would you like me to get you a translator?"

It was one of those situations. One of those situations when you're not wrong, but you *look* like you're wrong because nobody really wants to get to the bottom of things. I just slung my jacket over my shoulder and started to walk out. When I got near the front door of the bank, I heard a thud on the carpet. I looked down and watched my Mace canister roll right across the floor to the security guy. He picked it up and started reading the label. That's my luck. Two cops in one day get a hold of my Mace. Somebody wanted to see me land in jail. If there's a God, He was trying awful hard to get me behind bars that day.

I just reached out and took it from him and said, "Thank you," and walked the hell out the big dumb front door of that goddamn bank. It was worse in there than on the bus.

I looked at my watch, but it had stopped. It was one of those quartz deals that's supposed to last a lifetime. Its lifetime had been approximately six months. So I started walking north on LaSalle Street, and at Monroe I saw an insurance company clock. It was one-fifteen. It was already time to start going back to meet Lisa and I hadn't even had lunch. I was starving. I was so hungry I kept feeling like I was going to drop. You know how it is when all you've had is coffee and nothing to eat. I'll tell you how hungry I was. I was so hungry I ate at a Burger King. Burger Kings always give me diarrhea, but I ate there anyway. And there wasn't any-place to sit, so I ate standing up. Even though fast-food places make terrible food, it's probably safer eating there than it is at good restaurants. At good restaurants the cooks and the waiters spit in the food before they bring it to you if they've had a hard day or if they're in a bad mood. I knew this guy who was a camp counselor at a summer camp my parents used to send me to. He was a waiter sometimes, and he used to tell us about how they all—all the wait-resses and guys in the kitchen—used to spit big hockers into the food and then stir it up so the customers wouldn't see it. He said they do it almost everywhere, especially the good restaurants. At least at Burger King or McDonald's you can watch them while they make your goddamn food. If anybody tried to spit a hocker on a Whopper, you'd see 'em.

I ate a Whopper and had a Coke in about fifteen seconds. I set a new food speed record. Then I walked back outside to the noise and exhaust stink and all the mobs. It's really something when you can't see your own father for a goddamn minute. What the hell did she think would happen if I talked to him for one lousy minute? Did she think the goddamn ceiling of the bank would cave in? Or that Wall Street would crash? I hate regular people. I mean, people who all they can see is tweed and pinstripes and memos and money. God, do I hate them all.

I started walking back up LaSalle Street to a bus stop, but the stupid street was so crowded that it made more sense to walk than it did to get on a bus. You could make better time walking. So I walked. At least I had something in my stomach. When I got to Wells Street, I jumped on a bus and took a seat at the very back, where all the gang kids carve graffiti in the upholstery. I was thinking about Lisa. I was thinking that I should've been nicer to her when she said about playing at her mother's club. It's a dive, that club. It's called Scene II, and all these *hip* people hang out there. They all walk around like they own the place, being hip, after having just come out of Faces or someplace just as sickening. They talk during the music, and everybody gets drunk and makes fools out of themselves. Lisa's mother always hangs out with guys much younger than herself, guys that look like Mafia or something. But they pay the acts good. Well. And it's the only place in all of Chicago that would let guys as young as us play, on account of the booze laws. But I didn't feel much like playing. You have to really be in the mood to rock and roll. You have to be either real happy or very mad. I wasn't either of those, but I supposed I'd go ahead and play at the stinking club if Rick thought we should. Besides, it would make Lisa happy. I had Lisa on my mind.

Then I started reading the graffiti. I should say I *tried* reading the graffiti. Those gang guys can't spell. They have this kind of script that's very hard to read, too. Some guy named Shorty must have carried a power drill on the bus, because he carved his name right in the steel on the back of the seat in front of me. It said:

Allmitey Latin Cobra's Will
Overcom The World
—Shorty

As the bus was swerving all over the street and cutting cars off and almost running over old ladies with shopping bags, I started picturing people in Germany and Poland giving up to the Latin Cobras. I could just picture an office in the United Nations Building reserved for the Latin Cobras. There'd be a big summit meeting between Reagan and Yasir Arafat and Margaret Thatcher—and Shorty. Everybody would be in a conservative blue or gray suit, except Shorty, who'd be wearing green janitor baggies with an Afro pick sticking out of his back pocket and a transistor radio balanced on his shoulder. Reagan and all the others would be making speeches and signing documents, and Shorty, meanwhile, would be carving his name in a desk with a screwdriver. When it was his turn to talk, he'd get up to the microphone, walking the entire way like a pimp, and then he'd scream at the top of his voice, "Cobra love!" That's what those gangsters do. They say the name of their gang and then they say "love," because they think it means power or something. Then there'd be a cocktail party and all the world leaders would drink white wine from long-stemmed glasses. Shorty would whip out a bottle of Richard's Wild Irish Rose wine and propose a toast:

Yo' Mama.

And then there'd be a Grand Ball with an orchestra to celebrate the Latin Cobras, and everybody would be dancing a waltz, everybody, that is, except Shorty, who'd introduce his girlfriend, Rosa (whose nickname is Tiny) and the two of them would disco. Rosa would have purple nail polish, blue jeans, white socks, and pointy black high heels. Nancy Reagan would compliment her on her "costume" and ask if it'd been designed by Calvin. Rosa would chew her gum for a minute and then say, "Naw. I think it's Am-Vets." Then she'd sit on President Reagan's lap and tell him how cute white boys are, but they can't dance worth a shit. Shorty would've gotten the First Lady in a corner by then, fondling her rear end, and telling her he likes "older meat."

Yep. The Latin Cobras certainly will overcome the world. There's no doubt in my mind. I just hope it's televised.

Then something happened that took my mind off graffiti. I knew it was going to happen. I had to go to the bathroom. I had to go to the bathroom on account of the reaction I get to Whoppers. I knew it was getting close to the time I'd told Lisa I'd meet her, and I didn't have a goddamn second to lose. Believe me. I pulled that cord that tells the driver you want to get off at the next stop, and when the door opened, I *flew*. There was an Amoco station about a block up and I ran all the way. But when I got there, there was no attendant or nobody to ask where the bathrooms were. So I started to case the place, looking everywhere. I thought about the architect of Amoco stations and how he must be some kind of sadist, hiding the bathrooms for moments exactly like I was having. I went clear around to the back of the station and *there* were the bathrooms. But there was this thing on the lock of the door that said you had to put in a dime. Jesus. I checked my pockets and pulled out about fifty dollars in cash, but no dimes. I ran around to the front of the station and by then the attendant was back, but he was putting gas in somebody's car.

"You got change for a dollar?" I asked him.

He just looked at me, went back to pumping gas, and nodded. But he didn't give me any change. I had to stand there *dying* while he cleaned some schmuck's windshield and checked his oil. The guy was driving a Mercedes. If *I*'d've been driving a Mercedes, I'd've had change by then. But I was just a pedestrian. Pedestrians can wait. It's okay if pedestrians make in their pants.

I followed the guy back to the front office of the station and I *finally* got my dime. I ran all the way back to the washroom, put the dime in the slot, but the goddamn door wouldn't open. It was broken. People at that very moment were making business deals on LaSalle Street worth millions of dollars. Somewhere in the world someone was buying a new Ferrari, and scientists were discovering cures to diseases, but I couldn't get into the goddamn bathroom. That's why I sometimes suspect maybe there *is* a God. If there *was* a God, He'd be pissed off at me for not believing in Him, so He'd do things like give me a bitchy receptionist and keep me out of bathrooms when I really have to go.

I had no choice; I had to go to the front of the station and tell the attendant about how the door didn't work.

"The door doesn't work," I told him. "I put in a dime and everything, but the door won't open."

"Don't work," he said. "Gotta use the ladies' room."

"Yeah?"

"Yeah."

"It's okay, you mean? I mean, it's okay if I go in there?"

"Yeah."

So I ran back around to the bathrooms, but I had a hard time putting the dime in the slot. Somebody'd stuck some gum in the opening. I knocked first, but there was nobody in there. Then the door opened when I pushed the lever, but I was too scared to go in. What if some cop or somebody saw me going in there? They'd think I was a pervert waiting to rape some lady motorist who really had to go to the bathroom. I looked around real careful-like, but nobody was watching me. So I went in. I felt so weird, in a ladies' room. You could tell it was a ladies' room 'cause they didn't have one of those things you piss in on the wall. And was that place ever a *mess*. There was garbage all over the floor. (I won't tell you what somebody had left all over the floor because you might throw up.) I just calmed down and took care of business. I hate that phrase, like I told you, on account of Elvis, but that's what I did. No sense going into details. What kind of world is it when all the food either has hockers in it or gives you diarrhea?

By the time I got to Park West and Burling Avenue, like I told Lisa I would, I was ten minutes late, and she was standing around with Rick and Kevin and the bass player for our band, Pete Lower. We all the time kid him about his name by saying, "You can't get *lower* than that." He's okay. He's got like a genius I.Q. and is very quiet.

"It's about time," Lisa said.

"I had some business to take care of," I told her.

Rick said, "Where the hell have you been for the last two days, you sack of shit? I've only tried to call you about a million times. I left messages, too."

"I was out. Hi, Lisa," I said. She laughed and put her arm around my shoulder and started telling me I didn't look so good. Just what I wanted to hear.

Kevin asked me if I was going to graduate, and I told him I didn't know yet, but probably. I had to write a book.

"We're playing at Lisa's mother's club in two nights," Rick said. "I don't want to hear any excuses, Lenny. We open for fucking Lefty Dizz. Do you realize the publicity in that?"

"Yeah," I said.

"Record guys'll be in the audience and everything. Right, Lisa?"

Lisa nodded. She still had her arm around me. Boy, was she getting chummy. It felt sort of good having somebody's arm around me then. It could've been King Kong with his arm around me and I still would've felt a little better, but it was Lisa, which made it a *lot* better. I kept looking at her face when she wasn't noticing me so much. She has this real soft skin, like most girls do, but it was like even softer than most girls' skin. I thought I was falling in love all of a sudden.

"A guy from Arista will be there," she said, looking up at me. "You'll play, won't you, Lenny?"

"Goddamn right he'll play, if I have to throw him in the goddamn fountain again, he'll play." Rick has such a sweet way with words.

I said I'd play.

Pete asked in his high-I.Q. voice what we'd call ourselves.

"Frog Eggs was good. We were only Frog Eggs for ten minutes, once. I can get fresh frogs, too," Rick said.

Everybody groaned. Nobody liked that name much.

Kevin was thinking real hard and had his hand up to his chin, pacing around. "How about Rat Meat?"

"Why does everything have to be so gross?" Lisa wanted to know. It was a good question, but I wasn't thinking in terms of the band just then. I was thinking about dirty service station washrooms, fast food that gets you sick, newspaper headlines, and mothers being lesbians. It was a hell of a good question.

"That's the trend," Rick said. "You used to call yourself something like the Searchers or the Eagles. Now you gotta get a reaction like Puke on a Biscuit or something. We could go dressed as tampons and call ourselves Toxic Shock Syndrome. Or Herpes II. We could go dressed as tetracycline."

"My mother won't think that's funny," Lisa said.

"Why?" Pete asked.

"Because I think she's had them both."

Rick laughed. I got to admit, I even laughed. Jesus. It was the first time in about a month that I laughed. It felt good, too.

Rick told me that whatever we called ourselves, we had to practice the next night at this converted warehouse we'd rented in the factory section of Fulton Market. It's a rehearsal hall now. I told him I'd make it if he picked me up, and he said he would.

"Have a name, though," he said. "We gotta have a name by then."

Then I got this idea. I thought we'd call ourselves the Victims, and we'd come with all our clothes torn up and gashes on our faces and our hair all messed up. We'd make it look like we just got mugged, burned in fires, beaten, tortured, and things like that. I told them all about it and they liked it. Lisa didn't like it much. She didn't like it at all. She said it made her nervous, that I was too gloomy. I am pretty gloomy, I admit it.

Kevin asked, "How are we gonna look like we got all those bruises and things?"

"We'll just beat the shit out of each other before we go on," Rick said. "I'll get a crowbar and break your legs, and you set my clothes on fire, then we'll break a Coke bottle and cut up Lenny's face. How's that, Lenny?"

"Sounds good," I said.

Pete said maybe we should do all that as the opening number on stage, and then to see the end of the act the whole audience would have to get in ambulances with us and ride to the hospital, where we'd *really* get violent.

"We could all bring guns," Rick said, his eyes all wild. You should've seen him. He was going about a thousand miles an hour with his hands flying all over the place while he talked. "And then when we get to the hospital, while they're rushing us to surgery, we pull out the guns, and the audience figures we're gonna shoot each other, right? But we don't. We shoot *them*."

Pete said it was worth a try.

Lisa said it was sick.

I said we'd better just use makeup. "Can you do that?" I asked her. "Can you put makeup on us and make us all look wounded or something?"

"Coke bottles are more effective," Rick said.

"I can do it," Lisa said. "But we'll have to do it before the main band gets to the club, 'cause they get the only dressing room with a mirror."

"What do we get?" Rick asked.

"You have to use the staff bathroom. It's okay. Nobody comes in while you're there," Lisa explained.

The guys all made sounds like "Oh shit," and "Yuch."

"Well I'm *sorry*. But at least you're playing. We only have one real dressing room."

So everybody liked the Victims, and after a while they left to go watch the baseball championships at Oz Park. They asked Lisa and me if we wanted to go, but we said we didn't. Then it was just the two of us. Lisa was all excited about us playing, but I still didn't have my heart in it. The reason is, I feel like a victim almost all the time. It was something new for the others. I'd just as soon get on stage and just be Lenny Blake, not a victim. But it was my idea. I had to go along with it. Besides, nobody pays money to see a normal guy on a stage. They pay money to see somebody act weird and sick. I accept that part of it. I just don't like it much.

Lisa and me, we had a quiet afternoon, but it was nice. It almost made me forget about everything else. Almost. She had a car, a blue Toyota, and we drove down to Belmont Harbor. We parked the car and bought ice cream at this little stand they have there, and we watched people sailing out of the harbor in little boats. We sat right at the edge of the water, and you could see the Hancock Center and all the big buildings downtown where I live, only they looked *nice* for a change. When you see them in the distance on a sunny day from a harbor, they actually look *nice*. You'd never guess that the whole area was loaded with faggots and muggers and insane people. You'd just think it was a nice place to look at.

And I got to tell you about Lisa. The more time I spent with her, the better she looked. I kept getting that feeling I got back at school earlier that day, that feeling where I wanted to just kiss her or hug her. She was so pretty. Every once in a while a kid would zoom past us on a skateboard, or a bird would fly right over the water. Lisa kept putting her hand on my shoulder, or on my hand, and we talked about a lot of things. She was a very intelligent girl. The only problem was, she was almost as cynical as I am. But not so much. Pretty much, though. You know what we talked about? We talked about World War III. Not the most romantic subject in the world, but that's what we talked about. *I* brought it up, of course. One of the things I can't stand about myself is that I always bring

82

up horrible subjects and make everybody talk about them. But the thing was, everything was so nice, so pretty. It was *too* nice. I'm not used to it when it's *too* nice. It makes me start thinking about what could ruin it. There I was, having the nicest time I could remember, and what I pictured was a whole fleet of Soviet missiles heading straight for Chicago.

"It could just happen when we finish our ice cream cones," I told her. "All those people are getting on the Lake Shore bus, and they think they're gonna have dinner with their families, or they're wondering what clothes they're gonna wear to some play tonight, and then the missiles hit and everything is gone. This park, those boats, me, you. It's all gone."

Lisa was staring at the park. "I think about that sometimes. I think about all the time we spend on school and what college will accept us, and what it says next to our yearbook picture, and then one morning we wake up and the bomb hits. Boom. It's all over. No car. No colleges. No house."

"Oh, if it was just the cars and colleges and houses, I'd tell them to drop the fucker now. But I mean, like *us*, right now. There wouldn't be no more couples eating ice cream cones and not doing nothing else. That's the sad part. No more little kids playing hide-and-seek. That kind of stuff. But if it's just cars and colleges—"

"*You* know what I mean," she said, wiping the chocolate from her mouth with a napkin, "you know. I mean all the things we *rely* on. And then what about the people who aren't with their families? It would be nice at least if they could die together." She stopped. She thought a minute. "Would *everybody* die?"

I didn't answer right away. I tried to picture it in my head first. "Yeah," I said, "everybody. It would take them longer in the sub-urbs, though. They'd get all the radiation and they'd die slower. Their skin would fall off and they'd get cancer and vomit all the time. Me, I'd rather just get blown up than have my skin fall off. That's what they get for living in the suburbs."

Lisa said, "Don't you like the suburbs?"

"Oh, yeah. They're nice. But they're too snotty in the suburbs. Very hick, too. Green lawns. Quiet."

"Green lawns and quiet are nice," she said.

"Yeah, I know. But that's all they've got. I mean, they believe they deserve those things, and they start thinking *that's* reality. But it's not."

She was starting to get playful. She started messing up my hair, and she asked me, "Oh no? What's reality, according to the famous Mr. Lenny Blake?"

"Reality? Reality is rapists and gangs and crooked cops and plane crashes and faggots who try to get you to come up and listen to their records and black kids getting their heads cut off in slums and—"

"That's enough," Lisa said. "I get the idea."

I was making her sick. I do that to people.

I said, "But at least if they bombed us, all those things would be gone."

"But so would the nice things," she said.

"Yeah. But at least the bad things would be gone."

You can't win. If there's no bad, then there's no good, either. Sometimes the bomb makes sense to me. Other times it doesn't. What I wish, I wish they'd stop threatening. If they're gonna use it, then use it, already. If not, then stop threatening.

But we had a good time anyway. We walked around the harbor some more and then we picked up a pizza to go and brought it back to her house. Neither of her parents come home till real late 'cause they're both go-getters, or overachievers, or whatever you call someone who doesn't give a shit about having fun but only wants to make it big. They have this house on Fullerton Avenue in the Park West section of town—very expensive. The Governor of Illinois has a house around there, but he's never home. Lisa, she's got a great bedroom and a VHS video thing where you can watch old movies or new movies. We watched this old one, *Rebel Without a Cause*, with James Dean. It was pretty good, but corny. I wonder if things in the fifties were really that corny. If so, then Christ, it was almost the Stone Age. But it was kind of fun, in a way. Because if James Dean was supposed to be cynical, then I'm super-cynical. I mean, if that's as cynical as they could get back then, then they were doing all right.

I didn't eat much of the pizza, because I kept worrying about someone spitting hockers in it. I didn't tell Lisa that, though. I'd already made her sick once that day. I figured, let her eat in peace.

84

Hockers won't kill you. But I wasn't hungry. Then we played this game we made up called "I Hate It." The whole point was to say something you hate, and then if the person agrees with you, they have to say something *they* hate. If they don't agree with you, they have to make you explain why you hate it. If they still don't agree with you, they cancel your point. I was winning. I hate almost everything.

"Wayne Newton," I said.

"Icch," Lisa said. She was looking cuter every minute. She changed into these cut-off shorts and I couldn't take my eyes off her. "*The Dukes of Hazzard,*" she said. I agreed, of course.

"High school," I said.

"Preppy look," she said. Boy, did that girl hate the right things.

"Parents," I said.

"Why? Don't you like your parents?"

"What's the name of this game, Lisa? 'I *Love* It' or 'I *Hate* It'? I just gave my answer."

"But I don't hate your parents," she said.

"What about yours?" I said.

She just thought for a minute. You could see I never should've said "parents." It did something weird to her.

"I love my parents," she said. "I have to cancel you on that one."

"Okay. Your turn."

"No. Wait a minute. Why do you hate your parents?" she asked. She couldn't get off the subject.

"For very personal reasons. I shouldn't have brought it up. Your turn."

She kept thinking, and then she said she didn't want to play this game anymore. I said okay, we'd stop. But it made me curious why the parent thing bothered her so much. I don't really hate my parents, but I did then.

After we'd watched television (some dumb movie about a kid who's raised in a tank 'cause he'd die from germs or something) she brought it up again.

"Why do you hate your parents, Lenny? You can tell me. Honest."

"I don't really hate them," I said. "But can you keep a secret?"

85

She said yeah, she could, so I told her my mother was a lesbian, and about the lady who spent the night.

"Are you *sure*," she said, "or are you just guessing?"

"What's to guess about? The coat was there, the shoes were there, and they were both in the bedroom. What the hell is there to guess about?"

"Why do you hate your father?"

I told her about the divorce, and how he argues about how much money to send us, and about how I waited an hour to see him that day and he didn't even come out.

She just thought. She thought and thought and thought. Boy, can that kid think. Then, just when I thought the subject was good and dead, she kind of whispers something to me.

"What? What did you say? I can't hear you."

"I said, If I tell you something, would you promise to keep it a secret, too?"

"Sure. I won't tell anybody. Trust me."

Then what she does, she doesn't tell me. That makes me nuts, when somebody makes you promise not to tell and then they never tell you what you're not supposed to tell. I kept saying, "Come on, tell me. I won't say a word to nobody, not even if they torture me," but she wouldn't say a goddamn word. She just sat there staring into the TV screen and not saying anything. Then, when I think everything is fine and she's just changed her mind about telling me, I saw these big-assed tears come out of her eyes. Not separate tears, but just this whole flow of water, and the next thing I know, we're holding each other and she's crying. She's saying the craziest stuff. She says she's having sex with her father. She says he comes in her room every night and gets in bed with her and has sex with her and she hates him.

"I hate him! I hate him! I hate him!" And she's crying and I'm freaking, and suddenly I start wondering when the fuck those missiles are going to hit, and if it's in the next hour it won't be a minute too soon.

I said stuff like "It's okay, I won't tell anybody," but she wouldn't listen to me. All she could do was go into detail about how first he forced her and now she doesn't even put up a fight. Now, she said, sometimes she even *enjoys* it. I kept thinking, This is *Lisa?* That

86

cute little girl? Hell. Girl my ass. I thought about maybe I would
report the old guy, but then I remembered I promised not to tell
anybody.

"He won't let me go out with boys. Didn't you ever wonder why
I never have any boyfriends? He's jealous. He doesn't even like me
talking on the phone to them."

"It's okay," I said. I was still patting her back, like I was burping
a baby or something. Jesus. This was sicker than having your
mother be a lesbian. Much sicker.

Then I got the courage up to ask her something. "How long has
this been going on?"

Lisa, she sniffed, wiped her eyes, and said in this cracky voice,
"About a year? I don't know. About a year, I guess."

"A *year*? You've been having sex with your father for a *year*?"

Boy, was that the wrong thing to say. She went into flaming
hysterics when I said that, and then she got up and ran to the
bathroom and locked herself in.

I just sat on her bed. A whole fucking year. (I don't mean that in
a funny way, the way it sounds. The way it sounds is like I was
trying to be funny, but I'm not. I didn't mean a whole year full of
fucking, I just meant it was a long time, like a *fucking* long time.
You know what I mean.) The point is, you'd think that somebody
would've said something by then. I couldn't understand why a girl
would let her old man do it to her for a year without telling no
one. But then I sort of understood. The whole thing was so sick
and tangled up that she'd look bad no matter what. People would
think she was a whore, even if she wasn't. People are like that.
They hate the victims more than they hate the people who make
them victims. It's true. You had to feel for Lisa, you really did.
Poor kid. Poor screwed-up kid. Then I realized I'd better get her
out of the bathroom before she did something stupid, like slash her
wrists or something.

"Lisa? Hey. Lisa? Come on out, will ya?" I said. I knocked on
the door once in a while. But she wouldn't say anything. I could
hear her sniffle every so often, but she wouldn't answer me.

"Lisa?" I knocked again. "Please come out. It'll be okay. I promise. Please come out. Lisa?"

Nothing.

87

I was going mad with the idea that maybe she was cutting her wrists or overdosing or something. I started looking around the house for something to break the door down with. I found this wooden chair, but I didn't want to break it. Besides, I've seen guys try to break down doors on television, and even karate experts have trouble with it. I'm no karate expert. I can't even win at arm wrestling, most of the time, unless the kid is undernourished or about five years old or something.

I went back to the door and I heard water running. I've heard how people who cut their wrists let water run on them for some reason. I figured this was it—call the police.

"I'm calling the police, Lisa. Unless you come out right now, I'm calling the—"

"No!" she screamed, and the door flew open. She had a towel in her hands and she was blotting her eyes with cold water. That's what all the water sounds had been.

I said, "Holy shit," and then hugged her. "I thought you'd cut your wrists with razor blades or something."

"I thought about it," she said, "but all we have is electric razors." That made her laugh a little bit, even though she was still crying, kind of. We just held each other for a while. Then she had to blow her nose. I was about to tell her to come back to the bedroom with me, to lie down, when I heard a door in the house rattle.

"My *father's* home!" she whispered. "You've got to get *out* of here!"

"Is there a back door?" I asked. I was shaking something awful. I grabbed my windbreaker and put my shoes on.

"Yes." She was still whispering and pushing me around, trying to hide me. "But it's locked and it takes too long to find the keys to open it. Get under the bed. Quick!"

"The goddamn *bed?*" I didn't think I could fit.

"Yes. Hurry!"

"Lisa?" this man's voice yelled from downstairs. "Is your mother home?"

CHAPTER 9

Probably the craziest feeling in the world is hiding under somebody's bed in a house you don't know so good when one of the people around doesn't know you're there. Even if you don't have a cold, you feel like you have to sneeze or clear your throat. And you keep picturing how bad it would be if they found you under there. I was so scared. I was so scared I started to wonder if it's true that you can die from fright. I don't think it's true anymore. If it were true, I'd be dead right now.

Her father climbed the stairs. I could hear him. He climbed them kind of slow, the bastard. Lisa was throwing things around the room, making it look like she was doing normal girl stuff. Makeup or something. I couldn't tell. I couldn't see a thing.

"Lisa?"

"Yeah."

"How was school, honey?"

"Fine. How was work?"

"Okay. Your mother home?"

I wondered why he wanted to know that. I could figure it out, though. Boy, could I figure it out.

"No. She isn't. Would you like me to fix you dinner?"

"In a bit," he said. "Aren't you tired?"

Uh-oh, I thought.

"No. I ordered a pizza and did some exercises. I'm not tired yet. Why don't you wash up and I'll fix dinner."

I could hear him start to walk away. Then he said, "Don't you want to lie down for a bit? Maybe just a nap?"

That lousy bastard. I considered Macing him. I didn't think I could get out from under the bed fast enough, though. By the time I would've gotten out from there and on my feet, he probably would've killed me.

"No. I'll fix dinner. We'll take a nap later. I got some homework to do."

"All right," the old man said. Then he walked away. I just lay there. I was trying not to breathe so loud. I heard the bathroom door close and Lisa whispered, "Okay! Get the hell out of here!"

I was wiggling out from under the bed when the bathroom door opened again and the old man started walking toward the bedroom. Shit! I thought, and started wiggling to get back under the bed.

"Did I get any mail today?" he asked. Lisa was kicking my feet to let me know they were showing.

"Yes. It's on the kitchen table. Want me to get it?"

Silence.

"No, that's all right. I'll be down in a minute." And then he walked back to the bathroom and the door closed and the water started running.

"Now! Quick!" Lisa whispered again.

I got out of there so fast you'd've thought I was on fire. We both tiptoed down the stairs together and when we got to the front door, I realized I forgot my jacket under the bed.

"My jacket!" I said, very quiet-like.

"I'll get it," she said.

Before I could stop her, she was running back up the stairs. I had the front door open and was ready to run if the old bastard came down the stairs. Lisa was nearly back when the water shut off.

"Lisa?"

"Just a minute, Dad," she called out. Then she was pushing me out the door. "Go on, run!"

"But will you be okay?"

"Yes. *Yes!* Get out of here, now."

But I didn't feel like leaving her there like that, with the friendly family rapist. "Hasn't your bedroom door got a lock or something?"

"Lenny, goddamn it, will you please get the hell out of here *now!*" And then she slammed the door.

Outside it was getting dark already. Cars had their headlights on and everything. It was a pretty warm night, but I put my jacket on anyway. You can catch a cold on nights like that when you think it's warmer than it really is. I looked back at Lisa's house and wondered if her father would have sex with her that night. It sure sounded like he was planning on it. I couldn't stand the thought of it. I don't blame her, I'm not saying I do. But wasn't there something she could've done? I mean, couldn't she at least have *done* something? If I were a girl and that happened to me, I think the first thing I'd do is run away from home. Or kill him. Maybe both. What a stinking night.

I walked east to Clark Street, wondering where the hell I would spend the night. I was so sad. I missed my room. I just wanted to go home to my room and close the door and never come out again. But it was like my room wasn't mine anymore. Like my mother had put some kind of fence around the whole goddamn apartment. Then I wondered if she was worried about me. She lets me come and go pretty much the way I want, but if she hadn't heard from me in a whole day, I'd bet she was worried. Let her worry. Let her worry a lot, I figured. If it bothered her enough, she could look up in her est manual what to do when your kid leaves home. Maybe she could get assertive or something. Or maybe she had an aerobic dance for that occasion. She'd probably call my father. Good, I thought. Let him worry, too. Let them call the fucking police and drag Lake Michigan for my body. If he ever wants to talk to me, he can leave a message with my receptionist and then wait about a thousand years, just in case I'm with a client.

I was watching all the deviates on Clark Street and Fullerton. You got those leather boys there, with their short haircuts and tight jeans that look like they haven't been washed in a month, and white gym shoes. They all look like clones. I remember that look when it was in style for about two minutes a couple of years ago. Mostly they all got bald heads, too. I wonder why so many faggots got bald heads? Then I got sick of watching them, so I hopped on the Clark Street bus and went south toward my building. I had no place else to go. I hoped James was on duty, so I could hang out with him, and maybe he'd let me go home to his house until I could make other arrangements. I was sure he'd let me. James wasn't like a parent or a teacher or anybody who's *supposed* to be responsible but really isn't. James is the real thing.

This was the third bus I'd been on in one day, and if you think I liked it you should get your head examined. The night buses on Clark Street are totally opposite from the day ones; there's hardly nobody on them, which is good in some ways and not so good in others. What's good is that you don't have to *smell* anybody and *listen* to everybody talk crazy and make a lot of noise. What's bad is, if there's just a few of you, then you have to like *deal* with each other. You stand out.

The bus was crawling because of the traffic being so bad. Traffic on Clark Street is lots worse at night than it is in the day because all the night spots, all the *hip* little restaurants and things, draw people from the suburbs the way shit draws flies. I'm not kidding. All these people, they move to the suburbs so they won't have to go to the city and the first thing that happens when the sun goes down is they all come back to the city to eat and see shows and movies. It's very hypocritical. I wish they'd all just stay in the lousy suburbs and watch how green their lawns get or something.

Somebody must've known I'd be on that bus that night because they left a newspaper in the seat I was sitting in. It was all wrinkled and it was an afternoon edition, but I read it anyway. Most of the stuff like Ann Landers was the same, but some of the news stories were different. There was one about the recession deepening, which made me laugh, because what did they expect it to do? Get better? When has it ever gotten better? There was also one that made me reach for my Mace. I should never have picked up that paper. I should've just sat and thought about something. Except then I probably would've worried about Lisa and how much I wanted to kill her father, so maybe it's good I read the paper instead. I don't know. I don't think so, though.

The story was about a man who attacked a passenger on a CTA bus. He came at him, for no goddamn reason, with a kitchen knife, and slashed his throat in front of everybody. Then he kept beating him up when he was losing blood all over the floor. He just kept kicking him in the face, probably trying to make his stupid head come off like that black kid in the slums. It's crazy. Everybody wants everybody else's head to come off. Then the story said that one of the passengers, who was a minister, stopped the guy from beating him up and tried to put his throat back together until the ambulance came. It took the ambulance about forty-five minutes to get there even though the hospital was only two blocks away. It was a nice story to read while you were riding a bus at night with a black guy directly across from you who looked like he could bend steel bars for a hobby. It certainly made me feel like relaxing. I kept hoping the traffic would get better and the bus would get going, but it didn't.

Goddamn Clark Street. I hate that street. I hate CTA buses too. I damned well just about started hating the guy who wrote the news story and the guy who left the newspaper in the seat. I was beginning to hate everybody including the bus driver. I put my hand on my Mace and it felt all sweaty, but I kept it there anyway, and out of the corner of my eye, I watched the black guy across from me. I thought I saw him look at me a few times, but when you look at somebody from the corner of your eye you can't tell so good. I was too scared to turn around and see if he was looking at me or not. So I stayed there, frozen like a statue.

Finally, after about two centuries, my stop was coming up. Oak Street. I stood up, when all of a sudden this guy who I'd been watching out of the corner of my eye, he says to me, "You got the time, brother?"

He thought I was his brother or something. I'd never met him before and here he tries to get into my family. I said, "No, I don't." And I was walking up the aisle then, and I felt a little bad, because the guy wanted to know the time and I couldn't help him out. So I turned around and said, "I think it's about nine-thirty, though."

He folded his arms and looked out the window and said back to me, "Thinkin' ain't knowin'."

How do you like that? Then I got mad that I even felt sorry for him not knowing the time. Me, my trouble is I'll feel sorry for somebody because they don't know the time, and so I'll try to help them. Then they get an attitude, like it's my fault I don't have a watch that works. Where was *his* goddamn watch?

I got off at Oak Street, and I was just waiting for the bus to move on, when the guy who thought I was his brother got off too. He got off hurried-like, like he'd almost forgotten it was his stop, or like he just decided it was his stop. I tried to ignore him, to act cool, like I didn't care if he got off there too, but I was nervous. I figured he was either going to mug me, stab me, or try to make my head come off because I didn't know what the time was. People are crazy; you never know.

93

I started walking east on Oak Street, and I didn't look or nothing, but I could tell he was walking behind me. I walked past the Newberry Library and this park they have there called Bug House Square, which sure has the right name, on account of all the perverts in the city meet there to discuss what perverted things they'll do next. I pictured two guys meeting there for a regular little session after a day of being perverted. One of them would say to the other, "Slow day. I only pulled my pants down twice in front of little girls, and the guy whose throat I slashed was saved by a minister."

And the other guy, who'd be all greasy from not washing and who had bad teeth and who smelled would say, "Me too. One home invasion and only two rapes and one murder. Nobody even screamed. They seemed like they expected it. They probably've been reading the goddamn paper again."

I shouldn't have taken that route. What's wrong with me? You'd think I *wanted* to die. I wondered what other way I could've taken, but one was as bad as the other. The Michigan Avenue bus would've taken me practically to my front door, but I would've had to wait for it in Lincoln Park. That's something you just don't do— wait for a bus in Lincoln Park at night. Unless you feel lucky, or unless you just get sick of waiting to get maimed and want to get it over with.

When I reached the lighted-up part of Oak Street I felt a little better. My "brother" had gone someplace else; there was no sign of him. Also, it's better when you have bright lights and a lot of people, except the people on Oak Street near Rush and Michigan Avenue are the pinstripe people all over again. Except now, now they have their hip clothes on, like they just came out of an ad for jeans. They think they're on TV, and they won't give you an *inch* of sidewalk if you look like me. They figure *they're* on TV, but *you're* not, like you didn't pass the audition. Sophisticated ladies in designer clothes with makeup and guys on their arms who look like TV anchormen. All their lives they try to look beautiful for everybody else. I can't stand it. They'd probably just had drinks at Hillary's and were on their way to a disco or a nightclub to see some other guy who looked like an anchorman. They'd talk about Wall Street or some fabulous play, like they wrote it or something. That amuses me. Anybody who all the time tries to look beautiful proba-

94

bly never wrote a goddamn thing in his life. No time. No talent. No brains. They just *look* good, is all.

When I got to my building, was I ever glad. James was on duty. He was talking on the phone when I got to the lobby, and when he saw me, he said something kind of low to whoever he was talking to, and then he hung up.

"Lenny!" he said. He said it kind of pissed off. "Lenny, where in God's name you been?"

"Miss me?" I said, kidding-like. James didn't want to be kidded with, though.

"Yo' mother called me up worried sick about you. Wondered did I maybe see you or somethin'. I tol' her, no I ain't seen you since the day before, maybe you was out with friends. She say call her if I hear from you." He tipped his hat back with his hand and said again, "Where you *been?*"

I didn't like seeing him all upset like that. I sat down on this little chair he has in the lobby. It felt like the day was catching up with me and I couldn't do nothing to keep it away. It was a little like getting hit with a tidal wave, and you had to sit down to take it.

"I don't know where to start," I told him. Then I remembered what I wanted to ask him. "Hey James, can I spend the night at your place? When you get off duty, I mean. You suppose I could spend the night at your place? I don't take up much room. I don't even snore."

James, he just sighed and started pacing. He told me I had to call my mother and stop her from worrying. I said I would, only could I stay at his house, yes or no?

"You *got* a home, Lenny. You got a home right here. Why you want to run away?"

"I don't want to run away, James. I just don't want to *stay*, is all. Please say yes. C'mon. Give me a break, James. Please?"

He saw how I wasn't kidding around and that I was upset, so he said yes, I could stay at his place, but he made me call my mother first. People were coming in the lobby and wanted their car doors opened, so James had to go back to work. We didn't have a chance to talk or anything, so all he knew was that I was crazy and wanted to stay at his house. I called my mother from the lobby. It took her about one second to answer. She must've been sitting on the phone.

"Hello?"

"Hi, Mom. It's me. Lenny."

Silence. You never heard so much silence.

"Lenny, where have you been? Are you all right? Are you in trouble again?"

She was making me nuts, and I'd only been on the phone with her about two seconds.

"I'm fine. Really. I'm just gonna spend the night with a friend. That's why I'm calling. To tell ya. I won't be home tonight."

"No you're not. No, you're not spending the night with a friend, young man. I want you home right now. Immediately. Do you understand? Lenny?"

How do you talk to somebody like that? Mothers always say the wrong things at the worst time.

"I'm spending the night at a friend's house, Mom. I'm fine. I just don't feel like coming home tonight. I'm not in the mood, I mean."

"You're not in the *mood*. Did you say you're not in the *mood*?"

"Yeah. I'm not, really."

"What does *mood* have to do with it? Hello? Lenny?"

"Yeah. I'm here. But I'm not coming home tonight."

She like must've switched the phone to another ear. There was this noise and then she didn't say anything, and then she started talking again. "Lenny, I'd like to know something. Let's get this straight."

"Hmm?"

"Since when do you give the orders in this house?"

I looked at the phone like it was crazy or something. Always the wrong thing at the worst time. Then I said, "Ever since you and your friend started spending the night together," and then I hung up. I wanted to try and talk to her, but it was no use. There was no talking to her. All of a sudden she wanted to be assertive. She must've just come back from an est class. I wonder how many homes those self-help methods have broken up. Probably millions. Between corporations and self-help clinics and religions and hip clothes and nightclubs, families don't have a chance. I mean it. In the future nobody'll have a family. They'll just have a shrink and a health club and a corporation. They're already doing that in Japan. People are living in Toyotas right at the goddamn plant. They get

96

up in the morning and their family is the factory. That's the way things are going. That's supposed to be *normal*. But I'm the one who's sick. See how much sense that makes?

I watched James hike cars and open doors all night. They sure keep him running. It made me feel lazy just sitting there watching all the hipsters get waited on. By the time he was off duty and we were both in his car going to his house, I felt like if I ever saw another Mercedes I'd shoot it. I'd throw bricks right through the goddamn windshield, just so James wouldn't someday have to open its door for some fat-assed pinstripe.

"You nigger-lippin' it," James said, when he took the joint we were smoking back from me. Jesus, is that man funny. He said it just like that: *You nigger-lippin' it.*

"No I'm not. I'm white boy-lipping it. White people practically got no lips."

James, he laughed. "Where this little white boy be going to? Where you going to, Lenny?" We were on Lake Shore Drive then, and there were hardly any cars on the street.

"What're you talking about? I'm going home with you, James."

James took a hit from the joint and passed it back to me. He eyed the rearview mirror and shook his head. "No, no. That's not what I mean. I mean, where you be going to in this life, Lenny, when you can't even go home to yo' own house? Hmm? Where you be goin, you po' little white boy?"

God. I wished he wouldn't've said it like that. It made me feel like an orphan or something.

"James," I said, tipping the ashes from the joint in his car ashtray, "I don't know. But it just isn't my fault. Things keep *happening* to me, no matter how hard I try to make them *not* happen to me. Sometimes I just want to go in my room and lock the door and never come out. But then you get hungry and you have to come out for food, or you have to wash your clothes, or you have to go to school, or you have to see a shrink, or you have to play in a club. And as soon as you come out, all the killers and the nutty people, they jump on you and try to either make your head come off or to drive you crazy, or make you so sad you just wish the atom bomb would hit the goddamn Wrigley Building." I looked at James. We were at a red light. He was listening to me, you could tell, because it just shows in someone's eyes if they're

97

hearing what you're saying. "You know what I mean? I don't know. Maybe I *am* sick. Maybe everybody's right."

I waited for James to say something, but he didn't. He was much calmer now than he'd been when I first showed up at the lobby. He was listening, but it was like he'd heard it all before. It was like he'd been with me every step that day and he was just getting the replay. It's spooky how James all the time seems to *know* what you're going to say before you say it. And did I ever spill my guts. I had to, because he wouldn't say anything back to me. He just listened.

"You know why I can't go home? You wanna know?"

"You wanna tell?" he said.

"Yeah. It's 'cause my mother, she's a lesbian."

The joint was out by then, so I just sat back and waited for James to hear what I'd said. He didn't react or nothing, though, when I'd said it.

"She's a lesbian. She had a lady spend the night the other night and they were both in the bedroom together. She's a *lesbian*."

James turned on the radio and fiddled with the dial. Some jazz station came on and we drove through the night and past the depressing buildings that look like they should be torn down. "Everybody's got to be something," he said.

"They don't have to be a *lesbian*," I said, opening my window a little and watching how James just drove nice and easy-like down the road.

"Maybe they do," he said.

And then I told him about Lisa and her old man making it together. For a whole *year*. I told him about the lady who got raped and thrown off a cliff, the one I read about in the paper. I told him about how my father didn't even have a second to talk to me and about how I got diarrhea from a Whopper, but at least it didn't have a hocker in it. That made him laugh.

"Don't *laugh*, James! Jesus! I just told you about one of the worst days in my life and you're *laughing*."

"You *funny*; that's why I'm laughin'. You such a *funny* boy, Lenny. You scared to walk, you scared to talk, you scared to *eat*, even, and you want me to not laugh. You scared somebody gonna slip you a hocker all the time. I'm sorry, Lenny. But it's funny."

"I don't think it's so funny." I didn't, either. We sat quiet for a while until James talked again.

98

"You mad at yo' mama 'cause she bein' human. You mad at that pretty little girl's old man, and you got a right to be. But hell, Lenny, what you gonna do? You gonna shoot everybody you don't like? You gonna kill yo'self worryin' 'bout atomic bombs and rapists? You know who you is? You Saint Lenny. Saint Fucking Lenny, come down from heaven to keep everybody from makin' hockers in everybody else's food, for cryin' out loud. An' you wanna crawl under everybody's covers and make sure they put their things in the right places. They ain't yo' sex things, but you wanna make sure they be puttin' 'em where you like 'em to go. An' when you can't do that, you run away from home."

"Let me off here," I told him. I was beginning to hate *him*, too.

"What?"

"I said let me off here. This is as far as I'm going."

James laughed a little. "Okay, okay. Relax. I didn't mean nothin', sweetheart. I just tryin' to tell you 'bout the world. You calm down now. It's gonna be all right."

"No it isn't. It's not going to be all right and I want you to let me off *right now*."

What I was trying real hard not to do was cry. But I wasn't trying hard enough. You could tell from my voice and my stupid running nose that I was crying. I couldn't help it. Fucking James. The last person in the world I counted on and he was against me, too. He was making fun of me and yelling at me and not taking me serious, just like everybody else. Saint Lenny, he called me. What I wished all of a sudden, I wished a whole string of Mercedes had to have their doors opened and each one of them had tons of suitcases James had to lift. Then I felt so bad for wishing that I hoped I'd die. I wanted to open James's car door and jump right into the road. I wanted to just get run over by a semitrailer and be done with it. Because when even James goes over to the other side, what chance do you have?

I said, "If you don't stop, I'm gonna open this door and jump," and then I opened the door a little to show him I wasn't kidding. James, he slammed on the brakes, and I got out. I started running like a kid, just running into the stupid night by this bar that had a burned-out neon sign that flickered. I heard the other car door close and I heard James running after me, so I ducked in an alley and ran, but I slipped on something and went facedown into a load

99

of soggy paper boxes and garbage. It knocked all the wind out of me and I was gasping like a fish on a boat when you pull it in and it can't breathe anymore. I hate that feeling. With that feeling you think you're going to die.

"Lenny, hey babe—" James was holding me by the shoulders and trying to help me, but I couldn't get my breath. "Just take it easy, sweetheart. Relax yo' muscles and breathe light-like. It's okay, now."

But it wasn't okay. I couldn't get my breath back, and I thought I was having a heart attack. On top of everything else, I started crying again, so I hid my face in my arm so James couldn't see me. But what he did was, he picked me up, like, and leaned me on him and started patting my back. I couldn't stop then. Here's a guy trying to save my life and I'd just hoped he'd have to be a *slave*. Forever. I hated myself so much I kept hoping I *was* having a heart attack, and the whole time there's James, just holding me and talking nice to me and trying to make me feel better. I can still hear his voice. He was saying, "Lord, boy. It's all right. It's fine now. You a good boy, Lenny. I'm sorry I said those things to you. You just go ahead and cry now. You just go ahead."

The nicer he was to me the harder I cried. I felt so fucking stupid, garbage all over my clothes and in hysterics like I was about two years old or something. But it's a good feeling holding on to someone, and them holding on to you. It makes the pain go away, partially. I just held on to him until it was over. Until I was all cried out. I think it took an hour until that happened, though. Then, when I couldn't hear any more sounds coming from me, nothing at all, except rats crawling around in the garbage cans, and cars driving by making swooshing sounds as they passed, I got up and wiped the dirt from my jeans. Then James and me walked back to his car real slow in the night.

CHAPTER
10

ames lives way the hell on the South Side where all the train tracks and factories are. He lives in a big old apartment building on the third floor and you have to walk up 'cause they aren't no elevators. There's just stairs, and the hallways are dark and smell like somebody's always cooking in them. He's got a steel door, too, so nobody can break in. I liked that, the steel door. It made me feel better, being in such a crummy neighborhood. At least he had a steel door.

When we walked in, I saw a black girl, around fourteen years old, asleep on a salmon-colored chair that turned around if you wanted it to. James pointed toward a room I could sleep in and then he woke up the girl. Her name was Dana. He gave her some money and asked how the kids were. I didn't even know James *had* any kids. It's funny. All the time James, he knew about my life and who I lived with, but I didn't know anything about him. Dana said one of the kids had a cough and they didn't have no cough syrup, so she gave him tea and honey, and James said that was good, he'd get some cough syrup in the morning. Then he said he'd see her tomorrow. She looked kind of funny at me, like what was I doing there. James told her who I was and that I needed a place to stay for the night, but even while she walked out the door she was still looking at me kind of weird. Like, what would a white boy with garbage all over his clothes be doing here? But she left, and luckily I didn't have to tell her. She wouldn't have understood anyway. That's one of the reasons I don't tell many people about me. If I had to explain my life to everybody I meet, they'd think I was making it up.

"I didn't know you had kids, James," I said. He was busy unfolding a couch for me in the little room I told you about.

"They ain't mine. They's my sister's. Twins."

"Yeah?" I said. "She out of town or something?"

James, he shook his head. "No. She not out of town. She out of her mind. Don't take good care of 'em. She too much in the bottle all the time."

"You mean she drinks?"

"Yeah."

"So you keep them here?"

"Um-hmm."

"Doesn't she want them back?" I asked. I realized I was probably getting too nosy, but with James, he doesn't mind so much.

"Someday, maybe. When they old enough to look out for themselfs. Then, maybe. Till then, I got 'em. They ain't got nobody else."

That made me think. I was at James's place for the same reason. I mean, my mother, she doesn't drink. But I didn't have anybody else.

"This is the best I can do on short notice, Lenny."

I told him it was fine.

"You want anything, there's the kitchen. And the bathroom's down the hall around the corner. I'll leave the light on so you don't kill yo'self tryin' to find it. I bushed, babe. I gonna hit the sack."

"I'll be fine," I said.

"See ya in the mornin', sweetheart."

"See ya," I told him. Then he left, down the hall, and I heard a light click on, and all of a sudden I was alone in a place I didn't know so good. It made me real lonely.

There was a TV in my room, and what I thought I'd do, I thought I'd turn on channel thirteen and watch the lobby, but then I remembered where I was, and you couldn't get it from there. That made me wonder if James had a smoke alarm, so I walked around the room and then out into the living room, and then into the kitchen, but there was no smoke alarm. James should've had one. He should've. I couldn't even find a fire extinguisher. No rope ladders. That place was a firetrap. It made me so nervous, I wanted a cigarette. I only smoke when I'm really nervous, and I wanted one then. I found an open pack of Marlboros on the kitchen table. I was sort of thirsty, too, because when you smoke you just get thirsty, so I found a beer in the refrigerator. He had way more food in his refrigerator than we did in ours. All kinds of leftovers and pot roast and stuff. It'd been so long since I'd seen real food I forgot there was such a thing. But I wasn't hungry. I should've been, because I hadn't had any food since the Whopper, and even that didn't stay with me very long. If you know what I mean. So I just smoked and drank the beer.

Black people, they don't usually have real high-tech kitchens with the sink all empty and butcher block counters, but they have more of a homey thing. I mean, you can see pots and pans they cook in, 'cause they don't eat all the time in restaurants or have food brought in. They make it themselves. I can't cook, but I'll bet most black guys my age can. They probably do their own laundry and fix their own cars, if they have any, and they probably know how to fix something in the house if it goes wrong. They know how to survive. I don't know that kind of stuff so good. All I know is how to get out if there's a fire.

I decided I shouldn't smoke in a house that was a firetrap, so I put out the cigarette and ran water over it to make sure it wasn't still going. Then I sort of took it apart and washed it down the kitchen sink. You can't be too careful. I took out my Mace then and read the label. It had a little diagram of how you're supposed to use it. It was a picture of a person with a 1940s haircut holding his nose and spraying the canister at nobody. I started getting paranoid that maybe it didn't work. How did I know? I'd never used it. So I thought it would be a good idea to do a practice shot.

I opened the window in the kitchen and read the label again. I figured I'd just squirt a quick blast out the window to make sure it was working. I took off the cap and pretended someone was coming at me with a gun. I pictured one of the perverts from Bug House Square, all dirty and everything, coming at me to bugger me and take my money. He'd have one hand on his gun and the other on his zipper, and he'd have a big scar on his cheek from fights in bars with other perverts, and when he smiled his sick smile, his teeth

103

would all be broken and black and unbrushed. I said, "Come and get me, you dirty bastard bugger pervert," and then I stuck my hand out the window and lit it rip. I should've checked to see which way the wind was blowing, though, because as soon as I squirted it out the window, the wind pushed it all back in my face. And goddamn, does that stuff work! All of a sudden I was paralyzed, and I went blind. The last thing I saw before I stopped being able to see was a "YOU DESERVE A BREAK TODAY" button from McDonald's that James had hanging from the window-shade string. Then I started throwing up in the sink. I couldn't control my muscles; I just shook and puked and spun my head around trying to breathe. My hands, I couldn't feel them, and I couldn't stop puking, either. It was the second time in the same night that I thought I was going to die. There were like pins and needles in my throat. They kept stabbing me right at the back of my throat, and I was gagging all over the place like I'd tried to swallow a pillow or something. Then I fell on the floor and spun and kicked and wiggled and coughed and gagged some more. If you would've seen me you would've thought I was practicing steps to a punk dance, but what I was doing was dying. My eyes were stinging and tears were coming out like bastards. I tried to stand up. I grabbed one of the kitchen chairs and started to pull myself up, but then I was shaking again and I slumped over the seat with my head facing the floor and my legs in the air. I was caught like that for quite a while until I lost my balance and fell over on my head. I just stayed there until the stuff wore off, gradual-like. I was surprised I hadn't woke James up, but I'd tried to be quiet, even though I was dying.

First, I was able to breathe a little, and then I could see, but blurry. I kept trying to read this embroidered potholder over the sink. I thought it said, "Bet Your Ass," but when my vision got better, I saw it said, "Bless Our House." Yeah. That's what it said. Not "Bet Your Ass," but "Bless Our House."

"Bless my ass," I said, when I could talk.

When I was better, I got up and washed down the puke in the sink, and then I soaped my face and rinsed my eyes with cold water. I put the cap back on the Mace and looked at the picture of the guy with the 1940s haircut. They should've had a picture of what *not* to do, like a little illustration of him being stupid and

104

Macing his own face, so that you won't do that by accident. They could do it in little numbered squares, with first him Macing himself, and then him puking on himself, and then falling on the floor and nearly cracking his head open. The little fucker. I put the Mace in my pocket and went back to sit down on the bed James made up for me.

In the living room I found a copy of one of those scandal papers they sell in supermarkets, only I'm not going to say which one, because they sue people all the time. You know the one I'm talking about. Usually they have headlines like "Aliens from Space Kidnap and Rape 90-Year-Old Woman and Her Pet Cat." I took it along with me to bed for laughs. I figured I could use a laugh.

I turned on the TV, too, just for company. I was so lonely. All they had on this one channel was religious shows. There was one guy with a cheap toupee who was curing cancer victims if they'd say they believed in Jesus. First they'd say how their doctors told them there was no hope, and this guy, this master of ceremonies, would get all excited and start talking to Jesus, telling him to remove the tumor. What a bunch of crap. I wouldn't let that guy put a Band-Aid on me, let alone having him feel me up and trying to remove my goddamn tumor. If I had one, I mean. At the end of the show, they give an address where you should send money so this guy can work more miracles all over the world, and so he can spread the word about Jesus. If he wanted to spread the word, believe me, he could do it without poor people sending him millions of dollars. If he was serious, he'd get in a raft and go to Africa or someplace and do it for free. He'd wear crummy clothes and talk to natives and stuff, but instead, he's on TV asking for money. Someone should Mace *him* fast, before he makes his next million.

So that show went off the air and another one came on, but I wasn't watching it. It was all the same fanatical Bible crap. I leaned back on the sofa sleeper and opened up the newspaper I told you I found. *That* was mostly all crap, too, about Hollywood stars being alcoholics and screwing each other's wives and taking dope and murdering other stars. But there *was* one interesting story. It was about this Cuban guy in Miami who a few weeks earlier kept telling his employees that he'd dreamed a friend of his came into this little food store he owned and shot him. He kept telling them he'd

105

dreamed this, and then a few weeks later, that same friend walked into the little food store and killed him for real. *That* one was spooky. It made me start remembering all the dreams I ever had to see if maybe somebody I knew was going to kill me. I didn't have dreams like that, though. Usually I can't remember my dreams, but I've had a few I wouldn't mind really happening to me. I had one, about a very young actress whose name I'm not going to put down, but she's pretty young and all. In the dream we were having sex on a beach in California and the waves kept washing over us. It was a pretty good dream, until she turned into a fish and ruined it all. My dreams most of the time do that to me. They get all sexy and then somebody turns into a fish or Ethel Merman and it ruins it all. But I wouldn't mind that happening, that first part with the actress. I don't think she's too bright, but Jesus, is she beautiful.

When you start thinking about sexy stuff, especially if it's nighttime and everything, and you're all alone, and you're in the mood, it's kind of hard to think about anything else. I went right from thinking about that actress to thinking about Lisa. I started wondering what she looked like without her clothes on. I could picture it pretty good; as a matter of fact, I could picture it *too* good. She's got this kind of curly hair, light brown, but curly, and she has a lot of it. Makes her look glamorous, even in blue jeans. She doesn't have fantastic tits or anything, but I could picture them okay, and sometimes, if everything else is just right, size doesn't matter too much. And her ass. Her ass is her best part, except her face. Her face, it's beautiful. Real soft, real inviting and everything. That's how come I wanted to pull her in a corner and just kiss her that morning. And she has great legs. Perfect. She even has nice hands. I was so horny. All I did was picture her on a beach, swimming, or sunbathing. Then I daydreamed about rubbing suntan oil on her. I really did. We were sitting on the beach on a towel, like in a Coke commercial, except there was nobody but us, and I unfastened her strap to the top of her swimsuit and started rubbing suntan oil on her back. I rubbed gobs more than she needed, but who cares? I mean, I wasn't dreaming about suntans, I was dreaming about Lisa. Then I rubbed the stuff lower and lower, and then, well— those fantasies always end the same. I liked her; I did. And she drove me nuts, physically, but I don't know if you could say I *loved* her. I loved her in a friendly way, in a crush kind of way. But not the Romeo and Juliet kind of way. I just wanted to be friends with her, and every once in a while, I wanted to jump all over her on a private beach.

Then the guy on the TV ruined it all and snapped me out of my fantasy by yelling about how Jesus is coming, Jesus is coming, Jesus is coming. Hell. So was I, practically, by then. But he ruined it. All you need when you're hot and bothered is some fanatic yelling about Jesus, and things calm down pretty quick. The bastard.

I left the TV on, because as sick as it was, it was still company. What I wished I had was a guitar, because I felt a song coming on. Sometimes, if I'm just thinking, or waiting for a bus, or sitting in a classroom, I feel a song coming on, and I have to write it down. I write a lot of songs, sometimes in the bathroom, even. I can't read notes or anything, but I can picture where my hand would be on the guitar neck to get a certain sound, and then I just hum the melody over and over in my mind and put words to it. If I'm lucky, and if I have a piece of paper handy, then I write the lyrics down right away. That's what I did that night. The song is about Lisa and about how I didn't know how much she meant to me until that morning, and about how lonely I was then. It just came out like it had been in my head forever and just then got found. I call it "Rock Me, Roll Me, Hold Me," and I guess it's a making-love kind of song. That's what rock and roll really means. It means making love. Black people used to say rock 'n' roll when they meant having sex. Anyway, here are the words:

> I saw the sun for the first time
> Yesterday, yesterday.
> A night without love is the worst time.
> Won't you stay, won't you stay?
>
> Oh, rock me,
> Oh, roll me.
> Want you to hold me.
> There's nothing else to do,
> There's just me, there's just you.
>
> Deep in the heart of the evening

There's no time, there's no time.
Dream if you can, make it easy.
Love is blind, love is blind.

Oh, rock me,
Oh, roll me.
Want you to hold me.

'Cause I can't face the darkness alone,
Can't make it one more night on my own,
Won't you follow, follow me home?

Yeah, yeah, yeah, rock me,
Yeah, yeah, yeah, rock me,
Yeah, yeah, yeah, rock me,
Roll me,
Hold me,
Hold me, tonight.

That's for Lisa. That's Lisa's song. I never before wrote a song *for* anybody, but I did that night. I guess it was just time to do it. The way I heard it, I heard it being kind of a soft rocker, like a Buddy Holly sound, or a John Lennon sound, and then it sneaks up and Paul-McCartneys you over the head with a real loud ending. Those old guys, like Holly and Lennon, they wrote the real stuff. Not the opera kind of rock like is popular now, but real from-your-guts kind of stuff. Simple. I write like them. From the fucking guts. If you just write a song for money, then you're like a prostitute selling her ass. But if you write from your guts, then at least you know you've been honest with everybody, and at least if it doesn't sell, you still got a nice song you can live with. You can hum it to yourself three years from now and still know it's your song.

But then I got depressed thinking how my parents wouldn't care, or my teachers, how they wouldn't care that I wrote a rock and roll song. The preacher on TV, unless the song was about Jesus, he wouldn't care, either. Adults think rock and roll is stupid, just noise and a waste of time. That's why they think I'm stupid. That's why they think I don't *do* anything. They want me to know how to parse a fucking sentence, or to find a vector in a physics test, or to mem-

108

orize which general had a victory in World War II. But me, all I want to do is turn out a good tune once in a while. All I want to do is sing and play my guitar. Someday, when I'm rich and famous, and when they come to interview me, I'm just going to say one thing. I won't go on TV, because then I'd be like the preacher, selling his ass. And I won't do whole interviews, but I will say one thing:

You still think I'm sick?

And all my teachers will go to work and teach the same useless crap and talk about what junk rock music is. And they'll still think I'm sick. But I won't care then, because they'll have to listen to my records in restaurants and on the radio. Their kids will come home with my albums and stuff, and so I'll be a constant reminder to them that they were wrong. That I'm not wasting my time. Their kids will know. Kids are much smarter than adults.

I folded up the paper with Lisa's song on it, stuck it in my pocket, and then laid back on the sofa bed. I was tired, and I decided to listen to what the TV preacher was talking about. Maybe it would be laughs, like that supermarket paper was, I thought.

It wasn't, though. I was wrong that time. This guy was strictly out of his mind. He was talking about the end of the world, according to John in the last book of the New Testament, *Revelations*. He was going on and on about how the end of the world will be tomorrow, or the next day. He didn't know for sure *when* it would be, but it would be soon, he said. I sure hoped so. I hoped the end of the world would come before the end of his stupid program. That way it would at least shut him up. But, my luck. The world didn't end. He went on about this insane stuff, that a Beast was coming into the world and everybody would walk around with "666" on their foreheads, and then they couldn't get to heaven, 'cause they'd have this fucking tattoo. Give me a break. Jesus is going to meet you in heaven and if you have this tattoo, no go, Joe. Where was Jesus when Lisa's father had been raping her every night? Huh? Where was he then, I'd like to know. I mean, if he sees everything, then what did he do during all the times Lisa got it from her old man? Did he just *watch*? And this preacher guy, you could tell he believed it all. He kept talking about the European Common Market, and how it's supposed to represent ten united nations they mention in the Bible, and how monsters with horns on their heads are going to appear, and how Jesus would have a sword and kill everybody and blood would be in the streets up to your crotch or something. It was unbelievable. If this guy is on TV, it probably means people watch him. And if people watch him—not for laughs, like me, but for *real*—then they probably believe that stuff, too. That's scary. That's much scarier than even World War III, or rapists, or buggers.

I'm no Bible expert, but I do know that there were a lot of holy guys who said good things. But Bible people don't want to know about *them*. They're so scared and their minds are so closed that they only have room for one answer. It's like rooting for your favorite ball team. If you're a Cubs fan, you don't want to know what's good about the Mets, or the Pirates. You just want to know about the Cubs. That's stupid, in my opinion. I'm sure Jesus was okay, and it might've even been fun to hang out with him before they nailed his ass to a cross. But hey—don't give me any of this doomsday stuff from a book that's two thousand years old. They didn't even know what *shoelaces* were back then, and I'm supposed to take their word about the end of the world? Sorry. If I go to hell, I go to hell. But if heaven's got people like those crazed TV preachers in it, then I wouldn't want to go there anyway. Who'd want to sit around with a bunch of half-wits who've only read one book in their lives? Not me. I'd rather go someplace where you can at least hear some decent music. Some rock and roll, you know. Send me where they sent Lennon. Send me where Jagger's going, 'cause I couldn't cut it with Donny Osmond anyway.

I was thinking all this stuff to myself, just sitting on James's little sofa sleeper, when the end of the program came. You should've seen it. This guy, this sicko with the Bible, he closed the book he was reading from, looked at the camera like he was an angel or something, with this smile that sort of said, "I got the answer, you bastards, and you don't," and then all this dry ice kind of fog started spinning around him and he turned and walked up this big staircase like he was going back to heaven until it was time for the next program. That was the best part of the show. It had me in

110

stitches. I thought about how the director, once the cameras were off and everything, would yell, "Cut! That's a wrap," and then the fog machine would turn off, and the crazy bastard would be stuck at the top of a staircase that led nowhere except the ceiling of the studio. He'd climb back down, walk to his dressing room, and then someone would slide a report of how much money he made in phone pledges that night. That's religion in the 1980s.

After that, the TV station went off, so I turned off the TV. I was just sitting there in James's apartment feeling lousy. Four nights before, I didn't have any problems. Then I had that one problem about being thrown out of school. Then I had the problem of my mother being a lesbian. Then the girl I'm practically in love with, she tells me that her old man's been giving it to her for a year. Then there's the shrink who thinks my gestalt is crummy, and now I just Maced myself, had no home to go to, and I get told I'm going to hell by a guy who lives in TV heaven. See, that's the way it is. Problems don't go away—they *multiply*. The way I figured it, I could look forward to at least three fresh new problems in the next day or so. I'll bet if you live to be an old guy, by that time you're so up to your neck in problems you don't give a shit about dying. You're probably *glad* you're going to die.

I started walking around James's apartment because I was getting hyper. The clock in the kitchen said it was two in the morning. I couldn't sleep, I knew that for sure. What I needed was company, but I didn't want to wake up James, because he was real tired from working hard all day. It wouldn't've been fair. What I decided to do, I decided to give Rick a ring and see if he'd come and get me. We could spend the rest of the night talking in his room if he'd come and get me. I knew Rick had school the next morning, but it didn't matter, 'cause he mostly sleeps through all his classes anyway. Might as well give him a reason to be sleepy, I thought.

I dialed from the phone in the kitchen. Rick, he has his own line so I didn't even have to worry about waking up his parents. It took about a thousand years for him to answer, 'cause he's a very heavy sleeper. Even when he's up and around, you're not real sure if he's completely awake or nothing. Then he answered. He sounded dead.

"Hello?" he said, in this dead voice of his.

111

"Rick?" I said. "That you, boy? Are you dead or something?"

"Who the fuck is this?" He was angry, right away.

"This is Lenny. C'mon. Wake up. You gotta help me out."

"What the fuck time is it?"

"Nine in the morning," I told him. "There's an eclipse, so it just *looks* dark." Then he didn't say nothing because he was trying to figure out what I was talking about.

"*My* clock says it's fifteen after two, you bastard. Why did you wake me up?"

"Your clock must've stopped. Clocks sometimes stop during eclipses. It's a well-documented—"

"You lying bastard. What the hell do you want? I'm dead."

Then I told him about running away from home and being at James's place and how lonely I was, and how I Maced myself. I started to tell him about the guy on TV who said the world was going to end, but he didn't want to hear about it.

"No kidding, now. Come and get me. We'll go out for early breakfast and maybe split a joint or something. Whad'ya say? Huh? Come and get me. Please?"

"Where the hell are you?"

"At *James's* house," I said. "I told you that about twenty times already."

"No, no. I mean, where does he *live?*"

I had to think for a while before I remembered. "It's not so far."

"How the hell am I gonna come and get you unless I have an address?"

Good point, I thought. "It's Ninety-second and Halsted," I said.

"Fuck you!" Rick said. He kept saying that. I wished he wouldn't've. It's terrible trying to get someone to rescue you and all they'll tell you is "fuck you."

"Please. Please come and get me. I'm so lonely. Everything is going so bad for me. I'd do it for you, boy, if things were reversed."

"Fuck you," he said.

"Don't say that anymore, c'mon. We'll have early break—"

"Fuck you," he said, again.

It looked like I was going to be stuck there all night. But then I remembered how to make him come and get me.

"If I have to stay here, I won't sleep. And if I can't get any sleep, then I won't be able to play on Wednesday night. No opener for Lefty Dizz. No publicity."

He must've been thinking. I heard a match light on the other end of the phone. He was having a cigarette, probably in the dark. He shouldn't smoke in bed. He doesn't have a smoke alarm, either.

"I'll be right over," he said. "Be outside." And then the phone clicked and he was gone.

He would've come to get me even if I hadn't threatened not to play, I think. He just likes to give me a hard time. But I knew that part about not playing would get him over there fast, on account of he cares so much about the group. He really thinks we're going to make it. He likes my songs, which of course makes me feel good, but I just wished he wouldn't count so much on being a famous rocker. It hardly ever happens, and he should just do it for fun. But he doesn't. With him it's like a business. He knows I just do it for fun and he's all the time trying to get me to take it more serious. Poor guy. We're probably going to be ninety years old someday and still trying to make it. I'll have to help him carry his piano up on stage and he'll have arthritis and no hair, but he'll still hope he has a number-one record. It's the fame mania. I've seen lots of guys go through it. They get to the point where they'd sell their own mother for a chance at number one. It's stupid.

The next thing I did was sit down and write James a letter so he wouldn't be worried when he woke up and found me gone. I made him go through all that trouble and now I wasn't even spending the night, but I knew he'd understand. He knows I can't sit still sometimes. This is what I wrote in the note:

Dear James,

Thank you for saving my life tonight and being nice to me in the alley when I was covered with garbage. I don't know no one else who'd be so nice to me, and I owe you one. Thanks also for the little sofa sleeper which was real comfortable, only I couldn't sleep. I got hyper, so one of my friends is going to pick me up and go out to breakfast with me. I hope your kid's cough gets better; don't forget to get the cough syrup. Also, take the kid to a doctor

113

'cause you never know, it could be pneumonia or T.B. It's always better to know for sure. *You can't be too careful.* Thanks again.

Love,
Lenny

P.S. I puked in your sink, but I washed it down. I'm sorry, but I Maced myself by accident.

P.P.S. *Please* get a smoke alarm and a fire extinguisher.

I left the note right on my little bed so he'd know right away that everything was okay with me. Then I put my shoes on and my jacket and stood by the kitchen window waiting for Rick to come. I knew I said I'd be outside, but if you think I was going to wait on the corner of Ninety-second and Halsted at two in the morning by myself, you're out of your skull.

It took him forty-five minutes to get there, and by then I was starting to get impatient. I closed the steel door behind me when I left and Rick was laying on the horn, which I wish he wouldn't've done, because he might've woke up one of James's kids, or maybe James himself. Even when I got to the car door, he was still honking, just to be a pain in the ass.

"Shhh!" I told him. "James is asleep. So are his kids."

"So was I, until you called."

I closed the door and we drove away into the ugliness all around, the old buildings painted green, and the torn billboards, and the garbage all over the streets. What a depressing neighborhood. I'll bet there are thousands of rapes and murders every day around there.

We drove and drove, and an Eagles song came on the radio, the one about "Your Lying Eyes" or something like that. It's a depressing song. Rick handed me a joint, and when he breathed out all the smoke from his lungs, he said, "Long eclipse we're having."

"Yep," I said. "It's really a good one. Almost makes you think it's night."

"I hope you appreciate this, you bastard," he said.

I did, but I didn't feel like telling him so. This was the second joint I'd smoked that night, and I was way off on my own trip. I started thinking maybe I should go to my father's new apartment instead of Rick's house. I couldn't stay with Rick forever, and maybe it was a better idea to find a place for myself right away. A permanent place, you know. I couldn't stand all this temporary business any longer. It was like I was just hanging in limbo. Like my feet weren't on the ground.

We stopped for breakfast at a place called the Steak and Egger. They've got about a million of those places all over Chicago, and always in the worst neighborhoods. They're open all night, so they draw a pretty ugly crowd. Night people. Night people give me the creeps. All the decent people are asleep; even some of the not-decent people are asleep, so you can imagine what sort of person sits up all night in a Steak and Egger.

Inside, the lights were so bright it hurt. White lights. Fluorescent. I read somewhere that fluorescent lights lower your sperm count or affect your testicles somehow, so I wanted to eat and get the hell out of there fast. I probably got few enough sperm as it is. I hardly ever use my testicles.

We sat on two stools at the middle of the counter. To our left was a guy with a scraggly beard and no teeth and an ugly brown overcoat. He kept soaking something in his coffee and eating it, but I couldn't tell what it was. Or what it had been. Lovely visuals. To my right was a hooker and a guy with slicked-back, greasy black hair, and dandruff. He wore a dark shirt and you could see white flakes all over his collar. The kind of guy you'd expect to see with a hooker. They were the only people in the whole place except for Rick and me and the two guys making the food and washing the dishes.

"Too bad the Pump Room is closed," Rick said. In his hand he had the menu, and in his other hand he was fishing for a cigarette in his jacket pocket. His hair was all messed up from sleeping and his eyes were like little slits. He looked Chinese. He offered me a cigarette, and I took one.

We both ordered fried eggs and steak and then we just smoked. The greasy-looking guy with the whore was laughing at something, but she wasn't. You could tell that it was something that was sickening, just by the way he laughed. He probably just said something real dirty or perverted to her, just on account of her being a whore and everything.

"Practice tomorrow night," Rick said. He has a one-track mind.

"Yeah. Okay. Pick me up. I got a new tune I want you to hear."

"When did you write it?" he asked, squinting at me and smoking his cigarette real hard, till all the smoke made a big cloud over his head and hung between him and the fluorescent lights.

"Tonight," I told him.

"You got it on tape?"

I shook my head. I was starting to worry about what the lights were doing to my sex life. Not that it mattered. I didn't have much of a sex life, outside of my fantasies. But *those* were pretty good. I didn't want any stupid Steak and Egger lights ruining my fantasies.

"I got a cassette recorder in the car," Rick told me. "You can sing it in the car and I'll record it."

"I don't feel much like singing," I said, watching the cooks make our food. They were exactly the kind of guys who would spit something in your food if you didn't watch them. They had shifty eyes.

Rick said I'd feel more like singing if I had a good breakfast, but I didn't think so. I didn't say nothing, though.

Remember the old guy I told you about on our left? The old guy with like no teeth and the stuff he was dunking in his coffee? I'd pretty much forgotten about him because I was watching them make our food and listening to hear if they were clearing their throats or putting their hands anywhere funny, when all out of nowhere there was this noise—a crash—at the end of the counter. It was the old guy. He fell headfirst in his coffee and was sleeping in it. He was *drowning* in it. One of the cooks ran over to wake him up. He was shaking him by the shoulders of his ratty coat and yelling at him and saying he was a sonofabitch. The old guy woke up and you could tell he didn't know where he was. All he knew was that some greasy cook was hollering at him and telling him he was a sonofabitch. Then the cook, he told him to pay up and leave. It was a pretty sad scene. The old guy, who hadn't said a word to nobody, who'd only fallen asleep in his coffee by accident—probably because he'd been up all night with no place to go—he searched his pockets for some money, but couldn't find any. Rick, he was watching all of this with me, and he looked at

116

me then to see what the hell I thought. I got up, took a dollar from my pocket and gave it to the cook. The cook, he stared at the old guy, took the dollar I'd given him, and then he said the old guy had to leave.

"Get outa here now, you old sonofabitch" was how he said it.

"He doesn't have to leave," I said. "I just paid you. He's not hurting anybody. He's probably got no place to go, so why don't you just bring him a donut or something and put it on my bill."

"He's leavin' now," the cook said. What an asshole. He just didn't want the old guy around anymore, even if he paid. Just because he was old and couldn't stay awake.

"Why can't he stay?" Rick asked. Rick was in on it now, too. It was like two against one. Those are my kinds of odds, boy. The cook said we should mind our own business.

"It *is* our business," I said. "When you start getting rough with an old guy who can't even walk, then it *is* our business. He wasn't hurting you. You didn't have to shake him like that."

Then the cook, who had something in his hand, a spatula, I think (but it could've been a knife), he told us we had to leave, too. The greasy guy and the whore were watching us now. They thought the whole thing was very funny. A riot. Some people have weird senses of humor. The old guy sort of saluted everybody and was on his way out the door, but I went over to him and stuck a buck in his coat pocket. He just looked around, and then he saluted me again. Maybe he was a soldier once.

Rick, he drank his water and then let it all dribble out of his mouth on the counter. The cook started saying he was going to call the cops, so we left. I didn't need to see any cops on an empty stomach.

Back in the car, Rick pushed in the cigarette lighter, a joint hanging all bent out of his mouth. "That sure was a hell of a good breakfast," he said, patting his crazy hair down with his hand. "I don't know when I've enjoyed a breakfast so much."

I was just thinking about the way that crummy cook had treated that poor old guy who probably never hurt no one in his life. It's terrible. Then he was going to call the cops on *us*, for sticking up for him. Jesus. Everything is ass-backwards these days. It should be that if you're old and everything and can't take care of yourself, that places *have* to give you food, for *free*. But instead, they brutalize the poor suckers. That's the way it is. You take somebody who can't defend himself, and then it's okay to brutalize him. It makes me sick. James would say I did the right thing by giving the old guy the buck, but that I should've left it at that. Just accept it. That might be true, but I don't think so. If you start accepting stuff like that, then twenty years from now, if you were to see the same thing happen, then you might not do *anything* about it. So it's better to stay pissed off.

Rick and I drove to the lakefront, at Diversey Parkway, to smoke the joint and just talk. He brought out the cassette recorder and told me to sing my song so he could learn it at home. He can do that. He can just sit down with a guy singing and learn the piano part later. So I sang the fucker. Then he sang it with me a second time, and he even hummed a solo during the break, right off the top of his head. He's good. He did harmony and everything. The more I heard it, the more I liked it. It said everything I was feeling: just rock me, roll me, hold me. We sat there at the lake and I made Rick lock his door in case any perverts were around and might want to try to mug us or murder us. Rick, he thinks I'm paranoid. But I'm not. All you need to do is leave your car door open once, and *zap!* Some rapist or killer will get you. Especially at the lake at night. They're all over the place down there. They got squatters' rights or something.

"What the hell time is it?" Rick asked me, when we were both just sitting there listening to the radio. Some old, corny Beach Boys song was playing.

"I don't know," I said. "Don't you got a watch?"

"Nope." Then he sat there quiet for a while. Then he says, "Hey. How come you're not at home in bed like all good expelled boys?"

I forgot. I hadn't explained everything to him yet. Jesus. Where do you start? I wondered. Where the hell do you start?

At the beginning.

"What would you say if I told you my mother was a lesbian? Hmm? I mean, what would you say?"

He just stared. You could tell he thought it was a riddle or something.

118

"That's nice. Mine is a Capricorn. What's your father?"

"No," I said. "Seriously. My mother is a lesbian."

He was staring again. Sometimes his mouth hangs open like he's retarded or something. It was doing that then. He had his retarded expression on. Then he said, "Naaww, she isn't."

"Yes she is," I told him. I flicked off the radio. The Beach Boys are okay sometimes, but who needs "Surfin' U.S.A." when you're trying to explain that kind of stuff? It's like playing "Roll Over Beethoven" at a funeral.

Rick's mouth was still wide open. "But I know your mother."

"So what? What's that? A character reference? Does that make her less of a lesbian or something? Believe me. Take my word."

"Yeah?" he said.

"Yeah," I said.

"A butch dyke?"

"Yeah. That's how come I was at James's house. I didn't want to be around when she brought home her girlfriend. Her date." Hell. Just thinking about it was making me want to throw up. I don't know why that stuff bothers me so much, but it does. "I found out—when was it?" It seemed like a million years had gone by since I found out. "Yesterday, I think. She had some broad spend the night with her."

"Shit," Rick said, playing with his car visor, "*she's* doing better than *you* are."

It wasn't funny.

Then Rick turned the radio back on. This time it was a song by the Beatles, "Your Mother Should Know," which *was* kind of funny. We both cracked up then. It was so sick, we laughed. When things get too sick, that's what you have to do, sometimes. I remember once in drivers' ed class they showed us a film of people dead from terrible car accidents with their arms cut off and their bodies all bloody. It was supposed to scare us into being good drivers, but it was so sick that anybody would make that kind of movie and then show it to a bunch of young kids as part of school, just to upset them, that Rick and me laughed all the way through it. They threw us out at the end, because our laughing was going to ruin the finale or something, the grossest scene. I never did find out what happened at the end of that movie, but it must've been pretty awful. Two kids fainted.

Then Rick said, half asleep still, "How come nothing exciting ever happens to *me?* I'm graduating with honors and my mother's a Republican."

"Same thing," I said.

He asked me after a while what I was going to do. That was a good question. That was a hot one. I was asleep and I wondered if maybe I should've stayed at James's house. At least I'd've had a roof over my head. Then I remembered about my father. It was practically morning, but what the hell. You can't get in touch with him during business hours, on account of the guard dog of a secretary they have at the bank. At least if I walked in on him at four in the goddamn morning I'd be sure to find him. It was worth a try. I figured the two of us could live like bachelors, and then I wouldn't have to put up with perverted stuff in my own home.

"I could stay with my old man," I said, sort of to myself. I was watching the limb of a big tree blow in the wind above the windshield. Outside you could hear waves hitting the rocks. It's a lonely sound. Rick was lying back in his seat and trying to fall asleep.

"You think he'd mind?" he asked.

"I'm his son," I said.

"Your mother was his wife," he said back. "Nothing lasts forever."

"You're a cheerful guy, you know that? That's just what I wanted to hear." He was yawning and making wild animal sounds, stretching, sort of. "*Asshole.*"

"I'm hungry," he said, which had nothing to do with it. "I could eat a dead fish, that's how hungry I am."

I pictured him doing it. He would, too.

"I could just go down to the shore and pick up the first dead fish I see and bite its head off and suck on it for a while. That's how hungry I am."

He must be pretty hungry, I thought.

"Except there's no tartar sauce. Otherwise I'd just go down there and suck on an alewife."

An alewife is the kind of fish in Lake Michigan that are mostly dead all the time and wash up on shore. He was making me sick just listening to him, so I played the tape back and sat with the window rolled down, the lake air in my face.

"I *was* hungry," I said, "but you took care of that, boy." Then I turned the tape off. It was making me think of Lisa and how much I wanted to kill her father, and I could only handle one emergency at a time. I remembered how Lisa and me had been practically in the same spot yesterday afternoon, talking about nuclear war. Where's the goddamn bomb when you need it?

"I think he'd let me," I said, which sort of woke Rick up; he was just starting to snore.

"Who?"

"My old man."

"Let you what?"

"Stay with him."

"Wanna go there?"

I shrugged. "Not really." I thought for a while about where I'd like to be if I could be anywhere. "Where I really want to go is California. Live out on the beach. Sun in the morning. Surf. Cold beer in the refrigerator. Brian Wilson on my front lawn singing about how high the surf is and how big California girls' tits are. Yep. California."

Rick shook his head. "Mud slides. You'd hate it. You can't stand mud."

"Florida, then. I'd like to go to Florida and eat oranges in the sun. Wake up to the palm trees hissing in the wind. Give Anita Bryant my mother's phone number."

"Too many refugees. 'You don't have to live like a refugee,'" he sang.

I was running out of places I wanted to go.

"Maybe the French Riviera," I said. "Exotic women, the Jet Set."

Rick said, "Nope. You can't speak French. You'd order a hamburger and they'd bring you a soufflé. And they *hate* Americans. The waiters would piss in your food before they brought it to you."

"Hockers," I corrected him. "They'd spit hockers in it."

"That too," he said. "France is out."

"What the hell. Then I guess I'll go to my dad's," I said.

Rick said that was a good choice, on account of there was no mud slides, no refugees, and no waiters to piss on your food there. Then he asked where he lived.

"Sandburg Village," I said. "That bunch of high rises they got all sitting next to each other."

Rick, he said that was even better, that they had lots of stewardesses living there. Friendly skies.

I gave him the address, and he started the car and drove away. Just another little stop in the life of Lenny Blake, I thought. It was sort of like going off to find the Wizard. All I ever do is go looking for the Wizard. But all the time I know there isn't no Wizard. I didn't care then, though. I would've settled for anybody. Even my father.

When we got to Sandburg Village, I hunted for the right high rise. They all looked the same, especially in the dark. His is right across from the commissary, so after we found the commissary, we were all right. Rick asked if I wanted him to wait for me. I said yeah, I'd be back down to let him know if it was okay or not. Then I told him to lock the car door after me, but all he did was call me paranoid. Let the bastard get murdered, I figured. Then we'd see who was paranoid.

There was no doorman or anything when I got there; there was just a row of buttons and names. I found my dad's name. It said, "Robert Blake—709." He was on the seventh floor. I was willing to bet that he didn't have a rope ladder. I know my dad. Then I saw that the door wasn't even locked. Anybody could've just walked in and robbed him or murdered him and he would've been defenseless, because most bankers can't even *fight* good.

I didn't feel like explaining over the intercom from the lobby why I was there, so I just buzzed his buzzer and walked in. I was careful to make sure the door locked behind me, though. Rick would've said I was paranoid. Let the whole goddamn world in, who cares?

The elevator had an empty paper cup in it and chewing gum wrappers all over the floor. What kind of a dump was he living in? I wondered. When I got to the seventh floor, I had to walk all around until I saw which direction the numbers on the doors were going. The carpet was some ugly brown and orange job, in geometrics. Earth tones. Heavy. It made me dizzy if I looked at it, so I

122

didn't. But it still made me dizzy, like out of the corners of my eyes. Then I found it: 709. I knocked kind of softly on the door.

No answer.

I put my ear to the door to see if he was up and around. I should've talked to him from the lobby, just so he wouldn't have a heart attack about somebody knocking on his door at that time. There didn't seem to be anybody moving inside. If you know anything at all about apartment buildings, you know you can see if somebody on the inside is standing in front of the peephole. You can tell if it gets dark and light. There was somebody there, all right. I tried knocking again.

"Hey, Dad. It's me. Lenny."

Then there was more silence for a bit. Then he said, "Lenny?"

"Yeah. Open up. I gotta talk to you."

"What the hell are *you* doing here at this time?" He was surprised, but he didn't open the door.

"Selling Girl Scout cookies. Hey. Open up, why don't you?"

He wouldn't open up or nothing, though. I heard a rustling sort of sound on the inside, and finally, after about eight years, the door opened, but only a crack. I could see he was wearing only just his underpants and reading glasses. He looked hysterical.

"Sharp outfit," I said.

He wasn't laughing. He looked kind of sweaty and nervous. "Why aren't you home in bed?" was all he said, and still through only a crack in the door. It was starting to piss me off. What the hell did he have to hide? I've seen him in his underpants plenty of times. Without them, even. But not with his reading glasses. This was the first time I'd seen him with just underpants and reading glasses.

"Be a good host and invite me in or something," I said. But he just stalled.

"It's late," he said. I knew it was late, for Christ's sake. Didn't he think I knew it was late?

That's when it dawned on me. I knew something was wrong if he wouldn't let me in. I started getting crazy thoughts, that maybe there was a burglar inside with a gun to his head, and maybe he'd told him to get rid of me, fast. Or maybe it was a sick deviate who was going to tie him up and torture him and ask if he had any kids

123

or anyone to torture later. I thought maybe it was the guy who followed me when I got off the bus. So I acted fast. I gave the door one big shove and forced my way in. I nearly knocked my father down doing it, too, but when I was inside, there was no burglar. Dad was kind of shocked; he stood there looking stupid in his underpants. On the couch in the living room I could see a lady in a nightgown, a real *short* nightgown, and when my eyes adjusted, I saw she wasn't just a lady. She was the receptionist who'd given me such a hard time at the bank. What do you know. No Wizard there, either.

I leaned on one arm against the open door and rubbed my eyes. I was so tired I could hardly think. The lady had a highball glass in her hand; I could hear the ice cubes clink around in it. I sort of made a laughing sound. It was a weird sound and I didn't mean to make it at first, but then I just pretended it was a laugh.

"Excuse me," I said, and started to leave.

My dad, he caught me by the sleeve of my windbreaker and tried to hold me. "Lenny," he said.

"It's okay. It's all right," I said, trying to get away, but he wouldn't let go.

"I'm a single man, now, Lenny. You have to realize—"

"I realize it. My mistake. I should've waited till morning. Let go, please."

He was still holding me by the sleeve. I kept trying not to look in the apartment, because it was very embarrassing. I mean, it's one thing when your mother and father are together with no clothes on, but Jesus. It's another thing with your father and a receptionist. It's creepy to force yourself into a horny situation like that. It was plenty horny, too. Believe me. But it could've been worse. I could've forced my way in and found a *man*. It just pissed me off that it had to be *that* receptionist. The one who'd treated me like a piece of shit at the bank.

I took my arm back from him. I whisked it back kind of sudden-like and walked back into the hallway to the elevator. I pushed the down button and waited for the car to get there. The door to my dad's apartment was still open, and he just stood there staring at me. When the elevator came, I saluted him, the way the old guy in the restaurant did to me. Then the door closed and I was on my

124

way down. It was funny, in a way. It seemed like everybody in the world but me had who they needed. I didn't have anyone, except James. I realized then that I should've stayed with him. But even that wasn't what I was looking for. What the hell was I looking for? Don't ask me. I still don't know.

Rick was in his car with the motor off when I got downstairs. I rapped on the car window for him to let me in. He must've taken my advice, because the passenger door was locked. Smart boy.

"Is it okay?" he asked. I just got in beside him and closed the door behind me.

"It's *peachy*."

"Well? Are you gonna stay?" he asked. He was smoking a cigarette, so I asked if he had one for me. All of a sudden I felt like having one.

"You gonna stay or what?" he asked again.

"Can't. He's got a party girl up there." I lit the cigarette off of his and rolled down the window a bit.

"Your old man's doin' all right, it sounds like."

"Yep. It sounds like."

I wished it would've been anybody but that receptionist, boy. Some guys'll do anything for sex. Sex was ruining my goddamn life. And since I couldn't figure anything out anymore, I decided to throw in the towel.

"Take me home," I told Rick.

"What home?" he said.

He didn't know how right he was.

CHAPTER 11

t was around five or five-thirty by the time I got home. Rick left me off at the corner of Lake Shore Drive and Chicago Avenue, and I decided to go in the garage entrance so I wouldn't have to talk to the other doorman, or have him look at me suspicious or anything. Also, perverts, late at night, might've been watching channel thirteen if they were up and couldn't find anybody to do weird things to that night. Just because you live in a high rise doesn't mean there's no perverts living there, too. They could just be watching the lobby until somebody they like walks in, and then you never know what they're doing to themselves while they're watching you. You know what I mean.

It took me a few minutes to find the right key, and I was practically in the goddamn building when someone tapped me on the shoulder. I almost shit in my pants. Who the hell is tapping shoulders at five in the morning? I spun my head real fast (almost like that girl in *The Exorcist*) and I saw two huge guys behind me. It was like when I looked at them I was staring at their chests, on account of they were so tall and big, so I had to raise my head before I saw their faces.

"You got a light?" one of 'em says. He had a mustache. I figured he was about thirty or so, and a little drunk. The other guy, he put his hand on the door and closed it and took my keys from the lock. He was chewing gum real slow, and he had a sick smile. The kind of smile that lets you know you're in trouble.

"I said, *You got a light?*" the first one said again. I knew that was

126

it for me. I was going to be dead or buggered or both in a few minutes. I started wishing I'd never made fun of that Bible stuff at James's house. I figured God sent two deviates to rape me and kill me, 'cause I didn't believe.

I tried to answer, but my voice didn't work so good. It sounded like a kid's voice.

"No. No light," I said. They just kept smiling kind of sick. "I don't smoke," I told them, like they cared if I smoked or not. I'm so stupid. When you're in that kind of situation, though, you figure you'd better keep the conversation rolling or you've had it. "Maybe the doorman has some matches," I said.

The one who took my keys was like spinning them on his fat, dumb-looking fingers. Just twirling them around and around. I sized things up, to see if maybe I could make a break for it or grab my Mace in enough time to gas them. My guess was that I couldn't. I was so scared I was like petrified, and it's hard to move when you're petrified. And I was tired. Boy, was I tired. I almost wished if they were going to do anything to me that they'd get it over with quick, because I could barely stand up anymore.

"Maybe you got something else," the first one says to me, closing in around the doorway.

"Money," I said. "I got some money, if you want. About thirty bucks. You want it? I'll give it to you. For real. You can have it. I don't want it anyway. Really."

Then the one who took my keys grabs me by the arm and starts moving me away from the building.

"We're gonna take a little walk," he said, like one of those crooks on TV. "Keep your mouth shut."

So I kept my mouth shut. But only for a little while. They were like pulling me toward this little park on Chicago Avenue that has sleds for kids and stuff. I used to play there when I was younger, and my mother always told me not to talk to strangers. I always thought she meant when I was young. I didn't think some stranger would bother me in the playground when I was seventeen, which just shows you how wrong you can be.

"You guys can have the money, you know," I said. They were taking me to this dark little spot near the corner of the park. The whole time I was thinking how big they were and how much whatever they were going to do to me would hurt. I got a pretty weak constitution. I pass out from blood tests. *Keep 'em talking*, I thought to myself. *Just keep these two degenerates talking*.

"I was going to use the money to buy some medicine tomorrow for this very infectious skin disease I got. It's highly contagious. I get these sores all over my body with pus inside them and they hurt like hell, so I was going to buy that medicine. You can catch it just from touching me." They sure had strong grips. They'd stopped the circulation in my arms from where they were holding me. "There's no cure for it," I added.

Then the one who'd been doing all the talking pushed me up against a tree with his fist holding my sweat shirt near the collar. "I understand you got stuff."

What the fuck was he talking about? What stuff? I thought.

"And we want some. Now."

My heart was pounding like a mother. "Stuff?" I said.

He slapped me across the face with the back of his hand. It hurt so bad I could like *taste* it. You know that feeling when your face gets hit, and you can like taste the pain? That's the way it was.

"Don't play stupid," he said.

"Who's playing?" I told him. I could see blood coming from my nose, 'cause it was dripping on my sweat shirt.

"Hey, kiddo. This ain't nothing. That slap was just a teaser. Me and my buddy get rough sometimes. Know what I mean? You should save a little wear and tear on that baby face of yours and just give us a taste of whatever you're dealin' tonight."

They thought I was a drug dealer. I didn't even have an *aspirin* on me, for Christ's sake. I wished I had, 'cause I was getting a headache all of a sudden.

Then the one with my keys, he started frisking me while the other guy held me against the tree.

"We'll find it anyway," the guy who did all the talking said.

"You got the wrong guy," I said, while the other ape's hands were going through my pockets. "Honest. I ain't got anything. It's mistaken identity. Maybe you're just looking for a guy who *looks* like me."

That's when the ape put his hands in my pants. He searched *everywhere*, I'm not kidding. *Everywhere*. I don't know how I stayed sane. I just pretended it was like a doctor visit, sort of. I tried not to think while it was happening.

Then they went through my jacket pockets and found my Mace. They looked at the label real careful-like, the one with the little guy with the 1940s haircut showing how to use it. The guy with the mustache put it in his pocket. They both just stared at me, and then at each other.

"Who's your connection?" the talker asked.

What was the use of telling them I didn't have a connection? They wouldn't've believed me anyway.

"Guy named Fredericks," I said.

"Fredericks?" he asked.

"Yeah."

"Where does he live?" he wanted to know. When you lie to a gorilla, he'll believe you in a second. But if you tell him the truth, he won't. I just kept making up stuff about this Fredericks guy.

"The South Side."

Wham! He slapped me again, only this time, I must've passed out or something, because it was like time went by, and when I woke up I was on my knees.

"*Where* on the South Side?"

"Eighty-first and Western," I said, even though I didn't know what was happening anymore. "A big old apartment building. He's on the second floor."

"What's his first name?" he asked, his fist ready to smash me again.

"Lionel. Lionel Fredericks. He's got a scar on his forehead and he wears a long tan coat. Drives a Chevy. I don't know the license number."

They waited to see if there was more, but I didn't know what else to make up.

"Go on."

"Uh, he lives with this blond girl named Doris. About five feet tall. She works at the CTA. She's his cover."

The funny thing was, I was starting to believe the whole thing. I pictured Fredericks and his girl Doris being woke up in the middle of the night by these two Neanderthal men, and the big one would drag them out of bed and search them and beat them up. The talker would keep saying, "Where's the shipment for Lenny Blake?" And Fredericks would say, "I gave it to him already." And then they'd hit him and make his nose bleed, and the talker would say, "We searched Blake. He was clean. Where's the stuff?" And then the gum chewer would like strip Doris and do horrible things to her in front of Fredericks until he told them the truth. They'd torture them and bang their heads around. Poor Fredericks. I started feeling sorry that I'd spilled the beans on him. And then I realized how stupid I was being, 'cause there wasn't no Fredericks.

What the city should do, the city should invest some money in floodlights for parks. It seems like the whole thing wouldn't've been so bad if it hadn't happened in the dark. But even with floodlights, people wouldn't've helped me. They'd just watch me getting the shit kicked out of me the way they watch TV. Except they'd like it more, because there wouldn't be no commercials. And then the police would come around later asking questions about the offenders, and nobody would say they saw it. So forget the floodlights. The city's probably right. Why waste money?

I could tell the guy with the mustache had believed every word I said. He was talking real low to the stupid one, the gum chewer, and they seemed to agree on something. I was still on my knees when they threw my keys on the ground next to me. I thought they were just going to walk away, but what they did instead was, the big guy kicked me in the groin and laughed. I was going out of my mind. That's the worst pain in the world. I couldn't talk. I couldn't breathe. All I could do was hold my balls. It was awful. All I remember is the guy who did the talking said something like I wasn't out of the woods yet, and when I got my senses back they were gone. They didn't even give me my Mace back, the crooks.

I didn't have any energy or nothing, so I just stayed on the ground near the tree for a while. Your mind—when your body's all screwed up and everything—does some strange numbers. I was thinking about Lisa and how pretty she looked the day before at school, when I noticed her for the first time. I mean, really *noticed* her.

My mind was wandering all over the place, and I was thinking about another time, too, when I was about ten. Once I was depressed because I didn't have no one to play with, so I came to the

130

park on a rainy kind of day and just sat on the teeter-totter, pretending there was someone on the other side. I even talked to the guy, because I was so lonely. Some lady came by, a real pretty lady, and she saw me talking to myself all alone on the teeter-totter, and you know what she did? She got on with me and pretended like she didn't weigh so much. She had her feet on the ground the whole time, but she made the teeter-totter go up and down. What I liked about her was she didn't ask a whole lot of questions the way adults do when they're talking to a kid and trying to sound cute. She just made the teeter-totter go up and down, and then she said she was late for work. She said good-bye and left then. I watched her all the way to the corner; I remember it very well. I fell in love with that lady. When she got to the corner, she turned around to see if I was still watching and I was, so she waved. After that, I used to go to the park every chance I got, hoping I'd run into her again so she could play with me, but I never saw that lady again. What I used to do, whenever I was by myself and lonely, I used to picture her as my playmate. One day I even walked all up and down Michigan Avenue looking for her. That's what I was thinking about while I laid on the wet grass where the two pricks had left me. I was thinking about the teeter-totter lady.

I could feel the blood on my face all crunchy from where it had dried. I wiped a little away, but not hard. I didn't want it to start bleeding again. It's sad, when you're as old as I am, a *man* practically, and you're still looking for the teeter-totter lady. I started wondering what the hell was I doing in such a stinking, rotten world, when, like from nowhere, the sun came up over Lake Michigan. It made the birds go mad. They were chirping and flying, and the sunshine made everything bright again. A little even fell on my face; I could feel it because it was warm. I got up, dusted my pants off, threw my jacket across my shoulder and went to sit on the teeter-totter. I just sat there watching the sun, but not for too long, because you could go blind from it. I looked just a little. In the morning, when the sun comes up, it goes real fast. There must've been three inches between it and the water, and it had just come up a few minutes before. I was like measuring how much it came up with my thumb and my finger, when this little kid came wandering into the park with a brown paper bag that was his lunch. He was on his way to school. He was checking me out to see if maybe I was one of the strange men his mother must've told him to stay away from. He kept his distance, all right. He was a smart kid. If I were his age, and I saw a guy with blood all over his face, I'd stay away from him, too. But kids can sense things. He sort of knew I wasn't one of the guys who like to live in the parks, so he kept coming a little closer. I was still on the teeter-totter, just watching him.

"Ya want a ride?" I asked him.

He shook his head.

"It's okay," I said. "C'mon. I'll give ya a quick ride before school."

He looked at me a little longer and then put his lunch on the ground next to him. I lowered the teeter-totter so he could get on, and I gave him a pretty good ride. I didn't make it go too high, on account of I didn't want to scare him. He was the most serious kid I ever saw. He had short blond hair and glasses that looked real thick, and the whole time he just held on to the metal bar and didn't smile or nothing. Parents do that to kids. They were probably sending him to corporate kindergarten or something. Data processing school. Who knows? I told him a riddle about what state is round at both ends and high in the middle, but he didn't want to guess the answer.

"Ohio," I told him. "Get it?" It's round at both ends on account of the O's, and it's high in the middle, *h-i*. Get it?"

But he didn't get it. After a while I stopped and let him off. He picked up his little lunch bag and just walked away. He didn't wave or nothing. I don't know what's wrong with kids today.

Since there weren't any more little kids who needed rides, and since I was so tired I was almost delirious, I started walking the block and a half back to our condo building. People were on their way to work, and the place was lousy with Mercedes and Porsches whipping around the streets, and attaché case guys and ladies hurrying to catch buses. A couple of them stared at me as I walked, but I didn't care. Let them stare, I figured. I mean, I just didn't care anymore. What happens when you get real screwed up in life is, you don't care anymore. A guy could've jumped out from behind a parked car and put a gun right up to my ribs, and I wouldn't've cared. I'd just say something like, "Would you please just shoot if you're going to shoot? I'm tired and I don't have time for any terror at the moment," or something like that. I might even compliment him on his gun, or his holdup style, but I'd give him some pointers, too. I'd show him how to really get the most out of hurting people by either knocking their teeth out first, or grabbing their wallets so fast they don't have time to think about what's happening. If you're going to be a sicko, you might as well do it with some class.

When I got in the lobby, the doorman stared at me, too. He wanted to know why I was there. It wasn't James, it was the other guy who doesn't know me. I ignored him. I did it pretty good. I stopped at the stack of newspapers that had just been delivered, but I decided I didn't want to read one. It would've depressed me to take one upstairs and sit down to read about how many people had been raped and dismembered, so I walked past the pile of papers and opened up the lobby door with my key. The doorman just sort of followed me to make sure I was on the level. He waited by the elevators with me and stared and gawked.

"What flo' you want?" he said, when he saw I wasn't paying any attention to him. All you have to do to get harassed is live downtown and not look like an executive or a fashion model.

He said it again. "What flo' you want?"

I pretended like I didn't speak English. I said, "Esta mucho beat-uppo. Tengo no sleepo in de parko. Yo comer la Whopper, y gotta diarrhea-o."

He just looked dumb and said, "Oh."

"Si. Pero mi casa inhabito by-o lesbiana mucho loca y playo tenniso y aerobic dance-a."

He stared at me for a while longer. Then the elevator doors opened and a whole crowd of pinstripes walked off, and each one of the bastards did a double take at me when I got in the elevator. I must've looked worse than I realized. I pushed the button for the eighteenth floor, and just before the doors closed the doorman said, "Have-a-nice-day," real slow, so that I'd understand.

"Thanks. I will," I said. Then the doors banged shut.

It seemed like I hadn't slept or eaten for about a week. I couldn't

133

even fit the key in the lock or our door at first when I got there. It took me about ten minutes just to open the door. The first thing I did, I went to see what time it was on my alarm clock. It was eight-fifteen. Then I ran out to the refrigerator to see what kind of crap we had to eat. All there was was some leftover Chinese. I ate it in about two seconds. Then I started looking at stuff in the living room to see if my mom had any *friends* over. There were a bunch of highball glasses on the coffee table and on the dining-room table, but no clothes or purses or anything, so then I went to her bedroom door. The way things had been going, it didn't seem like a big deal to just walk in on her and see what the state of the world was. But her door was locked. I didn't care anymore. I didn't care if she had a whole women's tennis team in there with her.

I just walked back to my room and collapsed on the bed with my clothes on. I could feel myself falling asleep. Before I did, though, I got back up and looked in the mirror over my dresser. God! What a fucking sight I was. I looked like I was a corpse. I had blood all over everywhere, and a black eye, and lines under my eyes—the dark circle kind of things you get when you haven't had enough sleep. I could easily have passed for dead. But the weird thing was, it was like I wasn't the guy who was looking in the mirror. It was like I was somebody else looking at the guy who was looking in the mirror. I don't know. It was sure weird, though. I should've gone to the bathroom to clean up, but I was just too tired. I was even falling asleep while I was standing. So I went to bed, and put two pillows on top of each other to hold my head up, because it was starting to feel like my nose was bleeding again.

I'm no believer, boy. I'm sure no born-again Lenny Blake, but what I am is sick. I must be. Because before I completely went unconscious, I prayed. I prayed that while I was asleep no babies would get shot in the head, and that no more women would get raped and thrown off cliffs, and that Lisa's father would stop doing it to her. I even prayed that the little kid on the teeter-totter would learn to *smile* sometime. I made a deal with God. I said if He'd stop the craziness, I'd maybe someday stop in a church and take a look around or bring a priest some money or something. I told Him not to expect miracles or anything, that I wasn't going to stop drinking or smoking grass, or turn into a saint. Or stop having sex fantasies. I wasn't going to give those up for anything. But I'd do *something*. Boy, was I ever nuts. *Delirious*. I must've gotten a brain injury when that big guy beat me up. A blood clot maybe. I kept saying, "It's a deal then, right?"

But it takes two to make a deal.

CHAPTER 12

When I woke up, I couldn't tell if I'd been sleeping five minutes or forty years. You know that feeling, when you can't tell where you are or when you went to sleep or how long it's been since you've *been* asleep. And I had the worst case of the creeps I could remember, except for the time once when I was a kid and I saw *The Exorcist*. When I woke up I was the creepiest I'd been since then. The first thing I did, I went over to the window and peeled some aluminum foil away to see if anybody was alive besides me. I know it sounds crazy, but that's what I did. Outside there were people and cars and buses and road repair crews, so I figured it'd been a dream. Just to make sure, though, I went back to bed and turned on the little radio on my bedstand. I turned to the all-news station to see if there was still a world or not, but the hottest news item they had was about some dinner that night in Washington for a bunch of pinstripes from another country. Then I *knew* it'd been a dream. I searched my desk for a pack of cigarettes, found some Marlboros, and then lit one. I rarely smoke cigarettes, except when I'm nervous, and I was pretty nervous then. I thought the world had come to an end.

I looked at the digital clock on my radio and it said it was two in the afternoon. I knew my mother would be at her law classes, so I was alone. I tried to remember the dream, but it was all mixed up. I went and got my be-bop hat so I could think more clearly, and then I went to the kitchen to make some coffee. We got a Mr. Coffee machine, but I don't know how to work it, so I always make

136

instant. I sat watching the flame from the stove, and you know that old saying? About the watched kettle? If you watch it, the goddamn thing won't boil. It's true. I got that one from my mother. She's a walking cliché. No joke—listening to my mother is like pushing a button on a jukebox in the dark. You never know which familiar tune it's going to be, but you know you've heard it before. Anyway, I like my coffee and cigarette together, and I didn't want my cigarette to go out before the coffee was done, so I walked out of the kitchen so the water would hurry and boil faster. It may just be an old cliché, but it's true, too.

I was still walking around in a daze with a bunch of dream parts trying to stick together in my head. I went to wash my face in the bathroom, and you know what I found? A pair of woman's panties hanging on the hook of the bathroom door. I don't think they were my mother's, either, because they were too small. They must've been her girlfriend's. What bothered me was that I was getting used to the idea. I turned on the water and started washing the blood from my face. I wasn't just bloody, I was dirty. I hadn't had a shower in about two days. So I just soaked my head in the bowl and that's when the dream came back to me. It was so creepy I even got the chills.

First I remembered about the disco. I was sitting around in Faces, a disco in Chicago. I was just walking around with a drink, watching all the glitter people, only no one would talk to me. I tried to figure out what the hell I was doing in a disco. I *hate* discos. I can't even dance. (I guess that's because I'm white.) Then I went into a back room and it was dark and spooky, and when someone came in after me, I hid underneath the bed. There was a big bed in the room, and I could hear this guy who came in after me talking to somebody else. Then I realized it was Lisa's father. Dreams are weird, because like you can remember *real* stuff in them too. I remembered the first time I was underneath Lisa's bed, so I was kind of at home there. But this time Lisa wasn't there. Her father was talking about somebody, how he was going to get him, so I guessed he meant me. I figured he was going to have me knocked off, because the guy he was talking to sounded like the guy who stopped me at my building that morning and beat me up in the park.

137

I just lay there listening to them. I planned how I was going to kill them before they could kill me. I pulled this gun out of my pocket and tried to check if it was loaded or not, but there was a label on the bottom that said it didn't need bullets. Great, I thought. If it doesn't take bullets, then there wouldn't be no evidence. I just listened to the two guys talking and I planned how I'd jump out at the right moment and plug them both. With Lisa's father, I wanted to just *wound* him first and then kick him around a little before finishing him off. I'd make him confess about raping his own daughter and I'd get it on tape. I remember one of them said, "He'll get it tonight. He's no big deal." Or something like that. I was about to get out and shoot them both, but I was stuck. I couldn't get out from under the bed.

Then there was like this blinding light and a huge explosion, and all kinds of people started screaming. I wondered what the hell had happened. Then there was another explosion and the bed was blown right off of me.

The walls were falling down and on fire and everything, so I got up and ran for the door, only I couldn't find it. Lisa's father was under some plaster and stuff, so I started kicking him in the head, only it was useless. I could only kick in slow motion. Then I saw what the explosion had been. There was a huge mushroom cloud in the sky, a big gray cloud against the blue sky, and cars, little Japanese cars—Toyotas and Hondas—and trucks and stuff were falling all over the place from the air. They'd been blown up and swept away. That was it. It was World War III.

I let the water drip all over my face and then I reached for a towel. All the towels were damp, though, so I knew my mother must've left just before. My cigarette had gone out on the medicine cabinet shelf. I picked it up and tried puffing on it, but it was dead. So I went into my room and got another one. The kettle was screaming from the kitchen. I ran back there and poured some boiling water in my coffee cup. It was too hot to drink, but I drank it anyway. I like hot black coffee and cigarettes. I don't like the way they taste, particularly, but it always makes me feel like Al Pacino when I have them. At least I looked halfway normal now, except for a black eye. My hair was wet, so I just brushed it back and put

138

my be-bop cap back on. I'd forgotten to turn off the flame on the stove, so I reached from the kitchen table to shut it off, when I remembered more of the dream. It came in parts.

I don't know how I got back into Faces, but somehow I did, and nobody in there knew that the bombs were falling, that World War III had started. I was running around all over the place trying to tell somebody about the radiation and the explosions, but they couldn't hear me over the music. One couple was dancing in midair. I didn't know how they did it, and I didn't much care. She had nice legs, though, the girl who was dancing. It was kind of interesting to watch her, so I sat down at the bar and looked up her dress for a few minutes. I felt guilty doing it, because I should've been trying to find out where the people I cared about were, like James and my parents. (For some reason, my parents were out of town, staying in a resort that looked like my father's apartment.) (I just had that information; don't ask me how.) The girl who was dancing had great legs, though, like I said. You know how it is in dreams. You never say no to a little sex.

Then I noticed this guy sitting next to me, putting the moves on a black chick who looked like Tina Turner. He was a guy with a long beard and real long brown hair. He looked familiar. He had this long wooden cross leaning next to the bar, a huge one, and then I recognized him. *It was Jesus.*

I tried to get his attention, but he just ignored me. Finally, I walked between him and his chick and said, "I know who you are. I've seen your pictures millions of times. You're Jesus."

Jesus, he said yeah, that's who he was, all right.

"Could I have a word with you?" I asked.

Do you know what he said? He said, "No."

I couldn't believe it. It was noisy as hell, and Olivia Newton John was singing "Let's Get Physical," and Jesus was trying to ignore me. I told him off then.

"But there are atomic bombs dropping right outside. All these people are gonna die. You didn't help all those rape victims or murdered people in the *Tribune* and the *Sun-Times*. Aren't you at least gonna save somebody?"

He was just talking to this black chick and showing her the holes in his hands. She said, "Ooh. It must've hurt, huh?"

139

"Piece of cake," he said.

"Hey," I said. "Hey! People are dying. There's gonna be radiation."

"What do you want from me," he asked, "miracles?"

"Yeah," I said. "Miracles are your bit."

He just shook his head and went back to talking to Tina Turner. I don't blame him, personally. I mean, she looked terrific. I was jumping up and down and yelling about all the people who would die. I tried telling him what radiation poisoning was like. How your liver dies and your skin falls off and all you can do is puke all over yourself.

"Piece of cake," he said. That's just about all he would say all night. *Piece of cake.*

That's all I could remember for a while. I just sat at the kitchen table smoking and drinking my coffee and seeing in my head how the bomb explosions looked. They were so *real.* Did you ever have one of those dreams that were so real that when you woke up you still thought it really happened? That's how this one was.

I looked out the window another time just to make sure I wasn't fooling myself. But there were people all over, and no buildings blown away, so I had to get used to the idea that the bomb hadn't hit yet. In a way, it would almost have been better if the dream *was* real. Then at least the waiting is over. Now I had to wait again.

I went back to my room and turned on the educational channel, because all the networks have in the afternoon is soap operas. I know a lot of people like them, but I don't. The acting is so bad. You can tell when they blow their lines and then they stumble all over themselves trying to ad-lib and make it look natural, but it doesn't look natural. It just looks like they forgot their lines. And the scripts are all so terrible. Somebody's always getting killed in a car accident, or dying slowly of a blood clot in the hospital, and someone's illegitimate kid kidnaps or rapes someone else's illegitimate kid, and then the guy who raped them turns out to be their illegitimate father. Everybody is everybody else's brother or sister, only they don't know it until they get married and somebody gets drunk and the truth comes out. So I watched the educational TV station. They had a documentary on who killed President Kennedy.

140

I got into it for a while, but then it started to bore me with single-bullet and triple-bullet theories. This guy Oswald, some people say he was working for Cuba. Before I knew it, it was exactly like a soap opera, with everybody lying to everybody else, and things got so screwed up, nobody will ever know the truth.

I turned the sound off then and just watched the pictures. Shit. Everybody is so stupid. I figured out who-done-it in about two seconds. I'm good at that from watching and reading mysteries. I always know after five minutes who done it. It was Nixon. Nixon had Kennedy killed. I'm almost positive. In about two hundred years from now they'll discover that Oswald was Nixon's illegitimate brother and that old Dicky had a thing for Jackie and was pissed off 'cause he lost the 1960 election. It's so simple. What's wrong with people that they can't figure that out? Agatha Christie probably knew, too, only she didn't want to start any trouble. She knew about that kind of stuff. Why didn't anybody ask *her*? Or *me*? Nobody ever asks me anything.

I picked up my guitar and started to play it in bed, on account of I had to loosen up my fingers for practice that night. But they kept showing this film of Kennedy in a limousine, and they stopped it about every two seconds to show the building behind him where Oswald was supposed to be. That got me back into the Kennedy thing again. Nobody said nothing about Nixon, so I put my guitar down and went over to my desk. I figured what I should do is write a letter to somebody and let them know who did it. But then I couldn't figure out who to write the letter to. To the President? What does he care who killed Kennedy? He's a Republican. The F.B.I.? They probably already *know* and just aren't telling anybody. So who do you write to? I decided I'd write to the educational station that was showing the film. I looked up the address of the station and then wrote the letter—but I *typed* it, because I wanted it to be anonymous.

Dear Producer of the *Who Killed President Kennedy?* movie:

I'm watching your movie on TV right now and I want to tell you how good it is, only it gets boring when you

141

keep showing Kennedy in the limousine. But other than that, I think it's way better than a soap opera.

In case you guys still can't figure out who had President Kennedy killed, I thought I'd tell you who did it. It was Nixon. I don't have any proof, but it figures. Remember how pissed off Nixon was on account of he lost the election in 1960? We saw a film about it in school, in case you've forgotten, and take my word for it, he looked pissed off. Also, please consider how much madder it would make him to see a guy with someone as sexy as Jackie when he had to go home to Pat every night.

I'm not going to tell you who I am, in case Nixon gets me next. I read all about Watergate, and I know how that guy operates. He puts bugs everywhere and breaks into places. You might want to get a burglar alarm at the place where you work just in case.

Sincerely,
Your Average Viewer

Then I put it in an envelope and put a stamp on it. I wore gloves when I sealed it in case they check for fingerprints. Then I put the letter on the floor by my doorway so I'd remember to mail it when I went out.

For a while I just sat in bed drinking black coffee. The Kennedy program was over and they were showing previews of some ballet that would come on at night, but I'm not much interested in ballet. I just like rock and roll. I got up and switched the channel a few times, but there was nothing good on, just a bunch of soap operas, for a change. So I turned on channel thirteen and watched the Lobby Show. Even *that* was boring. James wasn't at his desk, so all I could see was a stack of newspapers lying on the floor. The newspapers reminded me of something else that had been in my dream. I thought I'd remembered all of it, but I hadn't.

There was this part when I was still in Faces, and now Jesus wasn't around anymore. I was at the bar by myself and a few other people were sitting in chairs next to me. One of the people turned around, and I knew who he was. He was the guy with the mustache who'd beat me up in the park. At first he didn't know that I was sitting right next to him at the bar, because he was too busy reading the newspaper. He was reading Ann Landers. What was stupid was that I got curious. I looked over his shoulder to see if the letter to Ann was the one about the lady whose husband wears panty hose, only the paper was in Chinese. The bartender came up to me and said, "What'll ya have, Lenny? The usual?" The bartender knew me or something. That was funny; I didn't know *him*. I also didn't know what the usual was, but I said, yeah, I'd have one of those. The mugger at the bar who was reading Ann Landers in Chinese, he heard the bartender say my name and then he looked up and saw me. *Blam!* He knocked me right in the face and practically sent me over the bar. He put the paper in my hands and made me read Ann Landers out loud to him. I thought that was kind of weird, making me read Ann Landers out loud while he listened. Kinky, sort of. And the crazy part was, even though it was in Chinese, I could read it. I said, "Ching lou vee nyung fling dung," and then he told me I missed a sentence and that I couldn't graduate from high school.

"But this is fucking *Chinese!*" I told him. But he just walked away with my diploma. Then the bartender brought me the usual. It was chop suey.

The bar had one of those projection-type TVs, where the picture is real big but fuzzy. I started watching it—it was the seven o'clock news. There was one of those women reporters dressed like she just came out of I. Magnin, and she was speaking into this real long, pointy microphone that looked more like a—well, never mind what it looked like. The reporter, she was interviewing a woman in a dark alley who was busy being raped. The guy who was raping her didn't have a face, and he didn't seem to care that there was a reporter around or that he was on TV or anything. He just kept going. The reporter said, "And now, miss, could you tell us how it feels to be raped?" She kept asking typical media questions, like, "Could you tell our viewing audience, who may never have had the experience, what it's like to be raped in an alley where no one will help you?" But the poor woman, all she could do was scream. Then the reporter said a lot of shit about how the interview was an exclusive, and that you wouldn't get to see it on any other channels. That was a relief.

I asked the bartender to switch the channel, and after he poured a bunch of drinks, he turned it to something else. It was a black and white movie about a carnival, but the carnival was on the top floor of a high rise in Chicago. It looked like one of the buildings in my neighborhood. You could hear all this spooky carnival music going, and there were lines of people coming up on the sun deck of this building and waiting to buy a ticket to do something. Then the camera started to move across the edge of the building and you could see what they were waiting in line for. There were a whole bunch of machine guns on stands, and if you gave the attendant a ticket, you could shoot pedestrians and cars down on the streets. All these idiots were waiting in line to shoot people on the street! The camera panned until you could see down below, where people were falling down and holding their guts from being shot by machine guns. It was a gory sight, even in black and white.

I asked the bartender to change the channel again, but he didn't hear me. He was running back and forth, pouring drinks right in people's hands, because he'd run out of glasses. I got up and changed the channel myself. This time Dan Rather came on with a special program about the end of the world. It was crazy, because Dan Rather looked and sounded a little bit like Mister Rogers. Jesus was sitting next to him in the studio, ready for an interview, but when Dan asked him (in his Mister Rogers voice) how long the end of the world would take, Jesus said you'd have to buy his new book to find out. The book was called something stupid like *Hitting Homers from Heaven.*

I must've been pretty pissed off, because I threw my chop suey at the TV screen, and I hit them both with it. They were trying to brush it off their faces and clothes, 'cause in this crazy fucking dream of mine it didn't matter that they were just on TV. They got chop suey all over themselves anyway. I said to Jesus, who was soaking in sweet and sour vegetables, "How can you sit there trying to sell a book when people are being killed?" He looked up and said back to me, very calmly, like a psychiatrist, "It's the *gestalt*, Lenny. It's just the *gestalt*."

144

*   *   *

That was it, I couldn't remember any more. I wondered for a while if I'd remember more of the dream all day long, or for the rest of my life, maybe, but that was it for then. I sipped more of my coffee and just watched the TV. I got to look that word up, *gestalt*. The problem is, I keep forgetting to. It probably doesn't mean anything. It probably just *sounds* like it's supposed to mean something. And that *dream*. If I had a halfway decent shrink to talk to—not that crazy Dr. Kollbisk, who's probably been brainwashed by the board of education—then he'd be able to take the dream apart and tell me why I'm sick. Dreams are very important. They tell you lots of stuff, but only if you got someone who knows dreams to explain what they mean. Me, I didn't have nobody to tell me anything. That's the problem. The people with the answers keep their mouths shut, so you have to find out everything by yourself, and that could take years.

That bothered me, that I might be fifty before I could figure out one lousy thing that I needed to know right then. I started thinking about how I wouldn't get the answers to anything until I was an old man. How depressing. Then I saw somebody on the TV screen in the lobby. It was a little black kid, around six years old. Then there were two of them, one boy and one girl. They were hanging around James's desk and coloring in coloring books. The girl, she had pigtails and a little sweater. The boy had a cowboy hat, and he kept wanting to color everything but the book in front of him. Then I saw James. He was leaning over the boy and showing him not to color on the floor tile, but to color in the book. The little boy, he didn't seem to like the idea. He started crying. James picked him up and for a second I wondered if he was going to hit the little nut, like you always see parents do in public, but he didn't. He just held him and rocked him until he stopped crying. James, he wouldn't hit no kid for something dumb. He might hit a kid for something big, or if like the kid was doing something that could kill him or hurt him, but not for anything stupid. James, he's all right.

I knew those two kids were his sister's twins. I wondered how come he brought them with him, on account of one had a cough and should've been home in bed. I decided to call him up. But

145

then someone was in the lobby asking James to do something, some pinstripe who probably wanted his car door opened for his fat wife or something, so I didn't call him after all. He had his hands full.

I cleaned up next. I took about an hour-long shower, because once I got in the bathtub, I didn't want to get out. What pisses me off is, once you're clean and get out of the shower, all you do is get dirty again. I think if you're a human being, you should probably just spend as much time in the shower as possible. You'll just get dirty again if you don't.

Then, when I was drying off, I found a note pinned to my bath towel. It was from my mother. She knows if she wants to reach me the best way is to leave something in the bathroom. When I'm at home, and when my life is *normal*, if it ever *is*, that's where I spend a lot of time. I like to be clean. The ink on the note had started to run, on account of I got it soaking wet before I found it, but I could still read most of it:

Lenny,

Not *dear* Lenny, but just *Lenny*. That's my mom for you.

> I don't want you running off again today like you have for the past few days. You are to stay home and begin your homework and your writing project for Dr. Kollbisk. I have exams this afternoon at school, and I won't . . .

The letter was runny here, so I couldn't make out too good what it said, but I think it said she wouldn't be home till a certain time, but I couldn't tell what time it said.

> . . . I left money on the table for you, so order dinner in and do some school work.
>
> I don't think it's fair for you to take advantage of the fact that I work hard at improving my life. Just because I can't be home to watch you every second doesn't mean you can go gallivanting off with your friends. Lisa Mankewicz called you several times last night. She is a rude girl. The

last time she called it was practically midnight, and she woke me up.

I'm not kidding, Lenny. There will be drastic measures taken if you don't get yourself in line, young man.

Mom

No one in my family ever signs anything "Love," and that's because we are real uptight. We are. I never even seen my parents *kiss*, for God's sake. I put the letter on the back of the toilet and started thinking. My parents, they don't understand. They always wanted me to play basketball and baseball and get involved in school government clubs. They don't seem to know that that's all right for some kids, but not for me. I don't *care* about any of that stuff, because if you do it, you end up exactly like everybody else. You never get to do what you really want to. You don't get to play on the same stage as Lefty Dizz by being president of your class. You don't learn to write rock and roll songs by bouncing a ball on a court. All you learn doing *that* is how to bounce a ball on a court, and what do you have to show for it afterward? Nothing. How the world ever got so full of idiots is beyond me. My parents, they got brains and all, but they're just like everybody else. They got to be *told* what to do instead of coming up with what they *want* to do. It makes me sick.

When I was getting dressed I thought about how much easier it would be if I just did what everybody wanted me to do. Maybe I could learn to shoot baskets or something; I don't know. It's kind of stupid always doing the things that are the hardest. It makes you feel tired. I was so tired of being fought against, I even considered going out and buying some Izod shirts at Marshall Field's and signing up at the Y for racquetball or something traditional like that. But I just didn't have it in me. Sometimes I wish I did.

When I looked at the clock it was already a quarter after three. What I wanted to do was find Lisa and go have a few sane hours with her, maybe get a hamburger or something. It was a good sign that she called me. Maybe Mr. Mankewicz didn't molest her, I thought. The bastard. If I caught a cab, I could go to where she parks at school and wait for her. Sometimes she stays late and watches a movie at the film club.

Before I left, I wrote a little letter to my mother so she wouldn't worry about me, even though she probably deserved to.

Dear Mom,

I know you don't want me to, but I had to go off *gallivanting* again. I want to see Lisa and then I got practice with the guys. I'd do what you said and stay home and do the boring crap Dr. Kollbisk wants me to, I really would. But tomorrow night we're opening for Lefty Dizz at Scene II. You're invited if you want to come and see us play. I'll be home right after practice, so don't go out and get a writ of habeas corpus or anything, whatever that is. I hope you did well on your exams.

Love,
Lenny

P.S. I'm not taking the money you left. Why don't you use it toward having some groceries delivered? I'm sick of pizza and Chinese. Maybe on Thursday you and me could have a normal dinner together or something.

I taped the letter to the refrigerator door, then I grabbed my guitar case, a spare canister of Mace, and the letter to the TV station about Nixon having Kennedy offed, and I ran out the door. It seems like all I ever do is leave home.

Down in the lobby, James was with his kids. He was playing jacks with them and he was pretty good at it.

"Hey, James," I said.

"Lenny," he said, like he didn't expect to see me. "You all right, babe? Got a gig tonight?"

"I'm fine. I'm sorry about last night. But I had to leave," I said. I put my guitar case down and picked up a newspaper. "I had the lonelies, though. You know."

"I be worried about you, Lenny," he said. The kids were like standing behind him, looking at me from around his legs. They were very shy. On James's desk I could see a bottle of cough syrup. He remembered to get it.

148

"Don't worry about me, James. You don't have to worry." Then I smiled at the little boy, and he hid his face. "These your sister's kids?"

James, he said yeah, that's who they were, all right. He said the baby-sitter was sick and couldn't make it, so there was nobody else to take care of them. He had to bring them to work with him. That kind of made me sad. Those poor kids would have to sit in the lobby all day, and James would have to do two jobs at the same time—being a parent *and* a doorman. Then James, he looked at me with his head tilted, like he was trying to see between something.

"Where you get that shiner, Lenny?"

I reached up to touch it. It still hurt. So did my nose. I forgot about the shiner.

"Listen, James. Can we talk? I mean, private-like. You got a second?"

James, he gave the ball and jacks to the kids and told them to stay behind his desk until he got back. Then we stepped outside for a minute.

"Last night, when I got back—actually, it was this *morning*, at around five or six o'clock—two guys, they asked me for dope and beat me up when they didn't get it. They took me to the park and wanted to know who my connection was. Isn't that crazy?"

He just shook his head. He put his arm on my shoulder and asked me what they looked like. I told him about the guy with the mustache and the other guy who was all the time chomping on gum.

"I seen 'em," he said. "I seen 'em hangin' around here the night befo' last when I was leavin'. Someone be trickin' on you, Lenny. Those guys is cops."

"No, they're not. They *can't* be, James. They wanted dope."

"They wanted somebody who *sell* dope, to make a bust. Don't you see, Lenny?"

I didn't really see. "I thought those guys were dope addicts."

"Dope addicts don't care 'bout no sources, Lenny. They go wherever they can get it. You bein' set up, my man. Someone done gone to the cops and tell 'em you a pusher. I seen them guys.

They cops. I *knows* it. A cop could walk around in *drag* and I still know he a cop."

"You sure?" I asked. It didn't make any sense to me. I don't sell drugs.

"I sure," he said, and then he looked around like he thought we might've been watched right then. "And if cops are beatin' you up, they sure you know something. They sure you hard-core."

"Whad'ya mean?" I said.

"The real thing, a dealer. Did you tell 'em anything?"

I started to chuckle. I remembered about Fredericks, the guy I made up. I told James, and he sighed and slapped the back of my head.

"You a *dummy*, boy. Lord, sometimes I wonder how *dumb* you can be. It ain't yo' fault. You just bein' white, I guess."

"Whad'ya mean? They would've killed me if I hadn't told 'em something."

"Maybe," James said, real dead certain-like. "Maybe they woulda, but after they find out there ain't no Fredericks, they gonna kill you for sure. They be back to get the boy who gave 'em the wrong information. You admitted to 'em that you got a supplier, and now they gonna believe you."

He was scaring the shit out of me. Why didn't *I* think of that? It's probably because James is right. I'm stupid sometimes. He was right about being white, too. If you're white, and you live on Lake Shore Drive, you don't know lots of things.

"You be careful 'bout how you come and go," James told me. He was giving me instructions like a football coach or something. "You get *driven* home, you don't just come walkin' in. That way, whoever drives you goes straight in the garage and drops you off at the service elevator. You understand?"

I said yeah, I understood. Only, then my knees wouldn't stop shaking. I went back in the lobby with James and picked up my guitar case. One of the kids smiled at me, the girl, and I patted her head. It felt nice. Little black kids, they got nice hair.

"You playin' tonight?" James asked me. My mind wasn't on things like playing, so it took me some time to answer him. My mind, it was on getting killed. Right where it always is. I pictured coming home and getting shot in the head or something. Fucking

150

cops, for Christ's sake. They got those magnum guns that would kill an elephant. You could come home in a tank, even, and all the cops have to do is shoot the tank. I was scared to death. I'm not exaggerating. I could barely move, I was so scared.

"Tomorrow," I said. "I'm playing tomorrow night. Opening for Lefty Dizz."

James, he said Lefty was the best bluesman in Chicago, except for maybe Son Seals. Then he said for me to be careful, and I said I would. I looked at the little kids playing jacks. They were having a hell of a time there on the floor. Then I looked at James, and he was looking at me in a way that made me want to cry. He was looking at me like I was going to die, like I was halfway to the funeral home and still warm.

I folded the newspaper under my arm without even reading the headline (because I knew whatever the headline was it wasn't going to be good), and I went out onto Walton Street and got the first cab I could find. I told him to take me to Harrison Godfrey High School, and then we drove off.

I had one of those drivers who thinks he's driving a roller coaster in an amusement park. The kind of guy who doesn't wait for red lights to turn green, and who takes corners at around sixty miles an hour.

"Hey," I told him. "Hey, if you don't mind, I'd like to get there in one piece."

But he didn't say nothing. He could barely speak English. He was one of those guys from Pakistan who goes crazy behind the wheel because all he ever rode when he was a kid was a camel. He took me way out of my way, too. I told him three times that he was taking the wrong streets, but all he would say was "Theez way eez queeker."

About ten times, we almost got into accidents. When he finally stopped at Burling and Halsted, I was ready to throw up. It was just like on a roller coaster, I'm not putting you on. I took my guitar case out of the back seat, then I walked over to his driver's window and gave him exactly the five dollars and seventy-five cents the meter said.

"Where eez teep?" he asked, very rudely.

"I'll tell you *where eez teep. Teep* is in my pocket, because you

151

went out of your way to get here and it cost me twice as much as it should have. And on top of that, you drive like an asshole. You could've killed somebody."

He didn't like that. During the whole ride he pretended not to know English, but when I called him an asshole, he knew exactly what I was talking about.

Then he drove off, but not before giving me the finger and saying, "Fuck you, jag-off pussy prick fucker!"

Jesus. Every time I turn around somebody else is ruining my day. I was going to hear that guy say, "Fuck you, jag-off pussy prick fucker" in my head all day, simply because it was the dumbest thing I ever heard. And I'd have to hear it in that stupid, funny voice of his, with the accent. It sounded more like "Jack-hoff poozy preek fuckah," the way he said it. I couldn't get it out of my head to save my life.

I found Lisa's car down on Burling, only about a half-block from where the Driver of the Year had left me. She has this nice little Toyota, the blue one that I told you about. I had no choice but to wait for her, and it was a pretty nice day; the sun was out and it was almost sixty-nine degrees. I heard the weather report in the cab. I had on a sweater and my windbreaker, and it was warm enough to take off the windbreaker and roll up my sleeves. I figured I'd get some practice in while I was waiting for her, so I opened my guitar case and sat on the hood of her car and played a few tunes. My fingers were in pretty good shape, considering.

I had this one tune about a girl I never met before, like a fantasy girl, and it was me telling her why she's screwed up, but in a nice way. I never had no girl's name to stick in there, so I didn't have a title yet. I figured "Lisa" would be a nice name for it, on account of it had the right number of syllables, and as far as I could tell, I was falling in love with her anyway—so why not? I thought about it, though, for a while, because if you name a song for a girl, and then something bad happens between you and that girl, then you're stuck with a song that will remind you of her and you may not play it anymore. But it was okay, I decided. Even if something happened between us, something bad, it was still okay for it to be called "Lisa." And she was just screwed up enough for the lyrics to fit:

152

Rivers flow and children grow
And planets dot the sky,
and Lisa's dreams aren't what they seem,
She can't imagine why.

Lisa, only time will tell,
Caught between what's real and what's a wishing well.
Believing
All your dreaming,
Scared to face the light,
Frightened of the break of day,
You don't have to tell me 'bout your fine tomorrow,
You just have to worry 'bout your sad today

Lisa comes like morning sun,
She shines beneath your door,
Then evening comes and Lisa runs,
She swears there must be more.

Lisa, so you didn't know
Love is only here a while before it goes.
Believing
All your dreaming,
Scared to face the light,
Running at the break of day,
You don't have to tell me 'bout your fine tomorrow,
You can live forever in your yesterday.

Pretty good, huh? I mean for a kid who's sick and doesn't even have a lousy diploma. Anyway, I got tired of playing the guitar with no amplifier, so I put it back in its case and took out the paper I'd got at the lobby. I didn't want to see any sick stories, so I refused to read anything until I opened to the horoscope. My mother, she reads the horoscope all the time, but usually I don't. Usually I'm afraid it will tell me something that will ruin my day, if I'm having a good one. Or if I'm having a shitty day, it will tell me all kinds of good stuff that *should* be happening to me, and I'll get twice as depressed, because I'll feel cheated. But today I was scared on account of the two guys who were out to get me, so I thought I'd open it up and see if it said anything about dying. My birthday is July third. I'm a Cancer. I don't know what that means, really, but that's what I am. I had the *Sun-Times*. Their horoscope guy is Omarr, this real creepy-looking guy with glasses and this look like he's just seen your future and doesn't like what he sees.

I read it, and it was just a bunch of stuff about how I shouldn't sign contracts for a while, and that I should watch my investments. It also said marriage could be on the horizon. I felt like asking for my money back after I read it—until I remembered that I didn't pay for the paper. In the first place, I don't have any investments. And I don't have any contracts to sign. And I'm barely old enough to get married—I'm not, in fact. Good going, Omarr. Nice job, kid. How do they let that crap in the paper? That's what pisses me off about horoscopes. At that moment in Chicago, about a hundred thousand people were expecting marriage, a contract, and something to go wrong with their investments. Jesus. When I'll start believing in horoscopes is when I can open up the paper and it will say:

> Oh shit! Are you in trouble! Two big cops are right now looking for you to tell you there is no Fredericks, and there is a large chance that they will beat hell out of you. Also, you have band practice tonight after you see Lisa, who, by the way, in case you're too dumb to realize it, you are falling in love with. Play your cards right and she will boogie with you soon. Play your cards wrong, like you probably will, and she'll go home and get it from her father. Don't eat any Whoppers, and stay away from your father's apartment at night, you jerk.

That would make a believer out of me. Then I could see some use in horoscopes. But don't give me any of this marriage-on-the-horizon crap.

Jack-hoff poozy preek fuckah. I couldn't get that cabby out of my head.

I was going to turn straight to the sports section, honest, just to see what all the guys with no necks would be talking about in bars

154

that night, when the paper flipped open and I caught the title of a story:

GIRL, 12, SEXUALLY ABUSED FOR NINE DAYS

Goddamn it. I *promised* myself I wasn't going to read that kind of stuff—but it was too late then. Now that I knew what the horror story was, I just had to read it. I wanted to know what happened to that twelve-year-old girl. I had to find out what the perverts were up to. Damn it. I was so pissed off at myself for seeing that headline that I tried putting the paper down and forgetting about it. I looked around to see if the two cops were anywhere in sight, but they weren't. I thought about playing another song, but I just wasn't up to it. I looked at the newspaper on the hood of Lisa's car. The front page was flapping in the wind, like it was teasing me or something. I looked at it. I knew I was going to pick it up and read it. I think the newspaper knew it too. It blew open practically to the right page.

I picked it up and read the goddamn thing. It was horrible. Three guys kidnapped a twelve-year-old girl on Clark Street and took turns raping her for nine days, until two of them were arrested. The guys were in their twenties and thirties, and the whole time they hardly even fed her. One guy did it to the kid three times a day. What an animal. I knew that people all over the city were reading about this animal and then flipping to the stock page to see how Dow Jones was doing. I pictured these sick, scuzzy guys, who probably never take baths, raping a twelve-year-old, and then some clean-cut executive downtown reading about it while he's sipping a Scotch and water on the rocks. And then, like what he just read was nothing, he flips over to the stock market page, checks his watch, sees that he's late for a meeting, and runs out of the place into a cab. All I hoped was, I hoped he'd get the same cab driver who'd just driven me.

I threw the paper on the ground and just sat waiting for Lisa to show up. It's weird having to wait outside of the school building while all the other kids can come and go whenever they want. It made me sad, a little, even though Harrison Godfrey High School is an insane asylum. It still made me wish that I could at least go *in*

155

if I felt like it. It was the same way with my own home. It would be nice to know that you could go in someplace and somebody would be glad to see you. I was like one of those guys they drag off to jail, and all the time he's screaming, "But I'm *innocent*, I tell ya!" Only, nobody will believe him. That's pretty much how I felt.

In the distance, coming out the door of the school and down the walk, I saw a girl with long hair and a nice little wiggle. It was Lisa. If I would've been two miles away with a clear view and a tele-scope, I still would've known it was Lisa. Honest. With some peo-ple, you can just tell.

She walked all the way to her car before she saw who *I* was, though. That didn't make me feel so hot. I mean, with her it's like harps and violins go off whenever she's close, and when she sees me, it's more like a washboard and a tuba.

"Lenny!" she said. She was at least surprised to see me. We didn't have a date or nothing.

"Hi," I said, like I just happened to be in the neighborhood. The problem with me is, I never say the right thing to somebody when I first see them. I'm always thinking that they'd rather not see me, probably. So I wait to see how they take it—the fact that I'm there. She was taking it pretty good. She was smiling, at least. Right up to the point when she put her hand up to her mouth and sort of gulped.

"What happened to your *eye?*"

I forgot about my shiner, and I didn't feel like telling her about it. If I would've, it would've been like letting those two gorillas who did it to me in on my private love life. Instead, I just made up a lie. I said it had been a stupid accident, which it was, kind of, so it wasn't a *total* lie. It was a sort-of, kind-of lie.

"What *kind* of accident?" she asked.

"A stupid one. Believe me. I don't even like mentioning it, really." Which was the total truth. She seemed to accept that as an explanation.

"That was a close call yesterday," she changed the subject. I didn't know what the hell she was talking about, though.

"Huh?"

"At my place."

I just stared.

156

"My father coming home, I mean." She looked to see if I thought so. "Lenny? Wasn't it? Why do I get the feeling one of us isn't here?"

"That was only *yesterday?*" That didn't seem right. My timing was all screwed up. "It feels like last year."

Lisa started looking at me, at my eyes, really. She probably thought I was buzzed or something. Then she was looking for her keys in her purse

"Are you all right?" she asked.

"Huh? Me? Yeah. Me? I'm fine. Okay, I guess."

She was still going through things in her purse. "I called you last night; you weren't home, though. Your mother answered, and I think she was a little pissed off that I called so late."

I just sort of waved my hand, like it didn't make any difference *what* my mother thought. Then we both sort of stared at each other and caught ourselves, and then looked away. Finally, she said, "Are you all set to play tomorrow night?"

"Yeah. That's why I've got my guitar. Practice tonight."

She opened her car door and asked me if I needed a ride somewhere.

"Not actually," I said, looking around. It sure is hard to break the ice with a girl. If you feel like I felt about *her*, that is. You try to act like you don't feel nothing, and then you end up looking like an asshole.

"Are you sure?"

"See," I said, trying to look in her eyes like Al Pacino, "I thought we could go to an early dinner or someplace, 'cause I have to—"

"Sure. That would be nice. Besides, I have something to show you."

"Yeah?" I said.

"Uh-huh."

"What?"

"Just get in," she told me. "It's a surprise."

I hate surprises.

I was sort of in the middle of explaining *why* I wanted to go for dinner, but it didn't seem to matter to her. I was talking with my hands, like you see Italian people do a lot (for effect), and I let one

157

of them fall to my jeans, right at the knee (for effect). Like out of disgust. I was disgusted because I was making such a mess out of things. See, the way I figured it, I'd tell her I had to talk to her and make it seem urgent, only then I wouldn't tell her anything at all, and then she'd sort of coax the truth out of me, the way the girl always does in television movies. But Lisa, she's no television girl. She didn't say what I thought she'd say.

"I sort of have to talk to you. I mean, you know."

"Okay," she said.

She wasn't supposed to say that. She was supposed to say, "About what? What's the matter?" And then I'd say, "Nothing, really. It's just something that I have to talk to you about." And then she'd bite her lower lip or something and try to wring it out of me. But it didn't work that way. I ended up just putting my guitar case in the back seat and climbing up front with her, wondering what the surprise was.

Lisa, she drives like a World War I pilot. She sped away from the curb and headed downtown. I looked around the inside of the car, but I didn't see any surprises.

"What's the surprise?" I asked her, very nonchalantly, like I didn't care. Like it was the eight-hundredth surprise I'd had that day.

"You'll see" was all she said.

"When?"

She giggled a little and said again that I'd see. I was getting impatient, because like I said, I hate surprises. Especially if I know I'm getting one. I opened the glove compartment, but all that was in there was Kleenex.

"You got me Kleenex as a surprise?" I held up the box.

She passed a bus on Lincoln Avenue and almost hit a car coming from the other way. Lisa has ice water running in her veins. Either that or she thinks what she sees out of the windshield is just a movie.

"Lenny, goddamn it, it's a *surprise*. Just wait, will you? We're almost there."

"I know what it is," I said. "You're gonna pass another bus and this time you'll hit the car coming from the other way and we'll die. That's the surprise, that you're gonna kill us. Right?"

158

She rolled down her window and said something about how she was a much better driver than most of the men she knew. Girls do that. They always say how females drive better than males, and it's usually right after they've almost had an accident. I looked at her. She was a lousy driver, but she looked so beautiful with her window down and the wind blowing in her hair, I felt like we were in a shampoo commercial. I expected to hear an announcer talk about lather.

We drove down to Rush Street, past Bug House Square. It must've been a national holiday for perverts, because there weren't any there. The park was empty. Maybe it was Richard Speck Day or something. When she turned the corner where all the nightclubs are, I was in a daydream. I was thinking about James's kids and how I hoped the people in the building would at least treat them nice, say hi to them and everything. It was something to worry about. The people in that goddamn building give everyone the freeze, and I was sort of hoping one of the old ladies who live there would turn on channel thirteen and see them and bring them some cookies or something.

Lisa stopped the car at the side of the curb, in front of her mother's club. She was smiling and looking at something out the window of the car.

"How do you like it?" she asked, motioning with her face toward the street.

"How do I like *what*?"

Then I saw it. On the marquee in big letters it said:

WED. THRU FRI.
LEFTY DIZZ
WITH LENNY BLAKE AND THE VICTIMS

At first I reacted like anybody on the street would. Who the hell are Lenny Blake and the goddamn Victims? Then I remembered that *I* was Lenny Blake.

"It's not 'Lenny Blake and the Victims,'" I said to Lisa. "It's just the 'Victims.' Christ!"

Lisa said she knew that, but she was thinking that it sounded better to have so and so and the somebodies. The front-man approach. Then she said, "What's the matter? Don't you like it?"

159

She looked a little hurt, and I realized that she probably had to twist her mother's arm to get her to give us billing at all, considering nobody ever heard of us before. So I tried to look appreciative—something I haven't perfected yet. I smiled like I meant it, like I was really happy, but deep inside I was shitting bricks.

"It's great." I said it smiling like an idiot.

"You don't like it," she said, and pulled away from me.

"No, no! I really *do*. It's great. Nice. Looks really good."

"Then how come you sounded like you were disappointed? Just a few minutes ago you sounded like somebody had just mugged you or something."

"Oh, I always sound that way. Even when I'm happy. I like it," I lied. I even leaned over and kissed her on the cheek and thanked her for going through the trouble.

It did sound kind of good, I have to admit it, now. Lenny Blake and the Victims. Not bad. The problem was, the guys were going to think I was trying to upstage them. And the other thing—if those two cops were out scouting for me, Lisa had just advertised where I'd be. It might as well have said.:

LENNY BLAKE IS IN HERE WEDNESDAY NIGHT IN CASE ANY NARCS WANT TO BEAT THE SHIT OUT OF HIM AND SEND HIM TO JAIL

All of a sudden I was feeling a little shaky and weak. I didn't know what the hell was wrong with me, and that made it worse. Not knowing what was wrong with me scared me, and that made me more shaky and weak. I thought maybe I was having a heart attack. Or a stroke. Don't laugh, 'cause it happens to kids, too. I had a story cut out of the paper once that was all about a fifteen-year-old kid who had a heart attack while he was playing basketball. That's the real reason how come I don't play basketball. Every time I even *see* a basketball game, I sit around waiting for one of the players to keel over and die from a coronary.

Lisa was looking a little twitchy, I guess because she could tell something was wrong with me. My breathing was all funny.

"Is something wrong?" she wanted to know. "Are you feeling all right?"

160

I tried to slow my breathing down, but it only got worse. My head got all light and everything, and my vision was starting to go white. It's hard to explain unless it's happened to you. It's like everything gets real light and you feel like passing out.

"I don't feel so good," I said.

"What is it? What's wrong?" She was leaning over me and looking worried as hell. That made me more sure I was having a heart attack. When somebody looks at you like you're dying, you figure that you must be.

"I'll be all right," I said, but I didn't think so. Lisa, she wanted to know if she should take me to a hospital. She told me I looked pale. Just what I wanted to hear. She might as well have told me I looked like I was having a heart attack.

We were about a half a block from Gino's, a pizza place. They have pretty good pizza, and right then I was thinking about how I'd much rather die eating pizza than having tubes shoved in me at a hospital. What they do in a hospital if you're dying, they shove tubes in every opening in your body—your mouth, your nose, your ears, your . . . well, your *other* openings too. No matter how small they may be, and mine is pretty small. I told her to leave the car where it was and we'd have pizza at Gino's.

"Are you sure you feel up to it?" she asked, very concerned and all. I mean, you could tell she cared, and that made me feel a *little* better, at least.

"Yeah. I feel like having a pizza."

Then she was worried about leaving the car in a no-parking zone, but I told her I'd pay the ticket if she got one. I didn't feel like looking all over Rush Street for a parking place, because I knew there wouldn't be any, and then I'd die without my pizza.

It was extremely embarrassing. She had to hold my arm all the way to Gino's so I wouldn't fall over. Anybody who saw us probably thought this very pretty girl was out on a nice day walking her retarded brother. I must've looked like a half-wit.

You have to walk down under curb level to get inside this pizza place, and it's dark as hell and nobody can tell who you are. Even the waitress can't tell. She can hardly see you, and you can hardly see her, that's how dark it is. I felt better right away. We sat in a booth across from each other, and I started playing with the candle they have on the table. Lisa, she was watching me very careful-like, to make sure I didn't fall over and croak. But I really did feel better just being in the dark. I felt like staying there forever. Sunshine is overrated.

"Lenny." she said.

"Huh?"

"How're you feeling? You feeling better?"

"Yeah. Jesus. I was passing out there for a second. But I'm okay now."

"You sure?" She asked, reaching across the table and touching my hand. I grabbed her hand and just held it. I might've been sick, but I was also alive enough to know it feels better to hold some-body's hand, especially if it's Lisa's.

"Yeah, I'm sure. Whew! That was spooky. Just hold my hand for a while."

"Okay," she said.

The waitress came then and gave us menus. We kept holding each other's hands, though. When she'd gone away, I started up the conversation again.

"Boy, am I glad you're here." She looked so pretty sitting there.

"I'm glad, too," she said. "Is there anything I can do for you?"

"There's a lot you can do for me," I said.

"What?"

There's no nice way of saying what I was thinking. What I was thinking was that she should run away with me and pull my clothes off and jump all over me. But you can't just *say* that kind of stuff. It sounds awful. It would be *nice*, but it sounds awful.

"Why don't you come over here and sit with me?"

"Over there?"

Then she got up and came over to my seat. She sort of put her arm around me and held my hand again.

"What's wrong?" she whispered-like, right in my ear. I started getting that shaky way again. Don't ask me why. Boy, was I screwed up. I was just starting to understand how screwed up I was. I felt like I should've been locked up in a mental institution. What I was, was *sad*. All the stuff that had happened to me in the last five days, even the *newspapers* I'd read, I didn't think I could take any more. When it was all happening to me, it got me mad and I could fight

162

back. But then, after a while, if I just thought about it all, it made me so scared and sad, I felt paralyzed. I mean, how long can you go on fighting everybody and everything in the world? Not long. Not very long.

I felt like that guy in the book *1984* by George Orwell, the one they made us read last year in English class. Everything he did he had to sneak, and everything he believed was completely different from what everybody else believed. Then he met this girl who he had an affair with, and she wasn't real bright or anything, but she was at least *nice* to him. I felt just like that guy—Winston, or whatever his name was. I think he got shot at the end, but the book isn't real clear about it. Other people I talked to said no, he didn't, but I think he did. I sat there in the booth feeling like Winston, and waiting for somebody to shoot me.

I was trying real hard not to, but I started crying, just a little. I mean, you couldn't tell. I just felt all watery in my eyes when Lisa put her arm around me. *I wasn't even horny anymore.* It figured. Leave it to me. Just when I'm about to get the girl of my dreams, I start thinking of her more as a sister than a lover. Maybe fluorescent lights had already ruined my testicles. It's possible.

She kept asking me what was wrong and patting my back and stuff, and that made it worse. By that time she could see that I had tears all over my face. She picked up a napkin and started wiping them away, but I took it out of her hand and wiped them away myself. What a man I am when I want to be.

"You have to promise me something," I told her. I wasn't looking at her when I talked to her. I was looking at the stupid candle. "You gotta stop sleeping with your old man."

She didn't say anything, and then I kept rambling. I said how she was the one person in the world I cared about, and that if World War III ever came I hoped we'd be the only two people left in the world. I said it would be nice, because there wouldn't be any newspapers with horror stories in them, and no more Ann Landers answering stupid questions, and no more Omarr with dumb predictions about our lives, and we wouldn't have to be afraid about perverts or murderers, and we wouldn't have to put up with parents. The only thing we'd have to worry about would be radiation, and I'd rather take my chances with that.

163

If she didn't know I was insane before that, she must've known then. But what she did, she listened, and kept her arm around me, and just waited until I was through talking. The waitress came to take our orders, and she ordered pizza with just cheese. I was listening to her while she was talking, and I could tell the waitress was staring at me, but I didn't care. For one thing, it's dark in there, like I told you, and for another, who cares what a waitress thinks about you?

I felt better then. The tears stopped coming, and then all I was was tired. I really felt better. It was like going to confession. That must be why Catholics do that. They must feel better or something. But I'm sure it's much nicer confessing to Lisa than some old guy in a black suit. Lisa should start a confession business. She's good at listening.

"Lenny," Lisa said, sort of turning my face with her hand. "I've thought about what you said. I thought about it after I told you what was going on. I didn't do it last night, after you left."

"You don't have to report to me," I said. It sounded colder than I'd wanted it to, but I didn't want to hear the crummy details.

"I know I don't. Nobody's saying I *have* to. But I want you to know it isn't going to happen anymore. I'm going to sit down and talk to both of them, my mom and my dad. I'm going to make sure it doesn't happen again."

I took a drink of water and played with an ice cube in my mouth. When it was all melted, I said, "You shouldn't tell your mother."

"I have to tell her *some*thing if I want it to stop. I won't go into detail. I'll just talk *around* it."

"She'll know what you mean," I said. I pictured her mother finding out. Lisa was being too naive about the whole thing. Her mother wasn't the type who would say, "Oh? Daddy's been fucking you for a year? Well, I'll have a nice talk with him and tell him not to do that anymore, and then everything will be fine." What her mother would do is throw the bastard out and divorce him, which is exactly what she *should* do. But Lisa, she somehow didn't realize that would be the result. She was still a little girl in a lot of ways. I liked that about her to an extent, except then there's reality, too, and she didn't come within a million miles of that.

164

"It may not be that easy," I said. "It's a very sick thing, and sick things have a way of getting sicker."

"Trust me. I'm going to handle it."

She was staring right in my eyes, and she must've known how I felt about her. You can't hide certain things (like, for instance, idiocy). And listening to *her* sound so brave made *me* feel like a fighter again. I felt almost up to punching somebody in the mouth, but I didn't know who. If I ever find out who deserves to be punched in the mouth the most, I'm going to do it, though.

I was in a better mood when we left Gino's. They got all kinds of graffiti carved in the walls there that you notice when your eyes get used to how dark it is. The whole time I was there I was reading that so-and-so loved so-and-so, and I was positive that all those people who carved their names and initials in the woodwork were either broken up or divorced or dead by then. I was even tempted to carve Lisa's and my name in a table or something, but I didn't know. I might've gotten yelled at by the waitress. And besides, someday in the future, if there *is* a future (which I doubt), I might come back and eat there, and Lisa and me may have broken up by then. Then it would just make me so upset to see our initials all carved in the wood, I'd have to leave, and I'd think about it all the way home. So I didn't do it.

Lisa and me walked down Rush Street not saying anything. Just holding hands and looking at the people and the signs and the sky. What I wanted more than anything in the whole world was to have my own family someplace in a small town. I saw Lisa and me getting married and having a couple of kids and a dog, and just minding our own business. It was a nice dream, while it lasted. But then I remembered about Russia and Iran and all those countries we're going to have nuclear war with, and that we'd be dead before we could ever get married. Maybe tomorrow, even. And if not, if the war *didn't* come by the time we got married and moved away and had kids all over the place, then I'd always be afraid that my kids were going to die when the bomb *was* dropped. So I made up my mind to hell with any of that happy kind of stuff. I could never have a kid as long as there was a bomb left in the world, and some jerk sitting with his finger over a button waiting for the word from the President. Some jerk who got twelve hundred dollars a month just to push a button when they told him to. What I'd have to do would be to kill the idiot who was waiting to push the button. Sneak up on him when he was eating lunch or something. But then they'd have another guy ready to do it. Half the people in the world would take that job and blow everybody up if the President told them to. They'd enjoy it. There's no way I'd ever get around to killing half of the people in the world, so I forgot about the dream. Why torture yourself?

I stopped in front of a game arcade and watched all these people playing with electronic screens and levers. They kept throwing quarters in the machines, and some of them looked like they'd been there for hours. It looked fun, though. I mean, if you just stayed for a few minutes and not your whole life. I was looking in the window of this place when Lisa said something. I didn't hear her, though, on account of my mind was so far away. "Hmm?" I said.

Lisa, she looked at my face and said, "Where'd you get the black eye, really?"

"Oh. That. I hit myself."

"You hit yourself?"

"Yeah. I hit myself in my sleep." I was going to use that old bumped-into-the-door routine, but it was overworked. So I came up with a new angle.

"Would you mind telling me how you hit yourself in the eye while you were sleeping?" she said, sarcastic-like. She didn't buy it.

"Well, *I* don't know. I was *asleep*, so I don't know exactly how it happened. I think I was dreaming I was a boxer, and I threw a punch at myself by accident. Something like that. I just woke up with my fist in my eye."

Even *I* wouldn't've believed that one. I was getting rusty at lying. I'd have to practice at it when I got the chance, I thought. Maybe I'll try to pass myself off as an albino Negro at the next Operation PUSH convention. Before she could say anything else, I changed the subject and asked her if she wanted to go in the arcade and play a few games. She said she'd go if I'd go, so we went.

The noise level in those places is incredible. It sounds like the inside of a lunatic's head. I'll bet that's the way the world sounds to

Jerry Falwell *all* the time. I found this one game nobody was using and put a quarter in it. It was a bunch of spaceships trying to blast the hell out of *my* spaceship, and they did, too. They were just blowing the shit out of me, and in no time they killed my ship with an atomic blast.

That game made me nervous, so I found another. It was like a Pac Man copy, a bunch of little guys running around trying to eat my guy. All those machines, they got little guys that want to either blow you up or eat you. And that's what people do for *fun*. It reminded me too much of my life, so I didn't enjoy it much. What they're going to do, I figure, they're going to make a Lenny Blake game, and after you put in your quarter, you got to make me run around a maze, because two cops will be after me, and if you get away from them, then a shrink will try to lock me up in a room and analyze me, and if you get me out of *that* mess, you'll have to try to keep Mr. Mankewicz from putting it to Lisa by making the little Lenny character shoot him or club him to death with a special lever. Then you make the little guy, who's supposed to be me, you make him go to a part of the screen that's his apartment, and when he gets there, if he's alone, you win. If his mother and a lesbian are there, you lose. Either way, you're out a quarter. Take my word for it, it would be a depressing game.

Lisa was at another game, blasting hell out of something, and there was this oldish kind of guy behind her, watching her ass. I walked right in back of her to cut in front of his view, and I told her I wanted to leave.

"Just a minute," she said, involved in the stupid game or something. "I'm winning."

I didn't bother to tell her that you *can't* win with one of those machines, or with anything else, really. I just let her finish the game. The guy was still staring at her. I think he was looking at her tits then, because he shifted his position as soon as I'd come up behind her. It pissed me off so much I almost said something to him. But I didn't know what to say.

Hey, you! Quit looking at my girlfriend's tits!

You can't say that. It sounds stupid. So I didn't say anything, but he sure was pissing me off. I hate when guys stare at a girl's ass behind her back. Wait—that's not exactly what I mean. What I mean is I hate when a guy stares at a girl's ass or any part of her, her tits, her anything, when she's not looking and just minding her own business. They think they're being suave, but they aren't. They're being douche bags. They must think that girls go for the pervert approach, but I don't know any girls who do. Perverts, they think the whole world is perverted, too.

I was glad as hell to get out of that arcade. I don't know how kids my age do that all day long. I mean it. I think if you added up all of their I.Q.s—all the kids who were in there—it would still be a double-digit number. Sometimes I think my whole generation is a bunch of idiots. Even *monkeys* would get tired of video games in about ten minutes. But not most teenagers. Most teenagers, if the place didn't close at night, would be forty years old by the time they got bored of the same old games. No wonder the fucking world is in trouble.

It was a one-block walk back to Lisa's car, and rush hour traffic had started by then. We were just walking and not talking much, when I spotted my old man across the street, coming out of Sweetwater's Cafe with that goddamn receptionist from the bank. She was holding on to his arm and looking in all the windows, and he was smiling, saying something to her that made her laugh. Maybe he'd memorized the obituaries from the paper that day. That's something she'd think was funny—death. I didn't let Lisa know that anything was wrong, because she tends to worry too much. I just kept walking toward her car and watching my dad and the receptionist. He looks like a monk from the back. I could see the little bald spot on his head as they got lost in a crowd of people, and I remembered a time once when he took our family on a trip out west. I was only around ten years old then, but I remembered real well when we were in the Badlands of South Dakota, up on a tourist view bridge. The Badlands are about a million miles of ugly dry hills that look like gigantic zits coming out of the ground. Geographic acne. He lifted me clear up over the railing so I could get a better view, and even though it nearly scared the shit out of me at the time, I knew he wasn't going to drop me or let anything happen to me. I trusted him.

168

I was thinking about that time on the bridge as he faded out of sight down Rush Street. Then I looked at the sign on Scene II.

LENNY BLAKE AND THE VICTIMS

Do you know that he walked right underneath that goddamn sign and didn't even see it? He just disappeared into a crowd like any other stranger on the street, with his arm around Miss Personality. Things sure have a way of changing. They sure turn around. When I got into Lisa's car again, the first thing I did was fasten the seat belt good and tight around me. I usually never bothered with seat belts, but I think I will from now on. They seem like a hell of a good idea.

CHAPTER 3

Me and the guys, we practice at this old warehouse on the corner of Morgan and Fulton Market, just southwest of the Loop. It's been converted to a rehearsal hall for rock groups and blues groups, and they got all kinds of rooms and stages, so when the place is full, it really rocks. You get to meet all kinds of other musicians that way, and you pick up some of their tricks, hear their new songs, and have an inside touch on what's happening locally. If an adult ever saw what the place looks like on the inside, they'd have it condemned. Or nuked. But adults aren't invited, so it's all right. If they had things their way, there wouldn't be any rock and roll. There probably wouldn't even be such a thing as an electric guitar. I wonder how come they haven't made guitars illegal? It'll happen. Just give 'em some more time.

That's where Lisa took me when we got off Rush Street. She parked in front of the loading dock and we just sat there for a while.

"You want to come in and watch us practice?" I asked her. But she said no, she'd just be in the way. She had a test to study for, anyway. So I started to reach for my guitar in the back seat, when she stopped me and kissed me. She was so small that when I put my arms around her I nearly lifted her out of the driver's seat. We sat and kissed for about ten minutes. She liked to put her hands through my hair, real gentle-like, and it felt pretty good. She had a thing for hair. No wonder her father was bald. Then, just when everything was happening between us, somebody pulls up next to our car and starts honking the horn. It was Rick and Kevin. I could've killed them. For about two cents I would've run them over.

"Gotta go," I said.

"I know." She sat back in her seat and watched through the window as Rick and Kevin unloaded the amplifiers. "Are you going to be all right?"

That was a funny thing to say, I thought.

"Who? Me? Sure. I'll be fine."

"I don't know, Lenny," she said, looking at the steering wheel. "Sometimes I think—"

"What? What do you think?" She was scaring me again.

"Sometimes I think you *aren't* going to be fine."

"What do you mean? You mean you get like premonitions or something?"

"No. Not that, so much."

"Well, what is it? Is it just a feeling?"

She said yeah, it was just a feeling. I knew the feeling. I get it most of the time, too. But Jesus. I didn't think other people got them about me. It must show. Like when your zipper's down.

We kissed real fast again, and then I got out and helped the guys with the equipment. Lisa drove off while I watched her, and then Rick tapped me on the shoulder. "You like 'em small, huh?" he said.

"So what?"

"Nothin'. You can have midgets together."

Rick can be a real asshole when he feels like it. Then he started saying not to feel bad about it, that if our kids were dwarves or something, we could sneak them onto airplanes and into movies for free, just by putting them under our coats. I picked up my guitar and went inside to see which stage we were going to get. It was going to be midget jokes all night. Rick, he does things in themes. Tonight he was going to Munchkin me to death.

I taught two of the new tunes to the guys in the bathroom on the first floor. The reason for teaching them the song in the bathroom is so you don't look like an idiot when you're on stage trying to learn chords and stuff. Some pretty famous guys hang out at that place, which is one of the reasons we like to practice there, and you don't want to look like you don't know what you're doing in

171

front of them. Pete, the bass player, lit a joint and started passing it around, but I didn't take any. I still felt a little woozy, is how come.

"Lenny?" Pete said, handing me the joint. He had a whole bunch of smoke in his lungs and he was trying not to let it out.

"No thanks," I told him.

"Come on," Rick said, taking the joint from Pete, "it'll loosen you up."

"Nothin' will loosen Lenny up," Kevin said. "No kiddin', even Quaaludes make him hyper."

"You guys gonna learn these songs, or what?" I said. That's one of the problems with musicians. They're all the time stoned.

"Relax, for Christ's sake. Jesus. Someone should slip some heroin in your oatmeal, Lenny. Have a hit. You're too nervous." Rick was holding the joint for me.

"I sing off-key when I'm high," I said.

"You sing off-key anyway," he said. "You might as well have an excuse for it."

I guess I *was* a little uptight. I gave in and took a few hits, nothing major. Just a few hits. Somebody was knocking on the bathroom door to get in, and Rick asked them what they wanted. Some guy said he had to go, and Rick told him to go ahead and go, that he didn't need our permission.

Pete said something was eating me, what was it? Rick started with the midget jokes again.

"He's upset 'cause the next generation of Blakes will all be under four feet tall. And what with the price of stepladders these days—"

"You wanna know what it is, you bastard? You wanna know why I'm upset? Last night I got beat up by two cops who think I'm a junkie. And my doorman, James, he knows a lot of stuff. He told me they'll be back for me, because to get them to quit beating me up, I gave them a made-up name when they wanted to know who my supplier was. They hang around outside my building and just wait for me at night." There, I thought; I'd said it. I tried to say it matter-of-fact-like, but my voice gave me away. You could hear by the way I said it that I was scared.

"You mean that shiner is for real?" Rick asked.

I told him yeah, it was for real.

He said he thought Lisa had just put makeup on me like we
172

planned for the performance. Then he came over to touch it, to see if it was makeup or not.

"Ow! Get your finger outta my eye, you sonofabitch!"

"Huh. It *is* real" was all he said.

"I *told* you it was real. The cops were real, too. The bruise on my ribs is real, too."

"How come you didn't tell them you're not a pusher?" Rick said.

"I *did*, but they didn't believe me. I tried to tell them. They were convinced, though. Someone's setting me up, that's what James thinks."

"Well, don't worry about it," Rick said, tipping the ashes from the joint. "I'll drive you home tonight."

"You gotta drive right into the garage so they don't stop me again."

"I will. Now relax, will you please? I don't want you throwing up on the stage tonight. Rumor has it that Mighty Joe Young is here tonight."

Mighty Joe Young is this real good blues guy. He's famous, if you know anything about blues.

Somebody was pounding on the door again and shouting at us. "What the hell are you guys doing in there?"

"Cost you five bucks to find out," Rick said. Then he turned to me and whispered, "Isn't there a zoning ordinance or something against dating Munchkins within the city limits?"

We open our act with an a cappella song called "Do It." It's real street corner and funky, until it breaks into the instrumental part, and then it rocks out. There were already a few of the local new wave dipshits that just hang out sitting at a table in the hall we were using. These guys all wear glasses and little skinny ties and sport coats. By the time we were halfway through the number, though, the place started filling up. People were coming down from the stages upstairs to listen to us, and I was real surprised to see about three or four Puerto Rican girls walk in. They were dressed in weird outfits, and their hair was done up real freaky. They started danc- ing, and they were pretty good. They must've been professional, because they were doing worked-out numbers. I saw a couple of black guys walk in then, and I knew they were some blues group, but I didn't know which one. Someone killed the audience lights then and put a spotlight on us. It always makes me nervous when that happens, because I'm real shy. But I usually act enough like a pro to fake it. The truth is, though, I'm scared to death on a stage. I'd rather be in an electric chair, almost. At least then you don't have to face the crowd when it's all over.

We went from one number to the next, and the place kept filling up. Even Pete, who most of the time looks like the Statue of Liberty on a stage, was starting to warm up. He was jumping around more than usual. All the girls, they go for Pete because he's handsome. He was driving the little Puerto Rican girls nuts. We slid into "The Love in Your Eyes," which I wrote for a girl once, but never let her hear it. It moves. It's got nice harmony parts, and Rick and I shared the same microphone for the "oohs" like Lennon and McCartney used to do. Someone passed beers and joints up to the stage, and I was glad, because I was getting thirsty. I looked out into the audience, and about forty people were out there by then, shouting requests. Somebody wanted to hear "Louie Louie." Rick pretended like he couldn't hear the request, so the whole room shouted, *"Louie Louie!"*

"No, I'm sorry," he said into the microphone. "I'm Rick and this is Lenny. Louie's in the john at the moment." And then we played "Inside Out," another one of mine. It's a slammer. It's about how crummy love gets if you give it half a chance. I got to psych myself up before I sing it. It's an angry song. So I started thinking about Mr. Mankewicz doing it to Lisa, and then I was pissed off enough to do it well.

I didn't know about that crowd. I like audience participation and everything, but these fuckers were crazy. People were dancing on top of tables, and I saw a girl do a dance with a beer bottle that's kind of hard to describe. Two little blondes that couldn't've been over fifteen came right to the front of the stage and started making obscene gestures toward Rick's and my crotches. Four years ago they were probably home at that time of day watching kiddie shows. Where do they learn that kind of stuff? Maybe *Sesame Street* has a new curriculum. Who knows?

I was working the crowd good then. You get like a kind of control after a while. We played "Rock Me, Roll Me, Hold Me" and "Lisa" for the first time together, and there were some rough spots, but other than that, it sounded like we'd been doing those two

174

songs forever. Then we went into one of Rick's songs, "Habits," which is one of my personal favorites. By then everybody in the building was in our rehearsal hall, and they were clapping and dancing and screaming and drinking. We did about forty extra bars of the chorus because they were digging it. Kevin was slapping the shit out of his drums, and Pete and me shared a microphone for the harmonies, and Rick was out front working over the crowd. In the middle of a verse, I grabbed Rick's ass real hard and he hit a falsetto note by accident. The crowd liked that. I don't like to do that kind of stuff too much, though, 'cause then you get a reputation for being a fag band.

We ended with a soul number that we all made up, called "Een My Country," which is all about a Saudi Arabian guy who comes to America to learn how to disco, but then he misses his goats and gets pissed off when they won't let him wash his feet in the men's john of the Pump Room. I do the whole thing with an accent, until the break, and then we all imitate the Temptations' choreography.

Then the lights went up and we ran the hell out of there back into the men's room. Pete locked the door behind us, when we noticed that there was another guy in there taking a piss. He was a big black guy with a leather vest.

"Oh. Sorry," I told him. "We didn't know you were in here."

"That's okay, my man. Place is big enough fo' mo' than one. Hey," he said, real interested and all, "any of you in that band?"

We told him we were all in the band. He said we were terrific.

"You guys is the *cat's ass!*"

"We don't exactly look at it that way," Rick said.

"No, no. I mean y'all's really *good.* Burnin' 'em up. Just burnin' 'em up out there. What'cha doin' in here when ya had all that front-line *pussy* back there?"

Rick whispered to me, *"All this guy can talk about is cats."*

"Too young," I said. "They all look like they're ten or something. You know. This is just practice. We just want to get the hell out of here now. We got a gig tomorrow."

"Where you be playin' tomorrow?" he asked, and then flushed the toilet and took a sip from a beer bottle he had resting on the sink.

"At Scene Two," Rick said. "We're opening for Lefty."

175

"Yeah?" He was surprised or something. "Yeah? I know Lefty. Shit, you boys is gonna go far. Far. I know Lefty fo' years. I use' to play bass fo' Magic Slim and Eddie Shaw." He started rolling a joint in one hand. I never saw nobody do it with just one hand before. "Say, you boys wanna come on down to a club tonight? I getcha in fo' free. Striptease club. *You* know."

I didn't feel like doing it, personally. But Rick seemed to like the idea. "I've never been to a strip club," Rick said.

"No I.D. cards," I told him.

"Shit. Don't need no eye-dee if y'all with me. I getcha in. Just like *that*." He snapped his fingers with his free hand and then licked the rolling paper and closed it. All with one hand he did it.

That's how I got myself into that one. I didn't put up enough of a fight. The problem was, it didn't sound like a half-bad idea. It was too early to go home, and there was nothing else to do but wait to see if the bomb would drop that night, and to watch the other bands rehearse. Pete checked out early because of a chemistry quiz the next day, but Kevin stayed with me and Rick.

The black guy, it turned out, was named Bruce, and he was there with Jimmy Smith and his band. We watched them play two sets, and every time I turned around, somebody else was handing me another joint or another beer. Rick was talking to a redhead he met up by the stage, and Kevin sat at a table with me and pounded on it like he thought it was a drum kit.

"I think you better stop smoking this stuff," I told him. He looked like he was ready to fall asleep.

"Whad'ya mean? Who are *you*, Pat Boone?"

"I don't mean permanently or anything," I said. He thought I meant for good. "Just for now. Just stop for now, 'cause yer lights are almost out."

"Huh? What lights? What are you talking about?"

Christ, was he wasted.

"Never mind," I said.

A couple of minutes went by, and Jimmy Smith and his band were playing "Hey, Bartender." They were doing it pretty good, really jumping. That's when Kevin tapped me on the shoulder and shouted above the music into my ear, "Never mind about *what*?"

"About your lights being almost out," I said again.

"What lights?" he asked. He was being impossible.

176

"Just shut up, okay? Just dig your stupor."

"Whad'ya mean I'm stupid?" he said, like an idiot. There was no dealing with him anymore. About ten minutes later he fell asleep on the table, even though the band was playing louder than they had all night.

At around nine o'clock, Rick said good-bye to the redhead, and Jimmy Smith and his boys started to pack up their stuff.

"How'd ya do?" I asked him. I meant about the girl.

"Got a phone number. Jesus, is she dumb. We talked about soap operas for the last two hours."

"That's impossible," I told him.

"That's what we did. We did the impossible. What the hell happened to Mr. Energy?" he asked, pointing to Kevin with a cigarette in his hand.

"Died. About an hour ago," I said. Then I realized it wasn't so funny, on account of his mother committing suicide about two weeks before.

"Jesus. He can't die. If he died, we'd have to get another drummer. We'd be short a drummer. And speaking of short—"

"I don't want to hear any more midget jokes right now, goddamn it." He was getting on my nerves with those bastard midget jokes.

"Well, it's okay, because I'm a *little short* on those at the moment."

He was being an asshole again. At first it was kind of funny, but it wasn't anymore. Besides, Lisa isn't *that* short. I mean, she's no giant or anything, but she's not a dwarf, either. I wished he'd cut it out.

Bruce came by with another member of the band, the guitarist, and told us to follow him in our car. "It ain't too far from here. It's down on Seventy-ninth Street."

"Just a *short* ride, Lenny," Rick said.

"We'll be there," I told him. He said it was solid and then slipped me another joint, which I put in my pocket, because if I would've smoked it right away I would've been in the Twilight Zone or someplace.

We had to carry Kevin to Rick's car. We laid him down in the back seat, and I put a sweater under his head for a pillow. On the way to the club I started getting paranoid about not having started any of the homework I was supposed to do to graduate. Where I

177

should've been was home. Lisa might need me, I thought. You never know. I told Rick I didn't think I wanted to go anymore, but he said we wouldn't stay long, he just wanted to see one stripper and then we would leave.

"What are we gonna do with Kevin?" I looked back at him. He was snoring.

"We'll leave him in the car."

"We can't just leave him in the car! That's a bad neighborhood."

"Don't worry," Rick said, "we'll lock the doors. People don't steal passed-out drummers. They only steal wide-awake drummers."

Bruce's idea of a "short ride" took nearly an hour. When we got there, I sort of had second thoughts about the whole thing again. For one thing, the neighborhood wasn't just *bad*, it was a *disaster area*. There were newspapers and junk all over the sidewalks, and little kids were playing on fire escapes when they should've been in bed. What's the matter with their parents, that they let little kids hang over fire escapes when they should be in bed? What, are they crazy? If I were a judge, I'd give a parent the gas chamber for that. No I wouldn't; scratch that. I'd just take out a gun and blow their heads off, or push them off a fire escape so they could see why it might be dangerous. Idiots. The whole goddamn world is filled with idiots. They don't *deserve* to have kids.

Rick and me got out of the car and locked the doors and started walking down the street, behind Bruce and the other guy.

"Man," Bruce was saying, "I can't wait to see that Katrina. Watchin' her take off her clothes is like *art*, babe. She like the Picasso of strippin'. She makes me forget all about the blues."

Just then, a little kid on a wood porch about one floor above us shouted, "Go back home, you faggot white boys."

The kid must've been seven, no older. I looked up at him and shouted back, "You get to bed! Do you know what time it is? Where're your parents?"

And the little black kid, you know what he did? He leaned over the rail of the porch—this old rotted-out rail—and said, "Fuck you."

Bruce and his buddy almost collapsed when they heard him say that. They were laughing so hard they almost choked. But I didn't

178

think it was funny. I thought it was sick—little kids talking like that and hanging over porches at ten-thirty at night.

"Did you hear what that little kid said to me?" I asked Rick.

"The whole neighborhood heard it, Lenny," he said, slapping me on the back.

Some night. Some fun.

This strip place Bruce took us to didn't even have a sign out front, just a big wooden door that was locked until they pushed a buzzer to let you in. A guy at the door stopped me and Rick, but Bruce said something to him in his ear and then he let us in. The place was real smoky and it smelled like booze all over. A bunch of guys were sitting at the bar, black guys, and I searched the place to find one white face, just *one* white one, but I didn't see any. That must be how black people feel when they go to Lake Forest. It's a pretty scary feeling. Rick and me got looked at a lot, on account of we stuck out like sore honkies (I felt like I was glowing in the dark), but after a while people sort of accepted us. I was still pissed off about the kid saying "Fuck you" to me, but then Bruce bought us both beers and introduced us to some of the guys he knew.

"Like ya to meet some friends of mine, openin' tomorrow at Scene Two for ol' Lefty."

That impressed the hell out of them. They all bought us drinks even though we already had some. So then we bought *them* drinks and we had a problem finding room for all the glasses and couldn't decide whose was whose. They were pretty nice guys, when you got to know them. They had a bunch of stories about famous blues guys like Junior Walker and Koko Taylor and Son Seals. Everybody said how Son was the meanest-looking, but really he wasn't so mean at all; he just looked that way. Then the entertainment started.

Some comedian who thought he was Richard Pryor came out on the stage and told a lot of jokes about cocaine and sex. He swore a lot, used a lot of dirty words, but he wasn't funny. Some guys, they think they're funny because they talk filthy. That's not how Pryor does it. Pryor is funny *first*, and he's dirty second. I think you got to be *born* funny to be a comedian. Like Woody Allen. The minute you're born, you have to crack everybody up. If you don't do it then, you never will. Woody Allen, when he was born, he was

179

probably complaining and asking the doctor if he'd washed his hands first, or asking if it was necessary to get circumcised. The comedian on the stage just then, he probably just said, "Fuck you," when he was delivered. And it probably wasn't funny then, either.

Then the women came on. Most of them were black, but not all of them. Some looked like hookers, and others looked like school-teachers. I sort of felt sorry for the ones who looked like school-teachers. They looked too sweet to be taking off their clothes in front of a bunch of screaming men.

Every so often Rick would lean over and ask Bruce if the stripper on the stage was Katrina, the one he told us about.

"Naw. Not yet. You'll know her when you see her," he said, and then he had another drink. Boy, could that guy drink. We weren't there more than an hour and he'd already put down eight at least that I counted. I was only on my third beer, and the room was already spinning.

Once in a while, a group of guys would get up and go through this door near the back of the stage, and then they'd come out about a half-hour later. I figured it was the bathroom and that there must've been one hell of a line for it to take so long. Except when I asked Bruce where the john was, he pointed to a little room clear on the other side of the bar. It was weird.

Rick was going bananas next to me. He was getting drunk and screaming, just like everybody else, especially when this one Latin girl came on and took off her blouse. I'm not kidding you, she had the most gigantic tits I'd ever seen. It was like not *normal* to have them that big. If she turned around real fast in a crowded room she could easily kill three or four dozen people, that's how big they were. Rick stared like he'd just seen heaven for the first time. Me, I just laughed. I couldn't stop laughing. It was 'cause I was drunk, but it was also because it was kind of funny to see Rick and all those guys hypnotized, just because a woman had tits the size of watermelons. I wondered what the hell she did with them when she tried to get some sleep—tie them down? If one rolled off the bed it would pull her over and she'd go through the floor—really. She was a public nuisance. What she needed, she needed an oper-ation. Maybe that's why she was working as a stripper. Maybe she was saving up for an operation.

I'm not going to tell everything they did up on that stage, be-
180

cause some of it was pretty sickening. They had props with them and did all kinds of, well, *performances*. It was starting to make me feel funny. Funny-slimy, not funny yuk-yuk. Bruce, he kept slamming me on the back every time one of the girls did something obscene, and he screamed, "WHOOOOOOO!" real loud whenever they did something he really liked. I started wanting to go home. I just wanted to go to bed and fall asleep and wake up sane. Or just wake up. I don't expect miracles anymore.

Bruce's buddy came back from that little door behind the stage and said that some of the girls wanted to meet me and Rick. I thought he was kidding at first, so I laughed and had some more beer. But then he said no, he wasn't kidding, and that we should go back there. They thought white boys were cute.

Rick was off his stool in about a half-second, but I grabbed him by the arm. "Where the hell do you think you're going?"

"Let go! C'mon! They want to meet us," he said.

"Rick, listen," I said. "We gotta go home. We got Kevin in the car and I'm tired, and I know what's going to happen back there."

"Me too!" he said. "*I* know what's gonna happen *too*. What the hell are you waiting for?"

"Rick—" But he was gone. He was down toward the door in a flash.

Bruce, he took my drink out of my hand and sort of pushed me off the stool. "Yo' turn, junior. They gonna think you insultin' 'em."

"I'm not insulting anybody," I said.

"Well, good then. Just go on back and meet the girls."

"I would. I really would, but I've got this appointment tonight and I can't be late."

"Appointment?" Bruce said. He was like pulling me by the arm toward the door.

"Yeah, it's weird, isn't it? I got this dentist. He works nights because his eyes are bad and he can't stand the sun. What it is, it's glaucoma or something. Weird guy. Only night appointments."

"Yeah?" Bruce said, folding his arms in front of his stomach and looking down at me. "Dentist, huh? What's his name?"

"Fredericks," I said. "Dr. Fredericks." I even opened my mouth to show him some fillings that needed work.

181

Bruce, he had me by the door then, and he put his big arm around me. "Look. They ain't gonna *bite* you."

"I know, but—"

"Unless you ask them nicely."

And before I knew it, he was pushing me back into this real dark place behind the stage where there were lots more doors and girls walking around in their underpants. I couldn't see Rick anywhere.

"*White bread!*" yelled this girl with like a bikini that sparkled. It was a stage outfit.

"Mine!" called this one black girl. She was pretty, the one with tight white pants who I'd seen on the stage twice that night.

"Look, I got this appointment," I said, but they wouldn't let me talk.

"Where's the white boys?" I heard another one say. She was the one with the monster tits.

"Juana's got one," said the black girl in the white pants, "and I got the other. Ain't he cute?"

Then the girl with the big tits said I should have some say in the matter, and the black girl started arguing with her. She said she saw me first. Then they asked me who I wanted, and I didn't know what the hell to say. If I said what I felt, that I didn't want anybody, they might've thought I was a fag, or crazy. Or they might've gotten insulted, like Bruce said. Then, before I had a chance to say *anything*, they were flipping a coin for me. From behind a closed door I recognized Rick's stupid laugh. He was laughing real hard.

"You're ticklish!" the girl's voice said, behind the door. "Ain't you! You're ticklish!" Then I didn't hear either one of them again.

My luck. The girl with the Goodyear chest won me. The black girl, she went storming off somewhere, calling the other girl a lot of names and saying she was going to get her later.

The one who won me took me in this little room and started talking baby talk to me. She told me to sit down in this chair by a mirror, and then she started doing a strip act just for me. The whole time she kept talking to me like I was about three years old, and she had an accent, a Spanish accent.

"Que Bonita, leetle white boy," she said. "Teresita look pretty tonight? Verdad?"

"Yeah. Real nice. Muncho verdad," I told her. "Listen, though.

Why don't you just leave your clothes on. I'm not staying very long."

"White boy shy," she said, and giggled, and then she started playing around with her hands under my sweat shirt.

"White boy's name is Lenny," I said. "Listen, señorita. You should really just leave your clothes on and—"

Christ. They were the biggest things I've ever seen. I didn't know what the hell to do with them, and they were all over me. They must've weighed twenty pounds, each.

"You'll catch a cold," I told her.

"Then you warm me up, white boy."

"Lenny," I said.

Then I started getting paranoid about VD. What if she had VD? In health class they showed us movies of guys and ladies with sores all over their faces and arms and legs. There wasn't much to do about it, though. By then, if I was going to get it, I was going to get it. What I hadn't counted on was her being an acrobat. She should get a job in the circus. I've never seen things from so many different angles. And the whole time, while I was spinning around and looking first at the ceiling and then at the walls and next, the floor, and in between ducking tits so I wouldn't get knocked out, I kept seeing me two weeks from then. I'd have big crusty syphilis sores all over my face and hands. I'd go into a store to buy something, and all the sales people would run for cover. In about three weeks all my hair would fall out, and soon I'd need a cane to even walk. What would I do *then?* Sit at home and read the *Herpes Review?* And all because Rick never saw a stripper before.

CHAPTER 14

The digital clock on Rick's dashboard said it was two-thirty. I watched the red numbers change every minute as Rick drove north on the Dan Ryan Expressway. I looked behind me and saw Kevin, still sound asleep on the back seat. My eyes kind of burned from smoke, but I wanted a cigarette anyway. I pushed in the lighter on the dashboard and turned on the radio. It was the news.

"A twenty-three-year-old man is being held in custody without bond tonight. He's been charged with deviate sexual assault and murder after the body of a three-year-old child, who was left in his care by the girl's mother, was found in a home on Winthrop Avenue in Chicago. Police have not yet disclosed the cause of death pending an autopsy."

The lighter popped out and I let it sit there for a while before reaching for it. When I did finally pull it out, it wasn't hot enough to light the cigarette, so I put it back in. Rick handed me a butane lighter. I took it, had to turn it around in my hand to find the button, and then lit my cigarette. It was a little cool for a May night, so I turned on the heater and changed the radio station. "Imagine"—by John Lennon—was playing. I listened to it and started daydreaming about a dozen things at the same time. Lennon's voice and the piano faded out while we drove under viaducts and overpasses. I saw this one sign, this green kind of sign flashing something in the dark, but I couldn't read it. It flashed and flashed until we passed it, and then I watched the expressway lights up ahead; they stretched for miles and curved and straightened out again. I thought, as we drove, that I could open my car door and fall onto the street if I wanted to. I thought about how I'd bounce and wondered which part of me would hit the road first, and how long it would take to come to a stop. I sat and pictured me bouncing down the street and rolling like a ball. I thought about how Rick's car's taillights would disappear in the distance while I just lay on the road.

I kept playing and replaying that scene in my head all the way to my condo building, the taillights zooming away and getting smaller and smaller, Rick driving, Kevin in the back seat sleeping. Kevin would wake up and say, "Where's Lenny?" Rick would say, "Fell out of the car about three miles back. Bounced and rolled just like a ball. Watched the taillights till they disappeared."

Rick drove right into the garage like I told him to, but as we were driving in, I saw the two guys waiting by the front door.

"That was them," I said, "the two guys by the revolving door. *Those are the guys!*"

Rick said, "Are you sure?"

"I'm sure." I was shivering all of a sudden. "Turn the car around and get the hell out of here," I told him.

I jumped out of the car and grabbed my keys from my back pocket. I let myself in at the service entrance and rang for the freight elevator. When you ring for the freight elevator, nobody can see you, 'cause there aren't any windows there. It's just a walled-off little corner on the first floor. The elevator was already there and the doors opened. I pushed the "18" button about a thousand times, and then the doors slammed shut and I was on my way.

I had my apartment key ready so I could run right in when I got there. I counted the floor numbers as they lit up, and I imagined I was on the elevator an hour. It seemed like it took an hour to get to the eighteenth floor.

I had a little trouble fitting the key in the lock, 'cause my hands were shaking all over. I was still shivering. When I got inside the apartment I double-locked the door. I turned the hall light on and looked around the place.

There were the shoes, the jacket of that other woman. I picked them up, without thinking, even. I was like a computer. I was all

185

programmed by someone else. I found an outer jacket slung over the sofa, and I picked that up, too. I walked to my mother's room, but the door was closed. I tried to open it, but it was locked. I stood just looking at it for a few seconds, and then, like I was programmed again, I kicked it with all my might, and half the molding around the doorway came off when it sprang open. I turned on the light.

First my mother and then this other lady, this young *girl* with short black hair, sat up like little markers on a pinball machine. I threw the clothes on the bed.

"Get her out of here," I said.

"Lenny!" My mother said; her voice was cracking from being scared. Her face was like white, like she'd just plugged herself into a wall outlet.

"Get her out of here now, or I'm gonna kill her."

They both just stared at me for a minute, and then the girl, she started grabbing at her clothes and throwing them on like there was a fire in the house.

I didn't even have to think; I just knew what to do. I stood right in the doorway while she got dressed. She was scared to death. I didn't blame her. My mother started talking to me from her bed. She wouldn't come out from under the covers. It was quite obvious she didn't have no clothes on.

"You have no right to barge in here and—"

"Oh God, Mother. Be quiet. This is bad enough the way it— Just be quiet." I was staring at the girl as she pulled the coat over herself and picked up her shoes in the other hand.

"Sondra," my mother was saying, with this very shaky voice, "you don't have to go. You don't have to—"

"*Shut up!*" I said.

The girl, she was starting to put on her shoes, but I grabbed her by the arm and threw her out the door of the bedroom.

"Put them on outside," I said to her. "And if I ever find you here again, you won't have to worry about getting dressed first."

Then I followed her to the front door, unlocked it, and let her out. She looked back as she pressed the elevator button, still holding her shoes, and then decided instead to use the stairs. It was the smartest thing she'd done all night.

I closed the door, locked it, and heard my mother crying from the bedroom. I didn't go back, though. There was no use to it. She didn't have nothing to say to me, and there was nothing I could've said to her. I didn't blame her so much. It wasn't her fault she's human, like James said. It was just a lousy decision on her part. Like me, making the lousy decision to go to the strip club, or to jump in the fountain at school. It wasn't her fault. It just had to stop, was all. Somebody had to do something. It was just my crummy luck that I had to be the somebody.

I turned off the light in the hall, closed my bedroom door behind me, and fell asleep, with Rick's taillights fading away in my head.

CHAPTER 15

When am I going to learn? When am I ever going to learn? I keep thinking that maybe if I'm good and stay out of trouble, things will get back to normal. But they never do; they just get worse, is all. And I'll tell you a secret, too. I don't think there ever *was* a normal. What I think, I think they keep you stupid so long when you're a kid, you just *think* things are normal. Figure it out. When do you learn about VD and nuclear radiation? At about the same time you find out there's no Santa Claus. I was going to say, *at about the same time you find out there isn't any God,* but most people never find that out. My guess is, if people ever got hip to the fact that there isn't a God, they'd commit suicide, because they'd freak if they knew they'd been going it alone all this time.

My life was just rolling along. I looked outside from a taped corner of my bedroom window. I just pulled some aluminum foil away and took a peek. If you were stupid, you'd think it was a beautiful end-of-May day. I mean, there were birds flying around and flowers growing in the pots on the windowsills of the apartment building across the street. It was real nice, if you were stupid about it. But out there two guys were looking for me, to cripple me, and Lisa's father, Mr. Mankewicz, was on his way to work after sleeping—or trying to sleep—with his own daughter. Out there, somewhere, my own mother was sitting in some restaurant having coffee with a lesbian I caught her in bed with the night before. Out there my old man was probably copping a feel from his receptionist and

188

not even caring if I fell off a bridge into the Badlands. And asleep in some ratty apartment with no smoke detectors was a stripper named Teresita, who knew she did it last night with a skinny white boy. She won't even remember his name, just his color.

Life is a bowl of cherries.

I made it to Dr. Kollbisk's office with no problems. I had my guitar with me, 'cause I was going to go straight downtown to Scene II right after my appointment with him. I was dressed in my stage clothes: a red T-shirt and jeans, bowling shoes, and an Army camouflage shirt. Dr. Kollbisk wasn't in his office when I got there, so I made myself at home and took a chair.

On his desk were a whole bunch of forms and psychiatric case histories about screwed-up kids. There was one about a kid who set fires all the time, who Dr. Kollbisk was recommending should go to a state hospital for anti-fire therapy or something. I forget what he called it, but it was like fire extinguisher school. I was pretty much alone there in the office, so I figured as long as I was reading his personal junk, I should see if he had my file hanging around. After some digging, I found it. I read it, didn't understand it, and then read it again. At first I thought he must've mixed me up with some other kid. But he didn't. It was about me, all right. This is what it said:

Case 1187582   Lenny Blake

Subject referred after suspicion of drug use and vandalism. Exhibits extreme tendencies toward paranoid psychosis, resulting in fantasies and lack of ability to discriminate between reality and hallucination. Potentially violent, antisocial, and frequently under the influence of narcotics and alcohol. Criminal behavior suspected, particularly in the area of soliciting for and distribution of controlled substances, especially marijuana, among the student population.

He thought I was a paranoid criminal or something. And after all that talk about just wanting to listen to me, just wanting to help me graduate. I couldn't believe it, that he would say those things about me. I don't mind taking a little criticism from time to time, you know, like maybe some of my guitar playing is sloppy, or I sing off-key a bit, or maybe I'm a little too careful once in a while about rapists or muggers. But, Jesus! Psychotic? How could he *say* that about me? He didn't even *know* me, and he was going around telling people I was insane.

I folded up the report and stuck it in my back pocket, next to my Mace, and then I sat back down. I'm a terrible baby, like that time I slobbered over James in the alley, and the day before when I cried in front of Lisa. I was crying again, a little. I mean, not much. Not much. But a little. It sort of hurt my feelings to think that someone would write that about me when he didn't even know me so good. The lousy bastard.

Dr. Kollbisk walked into the office after about five minutes, and when he saw me he pretended to be happy I was there.

"Lenny!" he said, and then he came over to shake my hand. It was Lenny-this and Lenny-that for a while. Very cozy. Big pals, we were. The hypocrite. He *Lennyed* me to death with talk about how my book was coming, and what my home life was like. I didn't say anything the entire time. I just sat there staring at him like as if I was saying, "You rotten bastard. I don't believe a fucking word you're saying." I did it cold as hell. It started to throw him after a while. After about a thousand dead ends in the conversation, he loosened his ugly tie (paisley, the ugliest tie I've ever seen in my life) (psychiatric guys got no taste) and gave me his *can't-we-be-honest* expression. He should sell coffee makers on TV with that expression.

"Lenny, is there something troubling you today?" he asked, like he really felt for me. The more he did that kind of stuff, the more I hated him.

"Me? No. Why? Is something bothering *you* today?" I was giving it right back to him.

He brought his fist up to his chin and sat looking stumped.

"You have a lot of difficulties right now, don't you Lenny?" he said, like he wanted me to feel better. I would've been safer in quicksand, believe me.

190

"I've got my fair share. How about you? You have difficulties, too?"

"We all do. But I think *you're* the one who needs to talk about your own."

Then he got up and unbuttoned his sport coat, walked across the room, and hiked his stupid corduroys up an inch or two. He was the kind of guy whose pants were always falling down 'cause he's got no ass.

"I talked to Mr. Atkins about you yesterday. I want to tell you, Lenny, that the school has a serious concern about drug use among its student population right now. It's epidemic."

He made it sound like the name of a new quiz show for drug addicts or people with diseases—*It's Epidemic.*

"He let me in on something about you. About an activity you haven't told me anything about.

He was waiting for me to ask him what it was, the activity. But I'd read the report. I knew what he thought. I let him hang himself. I gave him plenty of rope.

"To be frank with you, you've been under surveillance by police youth officers who suspect and have reported that you are dealing drugs to other youngsters like yourself."

Youngsters. Yeah, when I get home from a hard day of pushing, me and the other *youngsters* skip rope and play cowboys and Indians. What a jerk; he probably thought he could relate to teenagers by calling 'em *youngsters.* What perspective. What insight. Dr. Kollbisk was another one of those guys living in 1940.

"Now, are you with me so far?" he said, like it was difficult to follow his train of thought or something. I just stared. "The point is, this has to stop. For your own good, for the good of the other students, it has to stop. Drug use is like a cancer that has to be cut out as soon as it emerges, or else it's too late to cure. The thrust of what Mr. Atkins had to tell me concerns your suppliers, your sources of these drugs—"

Then I knew it. I was positive. Those two cops, they were tipped off by Atkins. As a matter of fact, the one with the mustache, I realized, like out of the blue, was one of the cops who was called in that night when I got pulled out of the fountain. He just looked different without his uniform. This whole thing with Kollbisk was just to get me to spill my guts, whether I had anything to spill or not. It was the setup of the year.

"He feels," Kollbisk went on in his boring tone of voice, "that there would be no need to prosecute you if you simply do what is right for the good of the school and, more importantly, Lenny, if you do what is right for your own good. That is, tell us the name of your supplier, or suppliers, and make a clean start of things. If you do that, I can assure you of a June graduation. I can *assure* you."

See how he operated? Every time I walked into his office, a new condition for graduation popped up. At that rate, he'd have me signing away my own grandmother and the keys to my father's car by the time graduation ever came.

I was staring, looking cool, acting calm. The calmer I got, the more nervous he got, 'cause he didn't know if I was biting the bait or not. James told me. James told me to be careful about the *subtle* things, and now I could see what he was talking about. Everybody's got an angle. Atkins wanted my ass, so he leaned on Dr. Kollbisk. Dr. Kollbisk wanted to keep his job and shine like a company man, so he was leaning on me. Who the hell was *I* supposed to lean on? Nobody. Students are the bottom of the ladder. We're the peons.

"Who do I talk to?" I asked. "If I talk, who do I tell? You, or Mr. Atkins?"

He was a little surprised. Up until then, I looked about as cooperative as a brick wall.

"Why, you can have it any way you want it." He stopped, picked up something from his desk, and threw it down again. At first I thought maybe he noticed that my report was missing, but he didn't. "I do think it would be wise to have Mr. Atkins present, if you have something to say."

"Okay. Get him here," I said.

He turned his head real fast in my direction. "Now? Are you ready now?" He was picking up the phone before I even answered him. Jesus, was he ever ready to play ball for the boss.

"Sure. I'll talk. Get him here, now."

I had the upper hand in the whole thing. Once you figure out the angle, you get control of the situation. Now I saw what James was talking about.

Mr. Atkins was on the other end of the phone, then. I knew 'cause Dr. Kollbisk said, "I have Lenny Blake here in my office, and he'd like to talk to you about what we were discussing yesterday. Yes. All right. Fine." And then he hung up.

"He'll be right in," he told me. He sat down at his desk and started clearing all the papers away, making the place look good for when Atkins showed up. I just sat and pretended to look at things on the wall—posters, bulletins, that kind of stuff.

"I want you to know that you're doing the right thing, Lenny. Some things seem difficult while we're doing them, but if you know what you're doing is right, then it becomes easier."

"Oh, this will be easy," I told him.

"Well, I appreciate the maturity of your decision." He was putting pens in neat little rows on his desktop. I just sat slouched in the chair with one leg crossed over the other. I was programmed again, like I had been the night before when I found that girl in my mom's bed. I didn't even have to think about what I was going to do. It's funny, but a lot of what Kollbisk said was true. If you know you're doing the right thing, it's easy. You get confidence. I knew I was doing the right thing.

When Mr. Atkins walked in in his sloppy three-piece *plaid* suit, Kollbisk almost kissed his ass in front of me. He was all over him, trying to make him comfortable. Then he sat down and Atkins looked at *him*, not me, like as if I wasn't there. Atkins, he's got thin gray hair and that sort of dead skin color, like dead guys have.

"Mr. Atkins, I've called you in because Lenny Blake, who's been seeing me lately for counseling, has something he'd like to tell both of us. He requested that you be present."

Mr. Atkins nodded and then said, "All right." He took out an envelope from his suit pocket and a pen from his shirt pocket, and then they both turned toward me.

"Lenny," said Dr. Kollbisk, "it's all yours."

I just sat and looked at both of them. They got kind of uneasy when I didn't say anything, at first. Mr. Atkins crossed his other leg. Dr. Kollbisk pushed and shoved some papers around on his desk. Then I started.

"I got beat up two nights ago by undercover cops, right in front of my condo building. They gave me this black eye—you can't see

193

it so good now, but it was pretty bad yesterday—and they wanted to know, these two cops, they wanted to know the names of my suppliers. They're still there every night when I go home," I said, looking right at Mr. Atkins, "and I'm getting sick of it." He was squinting his gray dead eyes at me, trying to see where I was going from there. I played it cool, though. I stood up, grabbed my guitar case, and leaned on it. "I don't *have* a supplier. You could get a million cops to beat me up and I *still* wouldn't have a supplier. Why I called you here, Mr. Atkins, was to tell you and Dr. Kollbisk together to *shove my diploma up your big fat asses!*"

And then I opened the door and walked out.

I was halfway down the corridor before Atkins stuck his ugly head out the doorway and yelled, "You'll never graduate from *this* school, Blake!"

"This isn't a school," I yelled back, "it's an *asylum*. And you're the head sicko."

I was out of the building a few minutes later, walking down the steps. Goodbye, Harrison Godfrey, I thought. I wasn't even shaking. Usually when I get mad, I get shaky, but not this time. This time I was whistling.

I caught a cab on Lincoln Avenue and took it to Lisa's mother's club. For a change, I didn't get a Pakistani driver. I got a black guy who drove like a human being. He wanted to know if I played in a group. It was a real good feeling to be able to say, yeah, I did, and have him ask which one. I was getting out of the cab when he asked me, and I just pointed to the sign above Scene II.

"That one," I said. "I'm Lenny Blake."

Do you know what that sonofabitch did? He asked me for my *autograph*. He wasn't even kidding. I signed a receipt booklet he had and gave him a two-dollar tip. I was feeling like a hotshot.

Nobody was at Scene II, so I went to the Oak Tree restaurant and had a cheeseburger. I tried calling Lisa from there, but there wasn't any answer at her house. I just sat in a booth drinking Cokes until they were coming out of my ears. Then at about four-thirty I went back to Scene II, and one of the waitresses let me in.

"Can I help you?" she asked.

I pointed at the sign. "I'm Lenny Blake," I said.

"Oh," she said, and then she opened the door wider and helped

194

me put my guitar case on a table. "I'm the only one here, Mr. Blake, but you can make yourself at home. The dressing room is in back. If there's anything you need, just let me know."

I told her thanks, I would. Jesus. If you get your name on a sign, it's a whole different world. It's better than a diploma, even. For a while at least.

Then me and the waitress shot the shit for a while, and it turned out she was from Oregon and went to Loyola during the day. She told me I was kind of young to be in show business already, and that I must be good. I told her I was okay, not great, but okay. She said I should start taking the other approach, that I was great, not okay. She made me feel pretty good. She made me coffee and everything, and she wasn't bad looking. Take my advice: if you're ever depressed, go talk to a waitress, not a shrink. A waitress will make you feel a thousand times better than a shrink will, and she doesn't even charge you for the visit.

I sat in the dressing room for about two hours before anybody else showed up. I was psyching myself up for the performance. I played a bunch of songs and sang real loud to loosen up my vocal cords. I wanted it to sound like I'd been singing for a week, kind of hoarse, you know. At six-thirty, Rick and Kevin and Pete showed up with the equipment, and by then the house sound man was there, miking us with the P.A. system. We ran through a few numbers and practiced the a cappella parts for "Do It." By the time seven-thirty rolled around, I was hyper. I was all ready to go, but the audience wouldn't even be there for another hour and a half.

"Let's go run around the block," I told Rick. Lisa hadn't shown up yet and I was getting nervous thinking about what may or may not have happened to her at home if she'd told her mother what had been going down between her and her father. *Going down* sort of sums it up pretty good.

Rick said okay, he'd run with me, so we took the side entrance and started running down Oak Street toward Lake Shore Drive. We ran around pedestrians, around taxis, around dogs in the park, and even around buses. That's how hyper we were. I didn't even get tired until we ran across Lake Shore Drive to the Oak Street Beach. There were people riding bicycles there and couples holding hands, and weirdos listening to headphones while they skateboarded. Rick and me, we stopped at a bench and huffed and puffed for a while.

"How're you feeling?" Rick asked, when he wasn't panting so much anymore.

"I'm feeling great," I said. I really was. I had this glow, boy. No fooling around. I was like a walking glow machine. "I'm gonna be good tonight."

"You gotta be *great* tonight," Rick told me. "This ain't a high school dance."

"You got it. Great it is. I'm gonna be fucking great tonight. I'm gonna burn up the first row. There's gonna be fallout in that club."

"What got into you?" Rick asked.

"C'mon," I said. "I'll buy you an ice cream."

We bought ice cream bars from this guy with a truck at the beach. We sat and watched girls walk by for about twenty minutes, pretty girls in pastel shorts and tops. Girls look great when there's a sunset and you're at the beach and everything. Then we ran all the way back to the club. One guy almost ran Rick over while we were crossing Rush Street, and Rick hit his car with his fist, right on the fender. He said something about how no wonder they call it *Rush* Street. Everybody was all the time in some kind of hurry.

The club was filling up by the time we got back. We went to our dressing room and took off our shirts so we didn't get them all sweaty. Lisa was already putting makeup on Kevin and Pete. They looked like two beat-up fags.

"Kevin looks so good I could kiss him," Rick said. He went over to Kevin and held him in a clench, pretending like he was kissing him.

I asked Lisa how things were going. She was looking for an eye liner pencil, and she threw a towel over my shoulders.

"It's going good," she said. She pushed me down in a chair and put her mouth next to my ear so the others couldn't hear us while we talked. "I'm going to talk to my mother while you guys are playing. She knows something's on my mind, and she knows it's about my father. I told her that much at breakfast."

"You sure this is a good time?" I asked. It seemed like lousy timing for some reason. It was just instinct on my part.

She was holding my head in one hand and putting eye liner on

196

with the other. "Hold *still*, Lenny." She was being real careful not to hurt my shiner. "And *yes*, this is a good time. I've got to get this thing settled tonight."

"Why tonight?" I wanted to know. She pulled away and looked for eye shadow.

"Because you-know-who got a little out of control last night."

"Whad'ya mean? Ya mean he *did* something?" I was getting that hate thing for her father again. That killer feeling.

"He *tried*, all right? He tried. I'm not going back home until this is out in the open. Hold *still*, please."

"I'll kill the bastard," I said.

"Well, if things don't go like I hope they do, I'll kill *myself*," Lisa said. You could tell she was nervous as hell, and that's why she was trying to get her mind off things with the makeup job she was doing on me.

"Don't talk like that," I told her.

"Goddamn it, Lenny. Hold *still!*"

"All right! I'm holding, I'm holding!"

Mrs. Mankewicz—Lisa's mother—walked into the dressing room a few minutes later, as Rick and me were putting our shirts back on.

"How do you feel tonight, guys?"

We all said hi, we were feeling all right. Mrs. Mankewicz isn't bad-looking for a woman in her forties. She's a little short, which is how come Lisa is too, but she's very pretty. In a way, though, she's too tough. She looks like what you'd call a "tough broad." Kind of hookerish. She kept her hair short, but not in a dyke style. She was extremely feminine. She had a lot of sex appeal for an older woman.

She walked around looking at us and telling us how pretty we looked, and she mostly joked with us and stuff. She was trying to loosen us up before the show, you could tell.

"You get forty minutes, two shows. Time it exactly, because I got an act that shouldn't have to put up with a hammy opener. You know what I mean."

I told her we knew, and that we'd be off in exactly forty minutes. She winked then, and slapped me on the ass, which I thought was a little strange, but I let it pass. What else could I do? I couldn't

197

say, "Mrs. Mankewicz, keep your hands off my buns," or anything like that. Jesus. What a screwed-up family.

A waitress came back and gave us a three-minute warning before we went on. All of a sudden I got the heebie-jeebies. My stomach went all funny.

"You okay?" Rick asked, holding me by the shoulder.

For an answer I leaned over the toilet and puked.

I heard Rick say, "Oh, *great*," while I was throwing up my cheeseburger and ice cream bar. I couldn't stop. The guys were all watching me from a distance; they were huddled together in the doorway looking at their watches. I rinsed my mouth out a few times, and then I heard them announce us.

"Ladies and gentlemen, Scene Two is proud to present Lenny Blake and the Victims."

There was a lot of applause, and as I was climbing the stage with Rick, he whispered, "Use your own microphone for harmonies tonight—*please.*"

There were a few giggles from the front tables when they saw us with our makeup. I was snapping my fingers with the rest of the group huddled around me for the a cappella number, and just before we went back into the song I said, "You'll have to excuse us. We just did an Avon lady backstage," which got them going. Then we broke loose with the street corner schtick. The echo on the sound system made us sound like twenty guys instead of four. Rick noticed it, too, and it made him sing even harder. We were off.

Halfway through a number a strobe light came on and the background lights all switched to purple. I looked at the other guys and we all cracked up. I couldn't see a fucking thing; the lights blinded me.

Then we did "Maybe Baby," an old Buddy Holly tune that, for my money at least, is one of the best rock and roll songs ever written. They allow dancing at Scene II, and a few couples got brave during the second number and hit the floor. I looked around the club and noticed that the people in the audience were tapping their feet. But it was a mostly sophisticated crowd. They weren't going to storm the stage or go through the rafters. I figured that after "Maybe Baby" we'd do "Lisa," because it isn't wild; it's just solid. These guys needed to be stroked before we blasted them. It's

198

tough, sizing up an audience. The thing to do is not panic, just let out the line and string 'em along and then roll it back gradual-like.

We got some applause after "Lisa," but it was nothing that was going to put us in the Guinness Book. We did "The Love in Your Eyes" next, which hits a little harder, but still is filled with pretty harmonies. The light guy was helping us out. He did an orange and blue bit with the center lights and kept melting them into each other. The crowd was starting to come around, so I went right into "Inside Out" and knocked the shit out of them. Kevin's bass drum and crash cymbals were burning, and his veins were sticking out near his neck, and he wasn't looking at anybody. He was like in a trance, just him and his hands spinning over the tops of his drums. We got about two minutes of continuous applause after that one, when Rick stepped up to the center mike and rammed into "Habits." I knew it would work. That song had even the pinstripes in the audience out on the floor with their secretaries, or whoever the preppy snots were that they brought with them.

I said, "You're a wonderful audience, good night—" right at the last chord, and then we all walked off the stage while they were still clapping. I collapsed in a chair in our dressing room (which was really a bigger-than-average john) and caught a glimpse of Lefty as him and his boys took the stage. The audience went ape-shit when they saw him. We warmed 'em up, naturally, but it just goes to show that there's a reason for someone being a headliner. It made me a little depressed, but there was nothing I could do about it.

"Gimme a beer, will you, Susie?" Pete asked the waitress who had let me in earlier.

"All of us," Rick added. Susie said sure, beers coming up. Rick and me took off our shirts and hung them up. I was freezing, so I put a towel on and lit a cigarette. I was starting to wonder what happened to Lisa 'cause I hadn't seen her at all during the show— not that I could see much from up there—and she wasn't around by the time we got backstage, either.

"Anybody seen Lisa?" I asked.

Everybody said they hadn't. Rick was dancing around on the sink next to me and singing "Besame Mucho," which meant he thought we'd done a pretty good show.

"Hey, Lenny, next time puke on the stage for an opener. Not in the dressing room," Rick said, jumping from the sink.

"Yeah. What's wrong with you? Got the flu?" Kevin asked me. He was sitting on the floor and tapping his sticks on a table leg.

"Just a little nervous, I guess," I told him. I wondered where the hell Lisa was.

Susie brought in a tray full of beers and I asked her did she see Lisa out there or not.

"She's in the office with her mother. Door's locked and everything. Looks pretty heavy."

"Whad'ya mean? Ya mean like they looked upset or something?"

She said yeah, they were both not looking too happy when she saw them go in there. Somebody had come by to see Mrs. Mankewicz, a business guy, and he got told by one of the bouncers that she wasn't seeing anybody tonight. It sounded heavy, all right.

We weren't scheduled to go on again until eleven-thirty. We sat, mostly, just talking and playing cards. I put my shirt on at around ten-thirty and took a cruise around the bar to see if I could find Lisa or her mother. They were still locked up in the office, though. So I went back to the dressing room and waited.

Rick was pretending he was a fortuneteller with the cards. When he saw me he said, "Ah, sit down, my son. The cards show there is a very short woman in your life. Either that, or you have a very short life with a woman in it. I cannot tell. The cards, they are not certain."

Jag off.

The waiting went on until about eleven-twenty, when Lisa finally came back to the dressing room.

I almost jumped out of my chair. "Where've you been? You okay, or what?"

She walked to the far corner and asked if she could see me outside. She wasn't looking at me when she talked, and she kept putting her hands up to her face to like hide it, like as if she thought she was going to sneeze or something.

We walked outside, and all the guys stared after us, like—What the hell? What's eating her? I closed the door and then we were standing in the little hall between the bar and the stage area. She was crying. Her eyes were all red and she could barely talk.

200

"She didn't take it too well, huh?" I said, soft-like. (Mr. Understatement, that's me. I'm going to have cards printed up.)

Lisa, she had her face in her hands and was making gurgling noises. She shook her head, but didn't try to say anything. I'd been right: bad timing. How can there be good timing with a thing like that? I didn't want to rub it in, that I'd been right, so I just put my arms around her and held her. God, was she shaking. She was like an epileptic, I'm not exaggerating. What I can't stand, I can't stand it when a woman cries. There's nothing in the world that will make them stop, and there's nothing you can say, 'cause they won't answer you. You just have to sit there and let them cry. What you want to do, you want to shake the hell out of them and say, "Shut up! Stop the stupid crying!" but that just usually makes them cry harder. I know. I once did that to my next-door neighbor a few years ago. She was a pretty little girl whose parakeet died. All she did was cry, so I shook her and told her to knock it off, it was just a goddamn bird, but that made her go crazy. So I learned my lesson. Now when I see a woman crying, I just let her cry. Even if it's about something dumb like a parakeet.

Finally, though, about four minutes before we had to go on, she started wiping her eyes and catching her breath. She was getting to the point where she was going to say something, but I didn't hurry her. I just let her take her time. She mumbled something, but I didn't understand it.

"What? What was that?"

"She *slapped* me," she said. She was stuttering all over the place like in soap operas when girls lose their marbles over some guy. "She called me a whore, and then she slapped me. She blamed *me* for the whole thing. She said I—I, that I'm jealous of her, and that I have an Electra complex. And then she said she was going to—"

"What? What's she going to do? What the hell is an Electra complex?"

Susie walked past us kind of sheepishly, like she didn't know if she should even be around us, and then knocked on the dressing-room door and gave the rest of the guys the three-minute warning. She walked back past us again and held up three fingers to me, and I nodded.

"Lisa," I said. I was talking soft so I wouldn't upset her. She was

201

half insane. You could see it in her face. "Lisa, listen. I gotta go play."

She nodded.

"I want you to stay in the dressing room until we're done. You hear me? Just stay here."

She nodded again, and then I took her to the dressing room and put her in a chair.

"It's time, Lenny," Rick was saying. I motioned them all the hell out of the room with my hand. Then I poured a half-bottle of beer for Lisa and made her take a sip.

"I'll take you home after the show, just as soon as we're through. You understand?"

"Yes," she said. Then I kissed her on the forehead and made it to the stage just as they were announcing us.

The second show was pretty good, too, even better than the first one, but that was because we were warmed up by then, and the audience was half crocked out of their heads. I put all my problems out of my mind for that forty minutes and just did my best. I was feeling more confident on account of the applause. I talked to the crowd more. I got one heckler, but I took care of him. He yelled, right between songs, "How old are you, punk? Thirteen?" I said, no, I was older than that, but still too young to do what he had in mind. I did it with a smile, so he wouldn't get pissed off and so it just looked like I enjoyed morons interrupting my show. We knocked 'em out with "Rock Me" this time, and we left them clapping.

I ran straight into the dressing room, only Lisa wasn't there, like I told her.

"Holy shit," I said, when I saw that the room was empty.

"What's the matter?" Rick said.

I just ran out of the dressing room and went looking for Lisa. It wasn't very hard. There was a crowd of paramedics and staff girls huddled around the office. They must've come in the back entrance, 'cause there was no fuss during our set.

I had to push my way through the crowd to get in there. Lisa was standing just outside of the doorway, sort of pressed up against the wall by all the people gawking.

"What the hell happened?" I asked her. She was crying again and moaning something I couldn't understand.

Susie pulled us both by the arms and led us to the back exit.

"Her mother overdosed. They think it's downers, but she'll be all right. I don't know what the hell is taking them so long to get her out of here."

I looked at Lisa and she was just stunned-like. She probably felt guilty or something. I know I would've. I feel guilty about everything.

"Take her home, Lenny," Susie said.

"Yeah. I will. C'mon, Lisa."

Lisa just sort of went where I led her, like a sheep or something, and then I remembered to ask Susie if Mr. Mankewicz had been told.

"Yeah. I called him and he's going to meet the ambulance at the hospital." She opened the back door for us, and the air felt cold. It felt like somebody'd opened a refrigerator.

I asked which hospital, and she said Columbus, on Lakeview. I nodded and then took Lisa outside.

"Where's your car parked?"

She didn't say anything, though. She just pointed to the street, so we walked until I spotted it, and then I put her in the passenger seat and drove to her house.

What a night. The planets must've been weird or something, because everything was like bad vibes. Not that the astrologers know anything about it. All they think about is marriage on the horizon and contracts. I'm usually no good during emergencies. I freak out very easily, but that night was different. The planets were weird, probably. I was still in control. It felt like we were in a movie, on account of everything seemed like it wasn't for real. It seemed like it was all just a play or something, so I stayed calm.

Lisa was like a zombie when I got her home. She just sort of moped around like some kind of zombie, and I was afraid to leave her alone. What I did, I mixed her a hell of a strong Manhattan, the way my father used to when he still lived with us. I knew she'd drink it because girls like drinks that have cherries in them. They didn't have the right kind of cherries at Lisa's house, though. They had the *candied* kind, and you're supposed to have the maraschino kind. But she didn't know the difference. I could've put a walnut in there and she wouldn't've noticed. She was half gone.

"It's gonna be okay. Really it is. She's at the hospital now, and in a few days she'll be good as new. They know how to handle this overdose stuff real good. They got pumps and stuff. You wait and see. If I'm lying to you, I hope my teeth fall out. Really."

I was talking to her, to sort of like comfort her, but Lisa, she wasn't talking to me. She wanted another Manhattan. So I said okay, I'd make another one, but only if she went to bed, and then I'd bring it to her. What I was going to do, I was going to make sure she was sleeping, and then I was going to sit downstairs on the sofa until her father came home.

Then I started thinking. What if he came home and did it to her tonight? That would freak her out *forever*. She'd never come back from that. I got so nervous thinking about it that I mixed myself a drink, too. Scotch and soda. Mr. Mankewicz might have been a degenerate, but he had a pretty good bar.

When I took our drinks upstairs, Lisa was undressed and in bed.

"Have a sip of this," I said. She had some pillows behind her back and had to lean forward to drink.

"Too strong?"

"No. It's fine," she told me. Then she leaned back, took a deep breath, and sighed this horrible sigh, with like clicking things in her throat. Poor kid. Poor goddamn kid, I thought. It's funny, but every time I was with her, my life seemed *sane* compared to hers. What I bet is, I bet everybody's life is fucked up, only nobody admits it. Really. If nobody ever talks about it, then nobody knows their life is the same as everybody else's. They think they're the exception.

I was going to ask Lisa then if there was an aunt or somebody I could call to come and stay with her, 'cause I didn't want to leave her there all by herself when her father came home. Besides, if he found out that she'd ratted on him, he might do *anything*. He was a crazy bastard, and you don't take chances with crazy bastards.

But when I went to ask her, she was snoring. She was out like a light. No wonder. Hysteria is very exhausting. I know. I spent half

204

my life being hysterical myself, and the other half being tired from it.

Then I got an idea. I got up and grabbed her phone from the nightstand and pulled the cord over to my side of the bed. I took a big gulp of my drink and called Susie at the club. They made me wait about twenty goddamn minutes before they put her on the phone, though. Back at the club, I guess, everything was going like it was normal, like nothing had happened.

"Hello?" Susie said.

"Hi. It's me. Lenny."

"Oh, hi, Lenny. How's Lisa?"

"Fine. She's doing okay. I made her a few drinks and she's out like a light. Listen, Susie. The reason I'm calling, you don't happen to know if maybe Lisa has any relatives who could come over and stay with her, do ya?"

She waited for a second and then she said, "Mmmm, no. Not that I know of."

"Oh. Jeez," I said.

"Why don't you just stay with her until Mr. Mankewicz gets home from the hospital? He should be coming home in a few hours."

Christ. I didn't want to tell her that he was the whole cause of this. People at the club talk, and before you know it, Lisa's whole history would be in the papers. Really. Reporters and columnists hang out at Scene II, and I could just picture one of them going back to his office to write the whole goddamn thing up after overhearing one of the waitresses talk about Lisa sleeping with her old man, and that being the reason Mrs. Mankewicz overdosed.

"Okay," I told her. "Thanks, Susie."

"No problem. Good night."

"Good night."

Then I hung up and worked on my drink for a while. What I started doing was putting the whole thing together the way Sherlock Holmes would've. Elementary, my dear Whoozits. Lisa's old man had screwed up his whole family. His wife almost committed suicide because of him, his daughter was all emotional and screwed up because of him, and now he was going to take it out on her, all because he was a pervert. Maybe that's what they mean by the "nuclear family." The whole fucking thing just blows up after a while, and if the explosion doesn't get you, the fallout will.

I did one of the stupidest things in my life then. I stacked some pillows behind me and got comfortable. I started resting my eyes. I was only going to rest 'em, just to give 'em a break for a second. But what I ended up doing was falling asleep right there on the bed next to Lisa.

When I woke up, I was on the floor. I thought at first that I was at home in my bedroom, and that I'd fallen out of bed like an idiot. But then I looked around and remembered I was at Lisa's, and that's when this big black shoe kicked me right in the face. It sent me right against the wall, and my head put a dent in the plaster. Something wet was all over my nose and mouth, and one of my teeth was on the floor next to me. Some maniac was screaming, "*Sonofabitch! You dirty little sonofabitch!*"

It was Mr. Mankewicz. He was trying to kill me.

I got up from the floor like in shock. I couldn't even feel any pain or nothing in my head; I was just numb. I jumped up on the bed next to Lisa and blood started covering the pretty yellow sheets she had. I remember looking down at her, and her looking real wide-eyed back up at me. Then there was just this long scream as her father came at me. She was screaming like an insane woman screams, real high-pitched and everything. She was saying, "Daddy, *don't!* Daddy, please *don't!*" And then he like charged at me. I caught him with both hands, right over the back of his stupid bald head. He went sprawling face down, and then I jumped on his back with both feet. Each time I jumped and landed on his back, I said something to him. I said, "*Asshole!*" once. I got "*Pervert!*" in there about twenty times. I was trying to break his back, but it didn't work, on account of I don't weigh enough. (I'm about 116 pounds, soaking wet.) I only just knocked the wind out of him, but it gave me time to tell him what I thought of him. I was holding my nose and catching the blood while I talked.

"You know what I'm gonna do, Mr. Mankewicz?" I said. "I'm gonna tell all your business partners that you do it with your daughter. I'm gonna tell the school board and get you arrested." (I was kind of running out of breath here, so it didn't sound so hot, what I was saying, but he heard me. You can bet he heard me.) "And then they'll put you in prison, where your roommate's gonna be this big three-hundred-pound black guy. A big three-hundred-pound black guy who's *real lonely*. Every day when you come back from making license plates, you know what he's gonna say to you? He's gonna say, 'Hi, sweetheart. Feel like a nap?' And even if you're not so tired, believe me, you'll feel like a nap."

Then the room was looking all tingly, kind of. It was like points and dots and points and dots, and the blood was making me gag. I looked around for something to hit him with. Stupid me, I forgot I had the Mace in my back pocket. I crawled off the bed, because I was afraid if I jumped I'd pass out.

"Get out of here, Lenny! Just run!" Lisa was screaming. "Oh, *God!*" she kept saying. Over and over again, just, "Oh, *God! Oh, God!*"

Mr. Mankewicz was getting up off the bed, so I grabbed the quickest thing I could find, a picture from the wall in a metal frame. It was a Picasso print of some bent-out-of-shape lady who looked more like a guitar. I broke the goddamn thing over his head, but it didn't do nothing except cut him up a little. So I started banging his head with the frame. I just kept bashing him over the head with it, but he kept getting up again. I couldn't keep my mouth shut, either. I was insane. Totally nuts. "You old bastard," I said. "In Germany what they do with guys like you is they cut their things off and give it to 'em in a jar. We're talking kosher, buddy." Which I'm not certain about, but it sounds like what they ought to do. I think I read it someplace.

Then he called me a bunch of names. He said I was a little shit, and a bunch of other stuff, but I wasn't listening so hot. Whenever he called me something I reminded him about his roommate, and how when he got to Stateville, the guy would be *so lonely*, and *so big*.

Mr. Mankewicz was still facedown on the bed when the frame I was hitting him with finally snapped apart. I was going to die. I knew I was going to die unless I did something, so I jumped on the bed again, with blood running all down my shirt and my jeans, and kicked him as hard as I could on the back of his head, like a karate guy. Bruce Blake, that's me. But even *that* didn't knock him out; it just made him fall off the bed and onto the floor, where he crawled around for a while.

Then, I don't know. Then Lisa pulled me down off the covers on her bed and started pushing me to the doorway. I asked her what she thought she was doing, but all she would say was that I had to get out of there before somebody got killed. "Fast, Lenny! Before he gets up again," she said.

"But I'm *winning*," I said.

"Please," she said to me. It was kind of pathetic, seeing her all upset and crying and everything. So I told her okay, I'd leave, but only if she put her jeans on and came with me. Mr. Mankewicz was groaning on the floor, and even though I kind of knew how he felt—being pretty beat up myself—I couldn't feel sorry for him.

"You make me puke," I told him, while he was trying to catch his breath. As a matter of fact, I *did* feel a little like puking, but I didn't want to mess up Lisa's bedroom. It was so pretty. It had been once, anyway. So I held it. I didn't puke.

Lisa was dressed in about two seconds. She helped me down the stairs, 'cause I couldn't walk so good. Everything was spinning. I started thinking that maybe I should go back and look for the tooth that her old man had knocked out, but I didn't have the energy. When we got to the front door, though, Lisa stopped. She acted like she wasn't sure she was coming with me or not.

"Hey," I told her. "He's not *dead*, you know. In about two minutes he's gonna come down those stairs and kill one of us. Or both of us."

Lisa was like dazed or something. "I know," she said. "But what are we going to do?"

"We're gonna get in your car and get the hell out of here, that's what we're gonna do, unless you'd rather see how I look when I'm *really* messed up."

She looked around the living room and everything, and I know what she must've been thinking. She must've been thinking that it would never be her home again. I know that feeling. Boy, do I know that feeling.

"Lisa?" I said. Then she snapped out of it. She took my arm and put it around her shoulder for balance and opened the front door. We limp-walked all the way to her car, and then she started looking in her purse for her keys. She moved things around in there real fast, and then looked up at me like she'd just realized something very important.

"The keys! They're on the piano in the living room!"

"Okay," I said. "You stay here. Be ready to fly when I get back."

I walked back to the front door, which Lisa had left open, and all the time she was yelling for me to come back. She said we should get a cab, instead. Sure. With my luck, we'd get that Pakistani driver again, and this time he might *really* take me out of my way. Or he'd laugh about how torn up my face was. A cab was the last thing I wanted.

I went inside the house and looked around. Lisa'd been wrong about the keys. They weren't on the piano. I couldn't see so good on account of being dizzy, so I had to look real close at everything. Once I thought I saw them on the floor, but it was just some change that must've fell out of my pocket.

After ten years or so, I spotted Lisa's car keys on the bar, next to the bottle of vermouth I'd left out. I grabbed them and headed for the front door again, just as Mr. Mankewicz came around the corner, on all fours. He saw me and tried to stand up, but I kicked him in the face with everything I had, and sent him backwards against the wall.

"Good night," I told him when I left.

Lisa probably had around ten heart attacks by the time I got back to the car. I threw her the keys, and she hopped right in, started it, and we tore ass out of there. Usually she's a crazy driver anyway, like I told you. But that night she made James Dean look like somebody's grandmother.

"Slow down, hey," I told her. "It's okay now. We made it."

She stepped on the brake a little to slow us down, and let out a big sigh. For a long time neither of us said anything. Then, at a red light, she looked over at me as I was dabbing my sweat shirt to my face to keep the blood from ruining the interior of her car.

"I think we ought to go to a hospital, Lenny," she said.

"No, really. I'm okay."

She just kept looking at me and not saying anything. Then when the light turned green, she started trying to convince me to let her take me to a hospital.

209

"No," I said, again. "When you go to a hospital, all they have is stabbed drunks and babies with bullets in 'em and stuff." I sat and thought for a second. "What we ought to do, we ought to go to *my* place for a while. I could get cleaned up there. Change my clothes." I realized that my mother would probably be home, but I didn't care. I'd just tell her the truth. It couldn't be any worse than what we'd just been through, I figured.

Then Lisa, she started wondering about things. She was wondering about exactly the kinds of things I was wondering about. "What are we going to do, Lenny?" she said.

I was watching the traffic go by, and all the neon signs flashing. "I don't know. I'm just making it up as I go along. I'm improvising. When I find out, I'll tell you."

She didn't say nothing then.

"Okay?" I asked her.

"Okay," she said, but you could tell she was worried. I wasn't. I mean, maybe I'm crazy or something, but I just wasn't worried, not about that kind of stuff.

"You trust me, don't ya?" I asked her.

"Yes. You're the only one left that I *do* trust."

"Same here," I said. "You're the only one I trust, too." We were at another red light, and my vision was still kind of bad, but not bad enough to keep me from seeing a squad car and a bunch of people all standing around it. The police were arresting this one guy who looked like a bum, and they kept shoving him up against the car while they put the cuffs on him. Chicago seemed like the rottenest city on earth. Rottener than it normally is.

"Hey," I said, "you got some money?"

"I think so. I've got around twenty dollars in my purse."

"No, that's not what I mean. What I mean is, you got some money saved up in a bank?"

She said yeah, she did.

"Me too," I told her. "What we could do is, we could go away. To a college town or someplace, till things get better. I got about two thousand dollars in the bank, and I'll get a job, and you can go to college, and we can like, you know, *live* together."

Lisa, she looked worried then. And I understand why, too. It

210

wasn't the plan of the century, or anything. It wasn't going to win a Nobel Prize. But it was practically all we *could* do.

"You said you trusted me."

"I do," she said as she turned down Lincoln Avenue. We were still a couple of miles from my building. "But—"

"But what?"

She glanced over at my mangled face and looked real sad. "You poor thing," she said. "You're so bloody."

"Yeah, well. It's that time of night. You trust me though, right?"

She smiled, finally. It was like waiting for a hundred years to see the sun again, and it was worth it. "Right," she said.

Out the side window I could see a bunch of stars in the sky, just hanging there. It made me sort of wonder. I mean, what the hell are they *doing* there? It pissed me off that they just sit there and nobody knows how come. Then I wondered how many planets got intelligent life. There are *none* that I can think of. If there are space guys—you know, the green ones with octopus arms and nine mouths and three left tits, or whatever they have—then every time they come past earth they must lock their doors and duck. We're sort of the Bronx of the universe.

We took a corner and the stars were still there, waiting around for something. I remembered when I was a kid I used to wish on them. I used to wish for toys and stuff, and for things like snow for Christmas Day. There were about ten bright ones, all in a row. It seemed like a shame to waste them and just let a wish go by, but I was afraid that whatever I wished for wouldn't come true. And I didn't need any more disappointments that night. So what I did, I took a rain check. *"I got one wish coming to me,"* I said, aloud. I forgot I wasn't alone.

Lisa looked over at me from behind the wheel. Boy, did she look tired. Maybe she was still loaded or something; I don't know. "Pardon me?" she said.

"Nothing," I told her. "I'm just talking to myself. Must be the bump I got on my head."

Then I started worrying about the bump on the head I'd got when it hit Lisa's bedroom wall. I started thinking that maybe I had brain damage. Maybe I'd never be the same. I tried to think of little things, like dates and stuff. I gave myself a quiz. When is my birthday? July third. What street is the Merchandise Mart on? Wells Street. Who discovered the Pacific Ocean? Uh-oh. I couldn't remember that one. I couldn't think of the guy's name who discovered the Pacific Ocean. To be honest, I don't think I *ever* knew who he was, but just the same, if I did once, I didn't then. So I figured I had brain damage. I ran a bunch of names through my head, just in case I could stumble on it. Lindbergh, Edison, Washington, Roosevelt, Napoleon, Eli Whitney. It was none of them. Patrick Henry, John Wilkes Booth, Desi Arnaz. Yep. I had brain damage, all right. I was certain.

When we got to my place, I had Lisa drive around the block a few times, so I could see if Starsky and Hutch were hanging around waiting to kill me. I didn't see them, though. On the third time around, I told her to drive into the garage, fast. She did, too, right behind a Cadillac that had just gone in.

She helped me out of the car to the service elevator next. It didn't take long to get there, but it smelled like urine when we got in. Somebody must've taken a leak in it. You could see the wet spot. Don't ever tell me that people on the Gold Coast have class. They have about as much class as Cro-Magnon man. What they *got* is money, which is supposed to make it okay if they wet in elevators.

Then I tried warning Lisa about my mother. "She's kind of weird, you know," I said.

"Whose mother isn't?" she said, which is true enough. Jesus. She was starting to sound like me.

The elevator was squeaking like a bastard, and for a second there I thought that maybe the cable would break. You all the time read about people getting killed in elevators, how the cable snaps and they take the *pancake express* to the bottom of the shaft. But it didn't. Snap, I mean. It let us off right at the eighteenth floor.

"Stand in front of me," I told Lisa, "so that when she opens the door she doesn't pass out from my face. I'm warning you; she's gonna be hysterical."

Lisa said okay, and when she was in front of me, I knocked. I could've used the key and gone straight in, but I thought I'd be polite for a change, in case anyone else was there.

212

My mother came to the door and asked who it was. I said, "It's me, Mom. Let us in."

When the chain came off and the door opened, Lisa and me walked in. I kept my face pretty well hidden until we were a good way into the apartment. When she saw my face, she went nuts. She's very predictable.

"Lenny!" she screamed. "Lenny, what *happened* to you? Oh my God!" Like that, for about an hour. Lisa and me kept trying to *shhh* her, and I went to the bathroom to look for a Valium. (It's a good thing we live in the "Valium Age." If this had happened about a hundred years ago, I would've had to hit her over the head with a mallet or something.) She was following me all over the place, asking nearly a thousand questions a second. She was very upset, you could say. I sat her down on the couch and gave her the Valium with a glass of water. I waited for a while, until the pill did its stuff, and then I only told her what I had time for. My mother, if you give her an inch of question room, will take a few thousand miles.

"I got to get away, Mom. Lisa's father and two cops want to kill me, and the school won't let me graduate. Besides, you and me are practically driving each other nuts, anyway. So I'm leaving."

"Your face!" she kept saying, like a broken record. Then I remembered that I hadn't even cleaned up yet. For the next half hour, Lisa and my mother worked my face over with a washcloth in the bathroom, and I think they took off more skin than Mr. Mankewicz had. My mother said I should go to a hospital, that my nose was broken, and I got to admit it sure did feel like it. Every time she came at me with a fresh cloth, soaking wet, she'd turn her face and say, "Oh, Lenny!" Just to cheer me up. It was kind of nice, though, in a way—my mother taking care of me like that. But it was also kind of painful, 'cause she doesn't know her own strength. Two or three times I had to bite my lip to keep from yelling.

I had to change my clothes next. Lisa and my mother followed me to my bedroom, and I had to shut the door in their faces just to get a little privacy. When I had some pants on, I opened the door and they were still there. I took out a suitcase and started throwing things in it, not too careful either. I wanted to get the hell out of

213

there fast. I tried getting my baseball bat in, but it just wouldn't fit, so all I did was take my Mace. My old bedroom, boy. Was I ever going to miss it. I remembered how it used to be when I was just a kid, and I used to build forts in there and pretend Indians were coming to scalp me. I used to use a blanket for a tent and bring all kinds of stuff in there and just play-act. What a crazy kid I was.

My mother was watching from my bedroom doorway, with her arm on Lisa's back. She didn't really hate Lisa, you could tell. She just didn't know her so good.

"What did your father and I do wrong, Lenny?" my mother said. That's what all parents say. First they do everything in the book wrong, and then they want to know what it was. Poor parents. I'd rather be anything than one of them.

"Nothing, Mom. You didn't do nothing wrong. It's not your fault," I said. I had the suitcase closed by then, and I walked right between her and Lisa to the living room. It hurt my arm to lift the suitcase, on account of all the bruises and stuff I had.

"I told your father that a divorce would do this to you," she said. She had a one-track mind, honest to God. If it weren't for the Valium, she would've cut her wrists or something.

"It wasn't the divorce, Mom. It's not your fault," I said.

"Then what in God's name *is* it?" she wanted to know, pacing the floor like a maniac. She was making me dizzy, all of a sudden.

"It's the world, that's all," I told her.

On and on it went. Lisa got the Blake Family Story in slightly hysterical installments, all between nose blowings and sighs, until I couldn't take any more. I had to get out of there or go crazy. Then, from like the corner of my eye, I saw a pair of shoes sticking out from underneath the sofa. I hadn't noticed earlier, but her bedroom door was shut. Well. Some things you can't fight. Some things you just got to face. That's what I thought to myself then, anyway. And I think I was right.

I led Lisa to the door, and pushed my suitcase across the carpet. I probably shouldn't've packed so much. I'd got my bank book when I was in my bedroom, and as we were leaving I stuck it in my back pocket.

"I'll see you," I told my mother. Lisa, she was out in the hallway already, looking pretty uncomfortable about the whole thing.

"But where are you going?" she wanted to know.

"I don't know. I'll write. Maybe in a little while, when everything is better, we'll come back." Then my mother and me, we looked at the carpet. You've never seen such carpet lookers in your whole life. That's 'cause we can't look at each other's eyes so good. What I thought of while I was looking at the carpet was James. I wanted to say goodbye to him, and tell him all he'd done for me. But he must've known. He'd know I did the right thing. "Say goodbye to James for me, okay?"

She said, yeah, she would.

"But be sure you do, huh? Just say, 'Lenny says good-bye and thank you.' Make it sound like I said it like a gentleman."

She nodded. Then I saw the bedroom door open a little, 'cause I guess Sondra was waiting to see when the coast would be clear. It made me feel guilty to think that somebody was afraid of me, so I tried to make it up to her. I said, "Tell Sondra I'm sorry about the other day. I mean, it's really none of my business and all. Okay?"

My mother was just standing by the door. Boy, did I feel bad for her. First her husband, and now her son.

"Tell her I don't care. James was right. You're just a human being," I said. And then Lisa and me, we left. We punched the elevator button and waited, but my mother wouldn't close the door. She kept it partway open and looked, pretending she wasn't looking. I don't like to admit this, but she was killing me. I'm serious. When the elevator came, I slid my suitcase on and told Lisa to hold it for a second. Then I went back to the apartment, kissed my mother on the cheek, and told her to keep a stiff double chin. It was a joke. She didn't get it.

I guess it was around four in the morning before Lisa and me said anything to each other. We headed out on the Milwaukee toll road, cruising north in the darkness. It you kept your window open, the breeze felt good on your face, and you could hear a million crickets chirping, or whatever it is they do. Lisa had the radio on low in the background. Some station was playing "Slip-Sliding Away," by Paul Simon. It's not a song you should listen to at four in the morning, unless you enjoy severe mental depression. I looked at Lisa as she drove. I saw how her pretty eyes gazed out across the road, real brave-like, even though she didn't know what was out there. At night on the road, all you can see is the white line. I must've yawned or something, 'cause the next thing I knew, she was looking at me from time to time, and smiling.

"Feel all right?" she asked. Her hair was blowing in the wind, the way I like it.

"Yeah. I feel okay. I'll feel better in a few days. But this is okay. How about you?"

She laughed a little. "Fine. I'm fine."

I could hear the road seams under the tires as we traveled. I wondered what my father was doing, and who he was doing it with. And I pictured Mr. Mankewicz with an ice bag on his head, and Mrs. Mankewicz—I wondered if she'd move back in with him or not. I don't think so. Not if she has a brain. The only thing that seemed to make any difference anymore was Lisa and me. Everything else just seemed like a million years and a million miles ago.

"Lenny?" Lisa asked me, turning down the radio, and putting her hand on my shoulder.

"Yeah?"

"Where do you think we'll end up?"

"Someplace safe," I told her.

"Where's that?" she asked.

I thought for a second. Through the windshield, I noticed all the stars, how bright they were above us, and I remembered about my rain check. I closed my eyes, made a wish, and then I kissed her.

"We'll know when we get there," I said.

And when we get there, we're gonna stay.